...oo soon; thick
smoke was coiling up the stairs, and as
they ran towards the front door a sudden
fierce burst of flame shot out of Mrs
Bloodvessel's door.

'Reckon that's where it begun – in
there,' panted Dido. 'D'you think, mister,
that she's – that she –?'

Van Doon looked through the door at
the raging flames and shook his head. 'If
she is in there, child, she cannot be alive.
But you say that there are others – there
are children down below?'

'Yes, and I haven't a *key*!' Dido clenched
her fists. 'Pa told me to put it on the
mantel. We gotta bash open the door, else
they'll all be kippered in there, poor
brutes. Oh, if Pa hadn't gone off –'

"Quick!" she said to Is. "You gotta help me get out the lollipops – all those young 'uns locked in down there – the fire's downstairs, just smell the smoke! They came down none

DIDO AND PA

Joan Aiken

Illustrated by Pat Marriott

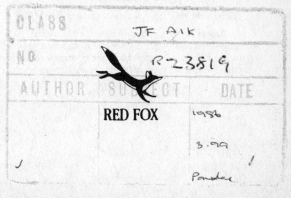

A Red Fox Book
Published by Random House Children's Books
20 Vauxhall Bridge Road, London SW1V 2SA

A division of Random House UK Ltd
London Melbourne Sydney Auckland
Johannesburg and agencies throughout the world

First published by Jonathan Cape Ltd 1986
Red Fox edition 1992

5 7 9 10 8 6

Text © Joan Aiken 1986
Illustrations © Jonathan Cape Ltd 1986

Set in Sabon
Typeset by JH Graphics Ltd, Reading

Printed and bound in Norway by
AIT Trondheim AS

RANDOM HOUSE UK Limited Reg. No. 954009

Papers used by Random House UK Limited
are natural, recyclable products made from wood grown in
sustainable forests. The manufacturing processes conform to
the environmental regulations of the country of origin.

ISBN 0 09 988850 5

To Ilse and Kit Barker

FAMILY TREE OF THE DUKES OF BATTERSEA

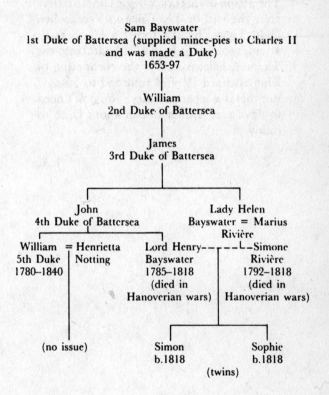

Sam Bayswater
1st Duke of Battersea (supplied mince-pies to Charles II
and was made a Duke)
1653-97
|
William
2nd Duke of Battersea
|
James
3rd Duke of Battersea

John   Lady Helen
4th Duke of Battersea   Bayswater = Marius
                                                    Rivière

William = Henrietta   Lord Henry-- ---L-Simone
5th Duke   Notting   Bayswater   Rivière
1780–1840   1785–1818   1792–1818
                        (died in   (died in
                        Hanoverian wars) Hanoverian wars)

(no issue)   Simon   Sophie
                        b.1818   b.1818
                              (twins)

Note to the Reader

The action of this book begins immediately after the end of *The Cuckoo Tree*, when Dido Twite, having foiled a Hanoverian attempt to slide St Paul's Cathedral into the Thames, has assisted at the coronation of King Richard IV and returned to Sussex. But this is a separate story; you don't need to have read earlier books about Dido to follow it.

J.A.

1

Dusk was closing in over the South Downs on a fine, bitterly cold, windless evening in late November, a hundred years ago, when the driver of a carriage-and-pair left his horses tied to a gatepost by the main Chichester to London road, vaulted over the gate, crossed a wide, sloping pasture, walked up a chalk track where the wheelruts showed white in the hazy twilight, and passed through a grove of beech trees.

Overhead the beech leaves, in colours of autumn rust and gold, seemed to glimmer with their own light; down below among the straight tree trunks it was almost dark, and very silent. The single snap of a twig could be heard for a hundred yards, and the goodnight squawk of a pheasant in the shadowy woods down below rang out loud as a hunting-horn.

By instinct, the walker trod with care, to make as little sound as possible. And while he climbed he kept glancing about him alertly, as if he hoped or expected to meet another person.

Beyond the beech grove lay an open space, a saddle-shaped triangle of rough downland turf. Now, in the shadow of a copse on the other side of this little meadow, a second figure could just be glimpsed, coming slowly in the direction of the first one – who called out eagerly, 'Dido – is that you?'

It was not possible to be sure. In the bad light no more could be seen than a smallish, shadowy shape, mooching along, rather dejectedly, head bent, hands in pockets.

'Dido?' called the carriage driver again. 'Is that you?'

From the small shadowy shape came a kind of astonished croak – not unlike the call of the pheasant. 'Simon?' – and then, after a pause – 'That's never *Simon?* Mussy me – I don't *believe* it!'

Then she hurled herself across the open grassy space. The driver had raced to meet her, and the two collided impetuously, laughing, panting, and hugging one another so energetically that they almost fell over.

'Is it really, really you? Oh, Simon! I reckoned I'd never, ever set eyes on you no more?'

'Hold up, girl – you'll have us in the blackberry bushes!'

'Why, Simon – how you've growed and filled out! Ain't you tall, though!'

'What about yourself? Not that I can see you in this light,' he said, laughing, 'but you feel twice the size. Puny little brat you used to be –'

'Reckon I growed on account of the whale oil – '

'*Whale oil?*'

'Croopus, Simon, there's such a *deal* to tell you. Oh, I've had such *times* since I saw you last – '

Arm in arm, still hugging one another, they

turned back through the beech grove, both talking at once.

'How in the name o' juggernaut did you know I was up here on the hill, Simon?'

'When I looked down this morning from the Whispering Gallery – and saw *Dido Twite* carrying the king's own train – in the coronation procession – you could have knocked me down with a quill. How in the world did *that* come about?'

'That's a long tale – that'd be a deal of long tales . . . But if you saw me there in St Paul's this morning, why in mux's name didn't you let out a holler then, to tell me as you was there?'

'In the middle of the coronation? I sent a message as soon as I could – but you'd gone by then; you see I had a lot of jobs to do after the service – getting red carpet laid along the streets from St Paul's to St James's Palace – '

'You gone into the carpet business, then, Simon?' said Dido, stopping in surprise. 'I thought you was fixing to be a painter?'

'Oh, I am,' he assured her. 'But, you see, when Uncle William died – '

'Hold hard! I never knew you had no uncle Will. Thought you was an orphan?'

'Yes, well, it turned out – You remember the Duke of Battersea?'

'Funny old gager in a wig what you used to play chess with?'

'It turned out he was my uncle. So – as he had no children – when he died of the quinsy last winter – that meant I was the next duke.'

11

'Holy mustard!' Dido exclaimed, thunderstruck. '*You*, Simon? You a dook? Come off it! You're gammoning me!'

'Fact,' he assured her. 'I'm the sixth Duke of Battersea. Loose Chippings Castle in Yorkshire belongs to me – and a big hunk of Battersea – and most of Wessex and East Humbria. And – on account of being the duke – that makes me Master of the King's Garlandries; which meant I had to see to all the decorations for King Richard's coronation, and get the red carpet laid; and a deal of other jobs. I'd just as lief be plain Simon, I can tell you,' he ended seriously.

But Dido, whose spirits had shot up as high as they could go, found the notion of her friend being a duke so exquisitely funny that she burst into whoops of laughter. She laughed so much she had to stand still – indeed, almost fell over, and had to hold on to him, laughing and coughing.

'Oh – that's plummy!' she gasped. 'You, a dook! I can remember when you first came riding into Rose Alley on a moth-eaten old moke.'

'But where have *you* been all this time, Dido? Last I saw of you – do you remember? – was when the ship sank, and we swam for a rock, and I must have fainted. When I woke, I'd been rescued, but none of the people who rescued me had seen you – or knew anything about you. I thought you were drowned. So did your pa. We put up a memorial to you.'

'A *memorial*? You never?'

This amused Dido even more. Then she said, more soberly, 'I thought as you was drowned, too. Lud

12

love us, am I glad you ain't! I got picked up by a whaling vessel, and carried all over – north, south, and rat's ramble – they dumped me on the Isle of Nantucket, and it took a plaguy long time getting back from there; it's umpty thousand miles across the ocean from England. And, coming home on a man o' war, we had to stop in at a place called New Cumbria – and then, after that, we got muxed up in the Chinese Wars – why, if I was to tell you the *half* of what's been happening to me, I'd be talking till Turpentine Sunday. – So you don't live in Rose Alley no more, now you're a dook?'

'No, my uncle left me a house in Chelsea – Bakerloo House. I live there with Sophie. She turned out to be my sister.'

'Well I'm blest! Come to think,' said Dido, 'anyone might 'a guessed it. You're as like as two blackberries – dark hair an' eyes. Why don't you live in Battersea Castle, where the old dook lived?'

'That – er – got blown up – ' Simon hesitated tactfully.

'Did my pa and his Hanoverian mates blow it up? I knew they was a-reckoning to, when the old king, the one before this one, came to eat his Christmas dinner with the old dook – '

'Well, yes, they did. And – I'm very much afraid – '

'Ma got blowed up too,' said Dido matter-of-factly. 'And my aunts, and a whole sackload of other Hanoverians.'

'How did you know that, Dido?'

'I run into my pa a while ago; he'd been a-sculling round here in Sussex, plotting away with a passel o'

13

jammy-fingered coves as reckoned to put a stop to this new king, King Richard, being coronated in St Paul's. But us put a stop to them,' said Dido with satisfaction. 'Me and a few Gentlemen put some ginger into *their* gravy. I'm right sorry about your castle, though, Simon.'

'Oh it didn't matter,' he said quickly. 'It was much too big. – Just fancy your running into your pa, though, Dido. Shall you – '

Shall you want to go back and live with him now? was what he had been going to ask. But he stopped, first because it seemed so unlikely that Dido would want to live with a father who had never taken the least notice of her, or been in any way kind to her; secondly, because, since that father had been mixed up in several Hanoverian plots against the last king and the new one, he would certainly be arrested for treason, if he were spotted by any sheriff or constable, and imprisoned in the Tower of London; and very possibly hanged.

At this moment they reached the road where Simon had left his horses tethered. By now it was nearly dark, so he pulled out flint and tinder and lit the carriage lamps. They gave but a feeble glimmer, in which he and Dido were able to see not much more of one another than they had on the open hillside. She could vaguely make out that he was bigger, thin-faced as he had always been, with a thatch of untidy black hair, but decidedly better dressed than when he had been a humble art student, living in her pa's attic and working at night in Cobb's coach yard to pay his school fees. – And Simon could dimly see that the puny, undernourished brat, who had teased and provoked him, and stolen his dinners, and saved his life, was now a girl of medium height, still very slight, but wiry and active-looking, with short brown hair, and dressed in midshipman's rig of wide blue duffel trousers and a tight-fitting pea jacket with brass buttons. The pea jacket was very thin and worn.

'Murder, but it's getting cold,' shivered Dido as she scrambled into the curricle.

'Winter's almost here,' said Simon. 'They say it's going to be a hard one, and come early. It might snow tonight; feels like a frost for sure. You'll not be warm enough on the drive to London dressed like that, Dido. We'll stop in Petworth and buy you a sheepskin or something to wrap up in.'

'I'd not say no to a bit of nosh, neither; haven't had a smidgeon all day. We didn't stop for the junketings after the crowning; one o' my mates as helped carry the king's train was anxious to get back to his sick dad here in Petworth.'

'We'll have a bite of supper then, before starting; I have to change horses too. Then we'll go to Bakerloo House. Sophie will be *so* happy to see you, Dido.'

Without the need for words, it had been accepted between them that Dido would stay in Simon's house; even if he were a duke.

In the courtyard of Simon's house in Chelsea, a group of ragged children had collected and begun to play a game. The house was an old one, built of crumbling stone; the courtyard, which opened on to the King's Road, was about the size of a tennis court and had a stone fountain in the middle, very useful for dancing rings round.

But the children were not dancing rings at the moment. They had formed themselves into two long lines and leaned towards each other, hands on the opposite person's shoulders.

They sang:

'Dig a tunnel, sink a mine
Under and out the other side,
Dig a tunnel, sink a drain,
In goes the king with his golden train –'

At this point two players, from opposite ends of the line, turned and ran under all the arching arms, passing each other in the middle.

'Who comes out?
Little Tommy Stout!
Ha ha ha, hee, hee, hee,
You're not the one I thought to see!'

Faster and faster ran the players, peeling off the end of the rank, diving under the arch, squeezing past each other in the middle, then joining on at the other end. There seemed little point to the game, except its skill and speed.

'Hey, all you young scaff and raff!' roared Fidd the porter, coming out of his lodge. 'Clear off! Clear off, I say! We don't want your like in here!'

They laughed and jeered at Fidd, but slowly began

to obey him. Just as the last few were skipping out of the big double gates, thumbing their noses at the porter, Lady Sophie Bakerloo rode in from the other direction, on a small, skittish mare. She was very pretty, with dark curls and eyes; she wore a fur-lined riding-cape.

'What is it, Fidd, what's the matter?' she called.

'Them owdacious young 'uns,' he grumbled, 'playing their capsy games in our yard . . .'

'But I like to see them, Fidd!'

A small lavender-seller, who had put down her tray of bunches and lavender-bags while she played, now passed Sophie, settling the strap again round her neck.

'I'll take two of your lavender-bags, my love,' Sophie called to her, and the girl curtsied, beaming.

'Thankee, my lady! They're a saltee for three, or a mag apiece.'

'I'll have three,' said Sophie, and gave her a penny.

'Walker!' exclaimed the little creature. 'Now four o' my mates'll have the money for a Lollpoops' Lodging! It's a farden apiece.'

'But what about yourself, my dear?'

'Oh, *I'm* took care of. *I've* got a dad. But in the Birthday League we all looks out for each other.'

'The Birthday League – what is that?'

'When's your birthday, my lady?'

'The tenth of April.'

'Mine's the fifth o' Febr'y. Now you're a member!' said the small lavender-seller, and skipped away, as Sophie stared after her, raising her small clear voice in a lusty shout of 'Swe-e-e-e-et Lavende-e-e-e-er!'

Sophie gave her mare's bridle to a groom, and went thoughtfully into the big empty house.

On the same day that Simon met Dido in Sussex, but several hours earlier, two other people had been talking about them.

In the great brick forest of London there is a district called Wapping. It lies a long way from Chelsea, eastwards of St Paul's and Tower Bridge. Wapping, north of the River Thames, was once a dank region of mud creeks and sandbanks. As the city stretched eastwards it became a maze of little narrow streets and alleys, twisting and turning in every direction between wharves and jetties, docks and creeks, inlets and boat basins. Keels of boats rubbed against doorsteps; masts and chimneys sprouted side by side. Warehouse gables and cranes hovered in the fog above the looped sails of schooners and the crates and bales on their decks. On this particular day the ancient dwellings, the granaries and storehouses, were hardly to be seen against the thickening sky, which promised bad weather before nightfall.

Among the counting-houses there were still to be found a few mansions from an earlier time, when rich gentlemen had pleasure-houses by the river, among the marshy fields.

One of these, known as Cinnamon Court, had been very grand indeed: a huge brick palace built by a merchant knight in the days of the first King James. Surrounded by a high brick wall, it still owned a spacious garden running down to the Thames; and it was still in private hands, owned by one single gentleman with his servants.

This man was not a native Londoner, but came from Hanover; he was the Hanoverian Ambassador to England, a nobleman of immense wealth and vast properties in Eastphalia and Saxony. His name was Wolfgang von Eisengrim, Margrave of Nordmarck, Landgraf of Bad Wald, Baron Blitzenburg, and first cousin to Prince George of Hanover.

Just now the Margrave was taking his lunch. He sat with his bare feet buried in a deep basket of flower heads – roses, carnations, violets, sweet peas – goodness knows what they must have cost. His doctor had told him this was good for the circulation. The lunch consisted of thirteen oysters, laid out like a clock-face on a Dresden plate, garnished with parsley and lemon wedges and a thin slice of black bread. By the plate stood a tall, narrow, green-stemmed glass of white wine. Glass and plate were on a small round table of rose-coloured marble.

The Margrave swallowed his frugal meal slowly, in tiny sips and small nibbles. He wore jacket and knee-breeches of black velvet and had a snowy muslin napkin tucked under his chin. The room was papered with red velvet and had a black marble fireplace. The sound of music, played on violins, hoboys and spinnet, came from the next room through an open door.

A wherry under sail crept past the dining-room window, which looked on to the river. The boat was low in the water and was evidently sinking. Voices shouted for help.

The Margrave turned his head slightly, and called, 'Play louder!'

Immediately the music doubled in volume.

Behind the Margrave's chair stood a servant, also dressed in black. With a slight gesture, his master directed him to go and look out of the window. He did so, opened the casement, leaned out, closed it again, and walked back, all in silence.

'Well?' said the Margrave, having despatched his thirteenth oyster. 'Did the ship sink?'

'It sank, my lord, with all on board.'

'Very good. That is very good. We have now disposed of Lord Forecastle, Sir Percy Tipstaff, and the Dean of St Paul's.'

The Margrave took a dried plum from a box the servant handed him, and thoughtfully nibbled at its black, wrinkled skin.

'So convenient for us,' he murmured, 'that King Richard is a stranger to most of his subjects. His having spent so much time abroad, hunting in foreign lands, is a decided advantage. Let me see, now, who remains to be despatched? Bring me the list, Boletus.'

With a kind of pecking bow, the servant lifted down a scroll that hung on the crimson-papered wall and laid it on the table in front of his master.

'And the ink, Boletus; and a pen. Aha; there still remains the Archbishop; and the Lord Chief Justice — no, that was Tipstaff; the Home Secretary, Lord Raven; and the valet — what is his name?'

'MacTavish, my lord.'

'He must certainly go. Now, who are these? Battersea, who is Battersea?'

'The duke, my lord; he is Master of the King's Garlandries; I am informed that he has been at various times in conference with his majesty –'

'*Ahem*,' said the Margrave coldly.

'I ask your pardon, sir; I should of course say, with the Pretender.'

'Indeed. Then he must be disposed of. And who is this Dido Twite? The name *Twite* is faintly familiar –'

'Er – excuse me, your excellency – your lordship's Chapelmaster, Herr Bredalbane –'

'Ah, so. Who, then, is Dido? A connection?'

'That I do not know. But I understand, my lord, that she is a young person who was – who was in some way involved in halting the St Paul's plot; furthermore she spent some time with the ki – with the Pretender, and carried his train at the ceremony.'

'Humph! Where is Bredalbane?'

'At hand, my lord.'

The servant assisted his master in putting on a pair of grey silk stockings and shoes with diamond buckles. The Margrave flicked a crumb from his velvet lapel and strolled to the window.

Cinnamon Court, built in an L-shape, had one wing at right-angles to the river, and the garden lay in the L. The Margrave could see spires, chimneys, cranes, and masts, appearing like the tips of trees out of the fog. Tideborne barges went silently past; the river was full and ran swiftly; the rattle of a chain could sometimes be heard, the clang of a ship's bell, the creak of an oar, the long hoot of a wherry. A distant boom came through the fog: St Paul's clock, striking one.

21

There was no sign of the wherry that had sunk.

Boletus, having left the room for a moment, returned.

'The young person Twite, my lord, set out for Petworth in the county of Sussex the very moment the coronation ceremony was finished. And it seems that the Duke of Battersea, having learned that she had done so, went after her.'

'Ah – and Bredalbane?'

'Is here, your worship.'

By the time that Simon and Dido had reached Petworth, dark had fallen, but the little town was a blaze of light, with bonfires on the outskirts, lanterns flaring, fireworks snapping and thudding, and dozens of voices raised in song.

'Reckon they're all a-celebrating,' said Dido. 'Well, the new king seems a decent sort o' cove; likely they'd 'a done a sight worse under that Bonnie Prince Georgie that my dad and his pals were so set on bringing over from Hanover. *I* say, why not make do with the king you got? Why fetch another in from furrin parts – as probably talks some peg-legged lingo that no one understands?'

'I did hear,' said Simon, guiding his horses with care through the narrow, sparkling streets of Petworth, where people were reeling about with ale-mugs in their hands, children were dancing ring-a-rosy by torchlight, and hot-cockle-sellers were doing a roaring trade, 'I did hear from Doctor Furneaux, the head of the Chelsea Art Academy – he's just back from Pomerania – that Prince George of

Hanover was mortally ill of an octagonal fever, and not expected to recover.'

'Oh well, poor devil, if he dies, that'll tie a knot in my dad's plots; he and his mates'll have to settle down and make the best of King Dick. – Where in mussy's name are you taking us, Simon, we've rid clean through the town?'

'I left my horses at a little inn on the outskirts. These are a job team. Mine should be rested by now, I reckon. While I have them put to, we can take a bite; we'll get served faster here than in the middle of town.'

Even at this small tavern, the Cow on the Roof, a humble thatched building at the junction of three roads, there were large numbers of festive customers. They had spilled out of doors, and were singing and dancing in the pub garden, and on the green beyond. The joyful sound of pipes and fiddles could be heard indoors and out.

Simon drove his carriage round to the rear. Trestle-tables had been set up across the inn yard, where an ox was being roasted over a bonfire, and great slices of beef were being carved and served to all comers.

'Here, Dido – why don't you sit at one of those tables and order us some beef,' said Simon. 'Wrap my jacket round you – I'll find you something warmer directly –' and leaving her he went off to make arrangements about the horses, returning soon with two brimming mugs of ginger-jub in one hand, while over the other arm he had a thick sheepskin jacket with brass buttons.

'There you are, girl; that ought to keep out the cold weather.'

'Why Simon – it's *naffy*!' exclaimed Dido in delight, snuggling into the thick warm garment and fastening its buttons. 'How the blazes did you come by it so quick?'

'Saw a boy wearing it, offered him a couple of shiners for it,' replied Simon, beginning to tackle the enormous plateful of beef that Dido had secured for him while he was gone.

'Croopus, Simon, are you as rich as King David now you're a dook?'

'I've enough to get by,' he replied cheerfully.

'Fancy! I can remember when all you ever had for dinner was a bit o' bread and a penn'orth of milk from Aunt Tinty.'

'And *you* used to eat most of that.'

'Things warn't bad, though, after you came to live in Rose Alley,' Dido said slowly, remembering. 'D'you mind how you and Sophie took me to the fair? And how all the Hanoverians used to come to Rose Alley and plot away with Pa, and drink Organ Grinder's Oil – and after they'd left, Pa used to play tunes downstairs on his hoboy – and you and me, upstairs, used to make up words to 'em?'

'Yes I remember that,' said Simon, remembering too how queer it had seemed to him that such an out-and-out villain as Mr Twite, who neglected his children, told lies more easily than he breathed, and never stopped plotting to do away with the king, should yet be able to make up such beautiful music and play it with such feeling on his hoboy.

24

'D'you mind one of his tunes,' Dido went on, 'you once put words to it that went:

> Oh, how I'd like to be queen, Pa,
> And ride in my kerridge to Kew,
> Wearing a gold crinoline, Pa,
> And sucking an orange or two –'

She stopped munching beef for a moment, swallowed a dram of ginger-jub, and then sang out the words in a clear, true little voice, pronouncing them with great and ladylike care, as Simon had taught her long ago.

Just at that moment there chanced to fall a brief lull in the general uproar, and her voice rang out into the silence; several people turned in surprise to glance at Dido, and one man in the crowd looked at her with particular attention; then he spun on his heel and walked off at a hasty pace into a shadowed corner of the yard.

'Yes, I remember that one,' said Simon, laughing. 'Another verse of it went:

> Oh how I'd like to be queen, Pa,
> Watching my troops at review,
> Sucking a ripe tangerine, Pa,
> And sporting a sparkler or two –'

'No, no, you're clean out, there,' corrected Dido authoritatively, 'it didn't go like that, it went:

> With slippers of crimson shagreen, Pa,
> And all of my underclose new!'

'My word, Dido, how much better you sing that you ever used! I can remember how you used to croak out the words, hoarse as a crow – now you carol away like a young throstle!'

'Guess it was all the whale oil they poured into me,' said Dido, gruff, pink and shy under his commendation.

'What *is* all this about *whale oil*, Dido? And how in the world did that lead on to your carrying the king's train at his crowning this morning? How in the name of Habakkuk did you get to *know* the king?'

'Why – it was this way –' began Dido, but at that moment an ostler lad tapped Simon on the shoulder.

'Beg pudden, master, but one o' those greys o' yours 'pears to be precious lame. D'you want to come and look at him?'

'Plague take it!' said Simon. 'I suppose that means I'll have to leave him here. I'll not be a moment, Dido; have some more beef, do.'

And he followed the ostler towards the stable.

Dido sat peacefully where he had left her, with her elbows on the table. She could not possibly have eaten any more; she felt full of beef, and very snug in her thick sheepskin jacket, and wonderfully happy. Just fancy me being here, she thought, and this afternoon I didn't think I had a friend in the territory, I can't hardly believe it; and she looked round at the crowded inn yard, fitfully lit by the bonfire, full of people eating and dancing and shouting *'Long live King Dick!'* Great yellow chestnut leaves drifted down from above, sailing over people's heads like birds joining in the rejoicing. Who'd 'a thought it,

26

mused Dido, Simon coming to find me like that, and him being just exactly the same as ever?

And she recalled how kind Simon had been to her during the time when he lived at her parents' house as a lodger, when she was several years younger, and often miserably ill, since neither her mother nor her older sister Penelope ever spared any pains to look after her.

Simon used to bring me a hot posset and make a fire in the grate and tell me stories about the wolves in Willoughby Forest, she recalled. And sometimes Pa's music used to come up from the room below, so beautiful: when Simon wasn't there, I used to lie in bed and hearken to the music and pretend that Pa was playing it for me. O' course I knew that he wasn't; Penny was allus his favourite; now and again he even bought hair ribbons for her, which he never ever did for me. But even for Penny he'd not play on his hoboy. I recollects her begging him: 'Play "The Blue Bells o' Battersea", Pa, do!' but the more she'd wheedle, the rustier he'd get, and tell her to shab off, or she'd get a clump on the lughole. Once in a blue moon, if summat had put him in a good skin, he'd play for her, but not if she asked. Never if she asked.

And he never, never once played for me. And oh, his music was so sweet! There was that tune I called 'Calico Alley', acos of the words I put to it, 'As I went dancing down Calico Alley'; and the one that went to 'Three Herrings for a Ha'penny'; and the one I called 'Black Cat Coming Down Stairs', because it sounded so solemn; and the one I thought was about rain, quick and tinkly. But the best of 'em all was

'Oh, how I'd Like to be queen, Pa' . . . Funny how that tune keeps a-going round and round in my head; and yet I haven't given it any mind for dunnamany years . . . I could almost think I hear it now.

And then it seemed to Dido that she *could* hear the tune, very faintly and hauntingly played — surely on a hoboy? — and coming from somewhere not too far off, out on the green, perhaps, beyond the inn yard entrance.

I must be dreaming — mustn't I? she told herself. But she could not resist standing up and walking a little way towards the gate, to see if the music grew louder as she moved that way. Yes, it did! I'm not dreaming, Dido said to herself. Some cove out there really is a-playing Pa's own tune.

Could it be Pa hisself, a-playing his hoboy? It just might be. After all, he was in Petworth not so very long ago. Wouldn't Pa be fair pussy-struck to hear as how, on this very selfsame day, I carried King Dick's gold-and-furry train, in his crowning procession, in St Paul's Church! Wouldn't Pa just stare to hear that! It'd be a rare joke to tell him about it, thought Dido — after he and his cullies tried so hard to stop the crowning . . .

Mindful of Simon, Dido turned back at this point, picked a charcoaly twig out of the edge of the bonfire, wiped her plate clean with a handful of grass, and wrote in big black letters on it with the charcoal:

DERE SIMON BAK IN 1 MINIT, DIDO

Then she walked out of the yard gate.

Beyond the entrance, on the shadowy green, people were dancing in circles. Another bonfire had been lit in the middle of the large open space, and carts were parked round the edge; some boys were letting off fireworks, and several different groups of musicians were playing.

But the hoboy music came from quite close at hand, from the big gnarled chestnut tree that grew on the hither side of the green, its high knuckled roots outlined against the light of the distant bonfire. A thin man was perched astride one of the roots, and was playing on a musical instrument; Dido could not see his face, but the closer she approached him, the more certain she became that he was her father.

'Pa!' she called softly. 'Is that you? It's me – Dido!'

The musician turned slowly towards her, lowering his instrument.

'I beg your pardon?' he said. 'I fear you are labouring under a misapprehension. I am nobody's pa; (thank heaven for that); my name is Boris Bredalbane, and I am a paid-up member of the National Union of Flintchippers –'

'Oh come off it, Pa, I can see you plain as plain, let alone I'd know your music if I heard it in Pernambuco. You ain't what'shisname Bredalbane, you're Abednego Twite – '

'*Hush!*' the thin man whispered imperatively, grasping her wrist and glancing warily around. 'Grass has eyes, bushes have noses and trees have ears, my chickadee! And the name of *Twite* is just a touch unhealthy since the constables picked up Godwit and Pelmet and Wily and some of my erstwhile colleagues – '

Indeed Mr Twite, Dido now observed, was wearing a ginger-coloured wig and moustaches, which looked incongruous on top of his tall thinness; and from somewhere he had managed to procure a gaudy Scottish kilt and sporran, in which he did not seem at ease; the kilt's hem dipped at the front, and the sporran had a tendency to slip round to the back.

Mr Twite finished the contents of a large pewter mug which sat beside him on the root – it smelt like Organ Grinder's Oil. Then, grasping Dido's wrist even more tightly, he stooped to pick up a set of bagpipes with his other hand.

'Gracious snakes, Pa, you taken to snake-charming, then?' she inquired, observing the bagpipes.

'Protect – hic - tive colouring, my jonquil,' he whispered, and began to draw Dido farther away from the tavern, towards a high hedge that bordered the green.

'Not that I amn't overjoyed to see you again, my sarsaparilla,' he went on in a low tone as they drew farther off into the shade. 'Welcome as jewels to jackdaws, you be! In fact – to tell the truth – I was hoping for a sight of ye – '

'Hoping for a sight of *me*? Why, Pa?' Though naturally pleased, Dido could not help being surprised and suspicious. When had her father ever wanted to see her? And she remembered him well enough to know that, when he spoke about *truth*, it was time to watch out for the biggest lie of all.

'Why, my duckling, for the sake of your poor suffering sister – Penelope.'

'Penny-lop?' gasped Dido, now really startled. 'Why, what in the world's amiss with Penny? And – if she does want me – which I can't hardly believe – it's the first time since Blue Moon Sunday. – 'Sides, I thought she run off with a buttonhook salesman?'

'Ah me, ah me!' Shaking his head, Mr Twite continued to draw his daughter farther into the shadows. 'These buttonhook salesmen – heartless scoundrels, to a man – naught but a nest of·adders! She should have known better than to listen to his wiles. And now your poor sibling lies at the point of dissolution – gasping in mortal agony – only struggling to keep alive in hopes of a sight of her sweet sis – and there's not a hand else in the wide world to tend her – '

'Hey, hold hard, Pa – Penny never tended *me*, that I recollect . . .'

31

'Calling out for her little Dido with every rattling breath,' continued Mr Twite — he was beginning to put considerable dramatic fervour into his account — 'with never a soul to give the poor wretch a sip through a straw, or to change her bandages — '

'*Bandages?*'

'Or to pick up her — hic — crutches if she drops 'em. "Only fetch me Dido, fetch Dido," she whispers, "if it's the last thing you do, fetch me Dido!" and I responded, "My angel, I will fetch your dear sister if it means dragging her between serried ranks of sabre-toothed tigers." Which is hardly more than the case, I'm that bothered and beset by ill-wishers and enemies — '

'But where *is* Penny, Pa?' demanded Dido, for Mr Twite had by now reached a closed carriage, quite a grand one, with a coat-of-arms on its door, which waited, with horses ready harnessed, in the shade of the hedge.

'Why, not too far from here, my dove; if we travel at the best speed our horses can command, I daresay you may just arrive before she breathes her pitiful last — ' and Mr Twite opened the carriage door. In the light of a silvery rocket which just then ascended, Dido saw that the coat-of-arms depicted an iron fist, holding a hammer, on a gold background.

Dido stood still, tugging back against her father's insistent arm, and said, 'Here, wait a mo, Pa, I ain't said yet that I'm a-coming with you — for one thing, my pal Simon's back there at the pub, and he'll be wondering where the blazes I've spooked off to — '

'Simon? Simon?' said Mr Twite vaguely. 'Ah, yes,

your young painter acquaintance; a fine, upstanding lad. – A sight *too* upstanding by half, as I recall,' Mr Twite muttered to himself under his drooping ginger moustaches.

'– Never trouble about your friend Simon, my larkspur; time presses too much for such considerations. I will instruct Ned here to give Simon your kindest regards and explain that you were called away on an errand of life and death – you'll see to that, Ned – hic – will you not?' he continued, addressing a villainous-looking lad who stood at the horses' heads. 'Make very sure that you find the correct person: a handsome stripling named Simon, who used to lodge with me in my house at Rose Alley in Southwark. Be sure to give him the message, as well as my own very kindest regards.'

'Aye, aye, I'll be sartin sure, guvnor,' replied the lad, emphasizing his intentions with an evil grin, screwing up his unpleasing face and laying one finger alongside his nose.

'Do so. That's my good boy.'

'But Pa – I don't *wish* to leave Simon – I haven't even said goodbye – I only just *met* him again – ' protested Dido, struggling in vain against her father's grip.

'No matter for that, my dilly; idle politeness must always give way when Necessity calls.' And Mr Twite picked up his daughter bodily and thrust her into the carriage. 'You will have *ample* time to see Simon hereafter, have no fear – perhaps – ' and he sprang into the vehicle after her, slamming the door. 'Give 'em their heads, then, Morel,' he called to the driver through the trap, and the coach started off with such a jolt that Dido was thrown to the floor.

'Saints save us, Pa, you sure are in a rush,' she gasped, picking herself up from among the rushes with which the floor was strewn, and thankful for the thickness of her new jacket, which had protected her bones from bruising.

'Never mind it, my sugarknob; the sight of your sister's joy will repay any such slight vexation,' replied Mr Twite, pulling out a pipe and a pouch of Vosper's Nautical Cut tobacco.

Dido said nothing. She was beginning to be more than a little aggrieved at this summary treatment. Pa's got no right to hale me off thisaway, she thought. Still, I'll make sure he don't keep me under his thumb once I've seen Penny. Soon as I see how she really is – prob'ly not so bad as Pa makes out – I can cut and run. But what riles me most is that poor Simon will be so put about; he'll be wondering where in herring's name I've got to. And he'll think it downright rude and capsy of me to light off like this without a by-your-leave.

That shravey-looking boy won't give him no message, I'll lay.

In this guess Dido was quite right.

She was so displeased with her father that she said nothing to him about having carried the king's train during the coronation ceremony.

When Simon returned to the stable yard, followed this time by his aged groom, Matthew Mogg, he found the table cleared, the plates removed, and a drunken carter sitting on the bench where Dido had been, with his head resting on the table beside a mug of Mountain Dew.

'Where's the young lass who was sitting here?' asked Simon.

'Lass? Lass? I never see no lass,' replied the man blearily.

'A skinny young girl in a sheepskin coat? Dressed as a boy?'

'Sheepskin coat? I hain't seen so much as a mole-skin coat,' yawned the carter, and, making a pillow from the folds of his smock, he laid his head down on the table once more and began to snore.

'Rackon thee's lost her, Mester Simon,' gloomily pronounced old Mogg. 'And dang me if I fathom why that lad yonder told thee the grey mare was lame, when 'er be fit and flighty as a flea.'

'Curse it! I hope no mischief has come to Dido!' worried Simon, looking vainly about the stable yard for her. 'Do you go that way, Matthew, and ask everybody you pass, and I'll try this way. Perhaps she just strolled out to look at the dancing.'

But, ask as they might, no word or trace of Dido was to be found. She seemed to have vanished like a bubble, like a drop of dew, as if she had never been there.

And, in the carriage beside her father, Dido, fairly tired out by her long day's adventures, and somewhat stifled by the copious, heavy fumes of Vosper's Nautical Cut, gradually slid down sideways against the lumpy horsehair upholstery of the carriage, and drifted off into uneasy slumber.

2

When Dido next opened her eyes, she was startled to see that the night was nearly over; the squares of black sky outside the carriage windows were now paling into a stormy grey. A high wind buffeted the coach as it rolled along, and rain slapped at the window-panes.

Sitting up straight, and peering out to her right, Dido could see, far away, a band of lemon-yellow light where the sun was half-heartedly trying to rise under a threatening pile of lumpy black cloud. The landscape faintly shown by the yellow light was also a surprise to Dido – and not a pleasant one: she had expected to see fields or woods, but what met her eyes in place of these was a desolate region of brick railway viaducts, small market gardens crisscrossed by black ditches and half-made roads; there were tall sheds, factory chimneys, and clumps of houses that seemed to have escaped briefly from the city and were now waiting for it to catch up with them.

In the light of a rainy dawn, this no-man's land, neither city nor country, looked wholly dreary and forlorn.

'Bless us, Pa,' said Dido, 'where in the world are

36

you taking us? Where's Penny? I thought you said we hadn't far to go? But at this pace we must 'a come forty mile and more?'

'Humph – awrrrk – aaargh – beg pardon? Whazzat you say, my chaffinch?' croaked her father.

Mr Twite, in the harsh morning light, presented almost as dismal a spectacle as the glum landscape outside the carriage window. His red wig hung awry, the moustache dangled sideways from his stubbly lip, his cheeks were drawn and grey, his eyes bloodshot and gummy.

'I said, Pa, that it's a plaguy long way you're taking me to Penny's place. I thought you said it was only a mile or so?'

He stared at her for a moment or two, working his face about as if getting it into order for the day while he collected his thoughts and put them in position.

'Ar, humph – y'r sister Penny – yes, quite so. That is to say – well. I must acknowledge, my eucalyptus – deuce take it, how I do *long* for a mug of Organ Grinder's Oil – '

'You must acknowledge *what*, Pa?'

Mr Twite said rapidly, ''N speakingof – y'rsister Penny – been guiltyof – very slight diggle-gression from fact.'

'You told a lie, Pa.'

'Not a *lie*,' said Mr Twite. 'No, not a lie. Different person, is all. Different deathbed. Arrrh hum. Oh, pisky bless us, how I do need a little something.'

'*Whose* deathbed?' queried Dido, now really cross and very puzzled.

'One o' myoldestfriends – dear, poor fellow – '

told him fetch m' daughter t'tend ailing brow – any-how, not far now,' added Mr Twite gladly, looking out of the window, where the rain was showing a disagreeable tendency to turn to snow.

After another half-hour's drive, Dido exclaimed, 'Croopus, Pa, we're a-crossing *London Bridge*! You never said as you was bringing me to London?'

'Did I not, my seraph? Ah dear me, what an absent-minded old fellow I am becoming, It is the power of music – the penalty of music.'

'Of music, Pa?'

'When I am engulfed in themes for a new serenade, a new suite, a new symphony – why, don't you see, that drives all other considerations out of my poor head. Tum, tum, terum, titherum, tarum, tarum, tiddle-I-dee!' And Mr Twite suddenly burst into vigorous song, the violence of which almost seemed as if it might shake him to pieces. He looked like an aged moulting thrush.

Dido, however, at this burst of musical activity, eyed him a little more respectfully.

'Are you making up some new tunes then, Pa?'

'I am always at it, my euphorbia. But, bless us, yes, my mind is at present engrossed – *engrrrr – osssed*,' he repeated, giving the word a slightly guttural, foreign accent, 'I am engrossed in a suite for a Royal Progress.'

'Like, you mean, when the king goes from St James's Palace to Hampton Court?'

'Just so, my poppet. I plan to call my suite the Royal Tunnel Music.'

'Why Tunnel Music, Pa?'

'Why, my chicken, you probably may not be aware, having been absent for so long on your travels, but the old king, King James, had, while he was alive, put in hand the work for a tunnel to be dug under the River Thames, running from Shadwell to Rotherhithe. This tunnel was, in fact, all but completed when he died, and the new king, King Richard – that is, ahem! – will open it at a grand opening ceremony shortly.' Under his breath Mr Twite murmured, 'And then, just won't there be fireworks! Oh, butter my whiskers.'

'So, is your Tunnel Music a-going to be played at the opening ceremony, Pa?'

'Well, my lovekin, that remains to be seen. But I hope so, I certainly do hope so.'

And Mr Twite gave several very emphatic nods, dislodging his moustache entirely. Dido thoughtfully picked it up from among the rushes and handed it to him.

Their carriage, having turned eastwards and gone past the Tower of London, now plunged into a maze of narrow streets that lay close to the docks – winding, slippery streets, littered with orange-peel, fish-heads and straw.

Children sailed boats in the filthy gutters, despite the worsening weather; tattered old women picked over dirt heaps, looking for bones or rags or bits of rusty iron; groups huddled round breakfast stalls, blowing the steam off mugs of coffee; little slattern girls carried baskets of water-cresses or shrimps, and shrilly called their wares.

'Juststopaminnit,' croaked Mr Twite, running all

his words together, as the carriage rolled past a corner tavern called the Two Jolly Mermaids; and he tapped on the panel and called out, 'Jarvey, jarvey, I say! Morel! Pull up, pull up. I *have* to wet my whistle.'

'His excellency gave me no instructions about stopping,' replied the driver.

His excellency? thought Dido. Who the pize can his excellency be, when he's at home?

'His excellency don't want a cove to die of thirst,' retorted Mr Twite, hastily ramming his moustache back into place. 'You stop here, and you can have a mug of Organ Grinder's Oil for yourself.'

'Oh, very well; tol-lol.'

The two men dismounted, the driver giving the reins into the hand of a boy who was pushing a wheeled coffee-stall along the road, presumably from its night quarters to its daytime position.

'Here, you! Mind these for a couple o' minutes and I'll give you half a jim.'

Dido made to follow her father, but he checked her.

'You'd best not come in, my dove; it's a sailors' tavern, not suited for your youthful innocence. I'll bring you out a mug of hot purl.'

Dido was about to protest that she had been in far wilder places during the course of her travels, but then it occurred to her that she might, while Mr Twite was in the public house, turn the time to good account. Accordingly, as soon as the two men had gone into the tavern, she stuck her head out of the carriage window, and said to the boy holding the horses, 'Hey, cully! D'you want to earn a brown?'

'I'd sooner a tanner,' retorted the boy, eyeing her shrewdly. 'Let's see the colour of your blunt.'

He was a stocky, round-faced boy, wearing a pair of leather smalls, rather too large for him, and over them a smock-frock which he had belted up with a dog-collar. His blue eyes were somewhat crossed, which gave him a carefree appearance; one of them looked hard at Dido, the other one stared over her shoulder. He was very freckled. Dido noticed that his coffee-stall looked neat and clean, and the brass urn was brightly polished.

She had a little money with her and was able to pull a silver sixpence out of her pocket and hold it up.

'Boil me! A real silver Simon. What d'ye want me to do?'

'You know the way from here to Chelsea!'

'Do I know my granma's patch box?' retorted the boy scornfully. 'Well?'

'Go to Chelsea, and ask for the Duke o' Battersea's house.'

'*Now* who're you gammoning? Go to the dook's house? He'd turn me over to the traps, sure as you're born. Who'd do that, even for a Simon?'

'No he wouldn't,' said Dido earnestly. 'He's a right decent cove, the dook – his name's Simon too – and he'll be glad to get word of me. You give him – ' she searched her person for something which she could send as a token, and finally pulled off one of the brass buttons from her sheepskin coat. 'You give him this here button,' she said, 'and tell him it's from

41

Dido Twite, that I'm with my pa on an urgent errand, I'm here in – where is this?'

'Wapping.'

'I'm here in Wapping, and I'll come to Chelsea as soon as I'm free. Got it?'

'I go to the dook, I tell him Died o' Fright's with her pa, an'll come to him as soon as she kin.'

'Right.'

'Let's have the mish, then.'

Dido handed over the sixpence, the boy took it, bit it, nodded sagaciously, and stowed it away among the folds of his breeches.

'Mind,' he said, 'I can't leave the coffee-barrer long enough to git all the way to Chelsea – that's a fair step, that be – but someone'll get it there.'

'What's your name?' asked Dido, wondering doubtfully whether she could really trust him, and wishing she had paper and pencil so that she could write Simon a note. How long would this business with her father take? Was he speaking the truth about this mysterious sick person? Did her father ever speak the truth?

Dido sighed.

'Name's Wally Greenaway,' the boy said, eyeing Dido with care, first out of one eye, then the other. 'Everyone round here knows me – my dad has the apple-stall yonder.'

He nodded to a barrow along the road, piled with russet apples. A tall, large-boned man sat behind it. Despite the cold wet morning he wore only a check waistcoat over shirtsleeves and drab breeches and a red belcher neckerchief. His hair was pale grey,

42

almost white. Dido thought that he was blind for he sat staring straight ahead without looking around him.

'Reckon I'll buy one of his apples,' she said, and scrambled out of the carriage. 'Pa's being mighty slow with that mug o' purl.'

A sign on the stall said '4 APPELS 1d.' On close inspection the apples looked rather wizened, but Dido was hungry and thirsty. Besides, if she bought the father's wares, the son might be more likely to do her business. Remembering a piece of advice that a sailor had once given her, she said to the boy, 'When's your birthday? Mine's the first o' March.'

When you talk to a savage or a native, Noah Gusset had said, *always tell him some secret about yourself – your birthday, your father's name, your favourite food – tell him your secret and ask him his. That's a token of trust; soon's you know each other a bit, then you can be friends.*

The question certainly had an electrifying effect on the boy Wally. He gaped at Dido as if she had told him that she was the Queen of Japan. He did not immediately answer.

Meanwhile Dido turned to the stall owner. 'I'd like one o' your apples, please, mister. Can I take this one with the leaf, in front?'

'They're four for a yenap, daughter.'

'I only want one.'

At that moment Mr Twite and the carriage driver emerged from the tavern, wafting strong fumes of Geneva spirit.

'Hey, cockalorum, what's this?' demanded Mr

43

Twite, in tones of strong disapproval, as he advanced. 'M'daughter hobnobbing with all the scaff and raff of London in the public street? That won't do, no it won't, by bilboes! Giving money and – and tokens – to barrow boys and crossing sweepers – chatting up louts and cads! Where's your sense of pride and propriety, child?'

And Dido's father, who must, she realized with dismay, have been watching through the tavern window, suddenly pounced on Wally Greenaway, shook him till his teeth rattled, and removed from him the button and the silver sixpence. Mr Twite pocketed the latter, and gave the former back to Dido, wagging his finger at her admonishingly and saying, with a knowing wink, 'Mustn't give coins and tokens to young lads in the streets, stap me, no, you mustn't! That's *flighty*, daughter, and owdacious – can't have ye demeaning the name of Twite, no, damme, we can't. Come along, come along now – bundle back in the carriage and look sharp about it.'

'*Hey* – leggo of me, Pa – ' Dido began furiously, but the driver was plainly prepared to assist Mr Twite in bundling his daughter into the carriage; she saw that resistance would be a waste of time and undignified as well.

But she was very angry indeed, affronted at being shamed in the presence of the boy and his father. Resolving to bide her time and to get away at the very first opportunity, she bit her lip, and climbed back into the stuffy conveyance.

The driver jumped back on to his box and Mr Twite was preparing to follow Dido when a voice called, 'Wait a minute! Wait just a minute, mister! You forgot something!'

It was the apple-seller calling after them – in a surprisingly loud, deep, resonant voice.

Mr Twite turned, startled and not pleased.

'You forgot her apple!' called the stall keeper, and he took an apple from the front of his stall and tossed it towards Mr Twite, who, more by luck than judgement, caught it in his left hand.

'Mister! You better watch out for that liddle maid!' called the apple-seller, warningly. 'She be a rare 'un, she be! I can see crossed sparkling lines over her head, an' a whole shower o' lucky stars. I can see a gold crown in her hand, look so, and a velvet carpet under her foot. So take good care of her, do-ee; or else the luck'll turn inside out for 'ee, and the shining lines'll turn to flint stones and sharp fangs, as'll strike and batter ye to the heart. There's a warning plain and clear for them as'll heed it!'

'Godblessmysoul!' ejaculated Mr Twite, looking quite pale and shattered at this unexpected harangue. Dismayed, he stared at the apple, then at the apple-seller, then, shaking his head from side to side as if wasps were buzzing round it, he clambered into the carriage and slammed the door.

'What next, I'd like to know?' he grumbled. 'Blind coster-mongers roaring out warnings – who the deuce do they think we are, King Solly the First and the Queen o' Sheep's Head Bay?'

But just the same, Mr Twite gave Dido a narrow, appraising look, as if wondering, perhaps for the first time, whether there might be more to her than met the eye; and he sat frowningly regarding her as the driver cracked his whip and the horses began to move once more.

'You better give me my apple, Pa, I'm hungry, and you never brought me that jossop you promised,' said Dido, and he absently handed her the apple. Noticing with interest that it was the very one she had asked for, the one with a leaf from the front row, she carefully polished it on her sheepskin sleeve and took a large bite. I never paid the blind cove for it, nor did Pa, she suddenly thought; soon's I can, I'll find out where he lives, or come back to his stall, and pay him a farden. I reckon he done me a good turn.

How good a turn, she did not realize.

But she did notice that the boy Wally was running alongside the carriage. Despite the inconvenience of his bunchy, belted smock and too-large trousers, he ran well, easily keeping pace with the horses as they broke into a fast trot.

Catching Dido's eye, he shouted something.

'What did the young ruffian say?' asked Mr Twite mistrustfully.

'He said his birthday's the ninth of December.'

'And what's that to the purpose? Why in daisy's name should we wish to know the birthday of a young guttersnipe like that? Does he expect us to send him a remembrance on the day?' peevishly demanded Mr Twite. Then, forgetting the boy, he stuck his arm through the handle, as the carriage gathered speed, and sat morosely observing his daughter as she munched her apple.

'He saw a gold crown in your hand – was that

what the fellow said? How the plague could the blind
rogue do that?'

'How should I know, Pa?' said Dido, nibbling
speedily round the core of the apple. 'But that's what
he said, sure enough. And a velvet carpet under my
feet. Maybe he means I'll go into the furnishing
trade.'

By now the boy, Wally, had fallen behind the
coach, but he shouted a word to another boy, a tow-
headed crossing-sweeper, who promptly dropped his
broom and broke into a run.

'Remember that song you used to sing, Dido?'
pensively remarked Mr Twite. 'Back in the dear old
days in Rose Alley when we all lived together in pre-
viousness and happy harmony, when your beloved
ma was still with us?'

Dido's chief recollection of that time was that her
ma used to feed her on cold fish porridge and thump
her with the fish-slice if she dared to grumble; that
her clothes had been too short and too tight, so that
she was often obliged to stay in bed for days on end
because she had nothing to wear.

'Which song was you thinking of, Pa?'

'Ah, many's the time we sung it together,' went on
her father with gathering enthusiasm. 'You a-sitting
on my knee and a-beating time with a pickle-fork in
your tiny fist. Didn't the words go:

> Oh, how I long to be queen, Pa
> And float in a golden canoe,
> Playing a pink mandoline, Pa,
> All up the river to Kew!

Was not that how the song went? I remember our voices used to mingle in it so happily!'

'The words didn't go quite like that, Pa,' said Dido, biting the last edible shred off her apple-core and tossing it out of the carriage window. It was pounced on by a skinny ginger-haired boy who had replaced the tow-head. 'But near enough, I daresay.'

'Perhaps those words foretold a Tremendous Truth!' exclaimed Mr Twite, on whom the Organ Grinder's Oil taken in the tavern had plainly worked a beneficial and reviving change. He gave Dido a tremendous smile, showing two sets of teeth the colour of Dutch cheese, then leaned forward and tapped commandingly on the panel.

'Not a drop more,' shouted the driver without turning his head.

'No, it ain't that, Morel. But I've changed my mind about going first to Cinnamon Court. Take us to t'other place, will'ee – Bart's Building.'

'My orders was to bring you to Cinnamon Court, with the kinchin. No other,' said the driver firmly.

'But, hang it, man, I've changed my mind. I don't *want* to go to the Court first. It's by far too early. His Nabs won't have ate his breakfast yet. He'll be all of a twitch. I want to go home and put on a clean cravat. Added to which, my dear little sprite here is tired and could do with a bit of shut-eye and a mouthful of furmenty.'

'Orders is orders,' replied the driver. 'It'd be as much as my neck is worth.'

'S'posing I was to tell Eisengrim about your little

affair in Fish Lane, that time when you'd orders regarding the garden gate?'

'You'd never!'

'Oh, wouldn't I, my game-cock? Don't bet your belt on that!'

'One o' these days you'll be found floating face down in the river,' said the driver sourly; but he turned his horses left, out of Wapping Lane, and made eastwards; this was a part of London wholly unfamiliar to Dido, but she noticed a sign that said Farthing Fields.

Soon the carriage rolled slowly down a narrow alley, and drew up outside a gaunt, blackened house that seemed to have slipped sideways at some point in its very long life, possibly because it had been built on a mudbank, for it stood close beside the swiftly flowing Thames. To stop the sliding tendency, half a dozen massive piles buttressed the riverside wall of the building, slanting into the muddy water like huge crutches. A rusty rail protected the house and ran down into the water. Most of the many windows were boarded over, and the doorstep was covered thick with green slime. The paint on the massive door was so blistered and flaking that it would have been hard to guess its original colour. A small court, a kind of bay, opened off the alley in front of the house; the driver halted his horses here, on the wet cobbles, having turned them first, as if anxious to get away from the spot as fast as he could.

'You'd best give me a chit for His Nabs,' he growled at Mr Twite, who pulled a notebook from his pocket, scribbled a few words, tore out a leaf, and handed it over.

'Tell him I'll be along in the wink of a cod's eye.'

'A likely tale!'

'And here,' said Mr Twite, scribbling on a second leaf, 'see *that* gets delivered too, will'ee? Send one o' the pages with it.'

Nodding gloomily, the driver took the second note. 'Won't there just be a spree when he gets your billy-doo, oh no! I wouldn't be in your shoes, my fine fiddle-guts, that I wouldn't!'

With which parting remark, the driver whipped up his horses and drove away, ignoring Mr Twite, who replied, unperturbed, 'His Nabs and I are just like brothers.'

At the entrance to Farthing Fields the coachman passed a small skinny boy who seemed particularly busy inspecting an apple-core he held in his hand, but threw a sharp look at the coach as it passed him, taking in the driver, the horses, and the coat-of-arms on the door panel.

Dido, chilled from the long ride, was quite eager to get inside, for the wet snow was now falling thickly. Her father was searching through all his pockets, apparently in vain, for a key. At last he rapped with the rusty door-knocker three times, at varying intervals: TAP, tap-tap; tap-a-tap TAP; tap-a-tap, TAP, TAP, TAP. There ensued a considerable pause, then, from within, a female voice cried, 'Who is it?'

'Desmond,' replied Mr Twite.

This surprised Dido, for her father's name was

Abednego; but it did not seem to surprise the person behind the door, for it began to open slowly.

Inside stood a raddled, sluttish woman, her dyed dark hair done up in curl-papers, which were partly covered by a large, gathered cap; she wore a frilly muslin wrapper, not very clean, over various petticoats, and greasy slippers on her feet; she held a heavy iron candlestick, which, as it contained no candle, Dido concluded was meant to be used in self-defence, if necessary. She was tall and plump, but her face was much wrinkled, especially round the pursed-up mouth; and her three-cornered eyes were extremely sharp and unwelcoming.

'Well, upon my word! It *is* you, Desmond! I thought you was meant to go direct to Eisengrim with the wench!'

The woman scowled at Dido, who scowled back.

'Changed my mind,' replied Mr Twite briefly. 'Let us in, Lily, and give us a bite o' breakfast. It's a devilish raw morning, I'm dry as a bone, and I want to collogue with you.' To Dido, he said, 'This, my dear, is Missus Lily Bloodvessel, as handsome and kind a lady as you'll meet this side o' Spitalfields.' He thought for a moment and added, 'Or the other side, either.'

Dido did not feel this to be much of a recommendation.

Nor did Mrs Bloodvessel appear to be at all happy to see Dido.

'Eisengrim won't be best pleased,' she observed shortly, making no movement to step aside and let them in.

'Fiddlestick, my amaranth,' retorted Mr Twite. 'Just you wait, and hearken to the bit of news I picked up from Polly at the Mermaids; and then see whether you don't agree His Nabs will be obliged to sing small. Plan B will have to go into operation – or my name's Othello Tudor. Come on, let us in, for pity's sake, we don't want to stand here parleying on the doorstep.'

'Oh – very well,' replied the lady slowly, giving Dido another resentful look. 'We'd best go down the area way, so's to clear out the lollpoops. It's almost their time. I was having a lay-in for I've a bad throat.'

For a moment Dido had wondered whether Mrs Bloodvessel could be the afflicted person that she was supposed to tend; but this did not seem likely, and she abandoned the notion altogether when Mr Twite said, as they descended the slimy steps that led to the basement entrance: 'You having a lie-in, Lily? That's not like you. I never knew you to be under the weather.'

'I got plenty to try me,' returned Mrs Bloodvessel darkly. She pulled a large rusty key from a bunch attached to her belt and opened the basement door.

'Everybody out!' she bawled in a voice so loud that it made Dido jump. 'Come on – out of it, you slummy little tadgers, you! And be quick about it! Time's up! One minute longer and you pay me another farden apiece.'

To Dido's amazement, out of the narrow door there began to appear what seemed like a never-ending stream of children, most of them barefoot, dressed in tatters, undersized, shock-headed, and bleary-eyed. They were yawning, rubbing their eyes, and shaking their heads as if to clear them, while they pushed past Dido and climbed the area steps. Some wriggled and worked their shoulders as if to relieve stiffness. One or two glanced curiously at Dido. Most still seemed half asleep. A strong reek of unwashed bodies came from them, and when Mrs Bloodvessel stepped through the door, beckoning her guests to follow, Dido found that the reek was even stronger inside.

'Eight-one, eighty-two,' counted Mrs Bloodvessel as the last yawning boy stepped through the door. 'There should be another, where is he? Come on, you — *get* out of there!'

The room they had entered was a dark, dank basement place, not large; Dido was astonished that so many children could have emerged from it. There was no furniture at all, not so much as a stool on the filthy floor. Dido was puzzled, also, by the forest of ropes that dangled from bacon hooks in the ceiling, with knotted loops at their lower ends, as if this were a kind of hangman's warehouse; then she guessed what their use must be as she saw Mrs Bloodvessel march over to a corner where a sleeping boy dangled motionless with his head, arms and shoulders through the loop of rope, and his feet dragging on the flagstones. He was so deep asleep that Mrs Bloodvessel exclaimed, 'Here, Desmond, roust this one up. Prod him, will you?' She extracted a long steel pin from her nightcap and handed it to Mr Twite, who jabbed it into the boy's arm. He woke with a yell, tugged his head and shoulders free from

the loop, and made off with terrified haste, as Mrs
Bloodvessel bawled after him, 'Six o'clock's striking!
Can't you hear Marychurch bells across the water?
Get out, you lazy young lollpoop, or you'll have to
pay for another night.'

When he had gone, Mrs Bloodvessel locked the
outer door behind him, and then proceeded to unlock
an inner one which gave on to a dark passageway and
a flight of steps.

'You go on up,' she ordered Mr Twite and Dido,
jerking her head at the stone stairs. As they did so,
she could be heard unlocking another door below.

'Look sharp and sweep the lollpoops' room and
sprinkle vinegar,' Dido heard her ordering somebody. 'And don't you dare drink any! There's just
half a gill in the bottle.'

Mr Twite and his daughter mounted to the ground

54

floor and entered a double room which ran from front to back of the house. It was rather dark, for the front window was boarded up, and so crammed with large mildewy pieces of furniture and piles of material that they had to edge their way slowly and with difficulty. By the back window, which gave on to a little muddy creek, a small area had been left free for occupation. Here was an armchair, a bamboo table, a frowsty couch, a pot of ornamental grass, a goldfish in a bowl, and dishes left from several meals on floor, table and mantelpiece. The whole place smelt strongly of cigar smoke. A fire, mainly coal dust, smouldered in a small grate.

'The comforts of home,' said Mr Twite contentedly, and sat down in the armchair.

Dido, who was beginning to feel exceedingly tired, looked around for somewhere to sit. The night had been spent in travel, the previous day had been a very active one; her legs ached and her head was heavy with sleep.

'Perch on the ottoman yonder, my sprite,' suggested her father. Following the direction of his nod, Dido saw what might be a sofa littered with books, bedroom ware and piles of linen. She had to climb over a sideboard, and past a pair of glass-fronted cabinets, to reach it. Shifting some books on to the sideboard, she cleared a space and curled up thoughtfully.

'Where's the sick cove I'm s'posed to nurse, Pa?' she croaked.

'We'll see him soon enough. Never mind that for now, my duckling. You rest yourself, taste a little of Lily's eggnog; that'll set you up like nought else.'

Just for the moment, Dido was glad enough to let go of her worries about Simon, and sink back into the soft grubby folds of the dustsheet that swathed the ottoman. She was so weary that her eyes began to close. Then she heard a thumping step as Mrs Bloodvessel entered the room and asked sharply, 'Where's the kid?'

'On the couch yonder. Make us a bit o' nog, Lily,' said Mr Twite in a wheedling tone. 'Look, I brought you a bottle o' canary wine from the Mermaids.'

'Oh – very well! Though with eggs at threepence a dozen – ' she grumbled. Soon Dido could hear the sound of eggs being broken and beaten, and the clink of a saucepan on the hob.

Wonder who His Nabs can be, that they all talk of, wondered Dido sleepily. He must be another o' these Hanoverians, working away to fetch Bonnie Prince Georgie over from Hanover land and tip King Dick off the throne.

Now and then she could hear the voices of her father and Mrs Bloodvessel.

'Pour in a drop o' wine, Desmond – not too plaguy much! A half cupful will do. Now the sugar. Now a pinch of – '

'Hush, my sybil. There! Nectar! Queen Juniper herself never tasted a finer brew. Here, my chickadee – put that inside you, and you'll soon be as spry as a new-born lambkin.'

Mr Twite actually exerted himself so much as to stand up and reach a long arm, holding a mug, across the intervening furniture to his daughter. Dido received the mug, which held a frothy yellow drink smelling of nutmeg and cloves. She tasted the liquid with caution, finding it highly spiced, but nourishing.

'Thank you, Mrs Bloodvessel,' she called politely, 'it's right tasty!' and received an ungracious grunt in reply.

Resettling herself, Dido sipped slowly and listened as much as she was able to the voices of her father and his lady friend. It's allus best to know what Pa's up to, she thought drowsily.

'So, tell me then, what Polly Tapster had to say? Though why you should pay any heed to *that* brass-headed mivey – '

'Polly's as staunch a Georgian as any, my love. We're lucky to have her in that ken, for Benge is a rabid royalist. And she hears all manner of tidings from seamen at that tavern. Now listen here – why, this very day – '

Mr Twite dropped his voice. Dido, listening with all her ears, could just catch the words, 'B.P.G. has stuck his spoon in the wall! Dead as a herring! News just come in from Bremen –'

'Lor!' said Mrs Bloodvessel. Even she seemed impressed with this information. 'Did he ever have any young 'uns?'

'Never wed. Neither chick nor child.'

'So what'll Eisengrim do now? You can't have a cause without a leader.'

'Eisengrim will have to fry other fish. Plan B.'

'What's Plan B? You can't have a party without a prince.'

A party without a prince, thought Dido. She imagined a party, a huge, marble-floored room filled with ladies and gentlemen in silk crinolines and satin breeches, waving their fans and drinking wine and waiting for the prince to walk in – waiting and waiting, waiting and waiting . . .

Heavy clouds of blue smoke began to fill the air as Mr Twite puffed on a pipe full of Vosper's Nautical Cut, and Mrs Bloodvessel lit a long brown cigar and smoked it.

'What about the kinchin?' Dido heard Mrs Bloodvessel say.

'Ah; we'd best put her somewhere where she can't wander . . .'

Dido fell asleep.

3

After several fruitless hours spent searching for Dido in the streets and environs of Petworth, and making inquiries of everyone he met, Simon had finally decided to return to London. He was very unhappy and worried about Dido, and left instructions with the Petworth constables that, if any word of her came through, he was to be informed at once. Then he drove off along the London road.

'I don't like it a bit, Matthew,' he said to his groom. 'Dido *wouldn't* just go off without a by-your-leave – it wasn't in her nature. Hang it, she was *pleased* to see me! And she was asking all manner of questions about our life in London and the house in Chelsea – I can't believe she went of her own accord. She wanted to come to London with me.'

'Happen she got snabbled,' said the aged groom gloomily. 'Someone see'd her with you – knowed you was the dook – reckoned as they could make a bit o' skin-money from her. Best you get back to the house i' Chelsea and wait; 'tis like you'll get a message asking for ransom.'

Simon frowned and shivered, shaking his head to dispel the horrible notion.

'Maybe! Yet I can't help wondering if her father has something to do with the business. She told me she'd seen him in Sussex not long ago – he was mixed up in the plot to stop King Richard's coronation. If *he* told her some tale – Yet Dido was never taken in by her father – '

'Maybe Miss Sophie'll have heard summat, time we gets home.'

They reached the house in Chelsea very late indeed for breakfast. Bakerloo House belonged jointly to Simon and his sister Sophie. It was really too large for them and their small staff of devoted servants, but by the terms of a Trust they were not allowed to do anything with it until Sophie came into her inheritance, on her eighteenth birthday. Then she had plenty of plans for it.

Sophie was bitterly disappointed and upset when she heard that Simon had found Dido and then, almost at once, lost her again.

'Poor little dear! How very strange! What in the world can have happened to her? Do you think you should advertise for her, Simon? Have her cried by the town crier? Or hang up placards in the streets offering a reward?'

'I am not sure that would be wise,' said Simon. He sat unhappily, nibbling without appetite at the enormous breakfast which the housekeeper, Dolly Buckle, had swiftly prepared and set before him. 'If we advertised – and someone who meant mischief had got hold of her – that would only add to her value for them – '

'Yes. I see. They would know how much *we* value

her. But oh – ' exclaimed Sophie, 'I am *so* disappointed! Dido Twite! To find her alive and well, after all this time we thought she was drowned! Where in the world can she have been?'

'*Every*where in the world, from what I could make out! The Galapagos Islands – and Nantucket – and New Cumbria – '

'How did she – ' Sophie was beginning, when Dolly Buckle came in again, curtsied, and said, 'Here's a note just come for you, Mester Simon.'

The note was short and to the point. It said:

> Dere Simon: I hav dissided that now you are a Dook I cant be your Freind. Ar stashins ar two far Apart. Good by will allus think of you.
>
> > Yrs affcctly,
> > Dido Twite.

Simon read this and bit his lip. Then he handed it to Sophie, who read it twice, very carefully, knitting her fine dark brows.

'Is this Dido's writing?' she asked her brother.

'How can I be sure? It is a long time since I have seen anything written by her. It could be, I suppose. Why not?'

Sophie turned over the paper and studied it.

'Why, Simon, look – this is music paper – ruled with sets of staves – the kind that songs and sonatas are written down on.'

'So it is! That makes me all the more certain that Dido's father must be mixed up in this business. He's a musician – he would be sure to have such paper.'

'Do you think he would hold Dido against her will?' asked Sophie doubtfully. 'Could he have told her that she must not be our friend? Might he have obliged her to write this? What is he like? You lived in his house – ?'

'Oh, he is a scoundrel. Yet somehow I don't see anybody obliging Dido to do anything she didn't mean to,' observed Simon with a grin. 'But then – could he perhaps have persuaded her that it would be opposing his cause to be friendly with a duke?'

'But Dido is not sympathetic to his cause! Not if she just foiled a Hanoverian plot to wreck the coronation – '

'No-o,' said Simon dubiously. 'But Twite *is* her father after all – '

'Who brought this note?' Sophie asked Mrs Buckle.

Unfortunately nobody had seen the messenger. The note had been found lying on the shelf of the porter's lodge.

'Why wasn't Fidd at his post?'

'He were a-reprimanding the children, Mester Simon.'

'What children?'

'The ones as allus keeps coming and playing may-games in the courtyard. Ten, twenty times a day he's obliged to chivvy 'em out. They're getting more cap-sical every week.'

'It is because the weather is growing so cold,' said Sophie in a troubled tone. 'Look, snow is falling now – in November! The children have to play games to keep themselves warm, poor dears.'

She spoke with deep sympathy; brought up on a

Poor Farm herself, until her noble birth was discovered, Sophie knew very well what it was to be cold and hungry.

'There now!' grumbled Mrs Buckle disapprovingly. 'They're at it again, this very minute, the young tinkers!' She pointed out of the breakfast-room window, which looked over the paved courtyard.

Sure enough, a party of about thirty ragged children was forming up to play some game, selecting one of their number to be It.

'Arminy, arminy, arminy,' they sang,
'My lover came over from Jarminy;
My lover came over from Bremen;
I gave him an apple, I gave him a lemon
And sent him off to heaven
One – two – three – four – five – six – seven!'

When the counting-out had been done, the girl chosen to be It went off and sat on the fountain with her back to the rest.

Fidd the old porter now came out of his lodge and was about to chase the group out of the yard, but Sophie flung open the window and called loudly, 'Leave them alone, Fidd, they aren't doing any harm!'

'That's as may be, Missie Sophie!' Fidd turned his aged tortoise head in Sophie's direction. 'Give 'em an inch, they take a furlong, *I* say! Let 'em in the yard, next thing they'll be a-scuttering all over the house like rats in a granary, before you can look two ways.'

'They can't play in the street, Fidd, it's too

dangerous there, with carriages galloping past all the time.'

Fidd retired to the porter's lodge, shaking his head dissentingly.

'I read in the paper, only today,' said Sophie, 'that there are ten thousand homeless orphan children in London — isn't that dreadful, Simon — ' She stopped, for Simon's eye had fallen on the newspaper she held out, and he gave a gasp of horror.

'Good heavens! The Dean of St Paul's, Lord Forecastle, and Sir Percy Tipstaff, all drowned on their way to visit the king — how shocking! The poor king will be so grieved! They were among his closest friends. Indeed, they were his only close friends. Poor man! I must write him a note of sympathy at once!'

Leaving his breakfast nearly untouched, Simon went off to the library.

But Sophie remained at the window, watching the ragged children in the courtyard.

Having chosen one of their number to be It, they were now leading her in solemn procession across the paved yard, chanting as they went:

'Bonnie Prince Georgie lies over the water
He don't rule over this land though he oughter
Bonnie Prince Georgie lies over in Hanover
Oh, why won't some wellwisher bring that
    young man over?
Our swords we will sharpen, our spears we will
    forge,
And it's up with the banner of Bonnie Prince
    George!'

The player chosen to be Prince George was now throned on a mounting-block and all the rest elaborately bowed and curtsied.

Then the actor playing Prince George toppled off the block and lay flat on the ground, while the others chanted, running round and round the fallen one:

'Bonnie Prince George, your breakfast is made!
He won't come down, he's dead in his bed.
Bonnie Prince George, your dinner is made!
He won't come down, he's dead in bed.
Bonnie Prince George, your supper is made!
He won't come down, he's stock-stone-dead.'

Each time they sang this the fallen figure twitched and then lay motionless again.

Finally they sang:

'Bonnie Prince George, your house in on fire!'

at which the 'dead' one jumped up and chased after the rest of them, shouting,

'Just wait till I catch you and I'll skin you alive!'

They all fled away shrieking, and the 'prince' caught one of them, and then the game started all over again.

Fidd the porter watched them, scowling; he thought it highly undignified that the Duke of Battersea's courtyard should be put to such a purpose. But at last the children became bored – or playing had warmed them enough to go back to their usual occupations. They began to drift away in clumps and groups, picking up, as they went, the trappings of their trade: trays of pencils, baskets of oranges or nuts, brooms, laces and ribbons; all the things they sold in the street.

Sophie noticed one of them, a small fair-haired boy, approach the front door of the house. She saw Fidd come charging out of his lodge, and she herself ran down the stairs to the front hall, so as to open the door and get to the child before Fidd reached him. She arrived just in time, as Fidd was about to pounce, growling '*Ho*, no! Not in there you don't go, my young warmint!'

'No, but I got a missidge!' gasped the boy. 'I'm on an arrant!'

'A likely tale!'

'Wait a minute, Fidd,' said Sophie. 'I wish to hear what the boy has to say.'

'And what are *you* doing, Lady Sophie, opening the door — that ain't dignified!' the old man scolded.

'Oh, pooh, Fidd! Go mind your lodge.'

'I gotta missidge for the Dook o' Battersea!' pleaded the boy.

'Have you indeed, my dear?' said Sophie. 'Then the duke shall be fetched. Tarrant!' she ordered a footman. 'Will you please ask his grace to step down here a moment?'

In a moment Simon came down. He was in the middle of his letter of condolence, had an ink blot on his finger, and looked rather put-about.

'What's the matter?' he asked.

'This boy has a message for you,' said his sister.

Instantly Simon became very alert. 'Yes? What is the message?' he asked the boy.

'Send them gummies away out o' hearing.' The boy jerked his head at Fidd and Tarrant. 'Now listen close.'

He brought his hand out of his pocket and opened it, disclosing a small, rusty, very chewed-looking apple-core.

'See this? It's all there were to bring. There were a token, but it got took back. And there were a Simon, but it got snabbled. And there were a missidge.'

'What did the message say?'

'Her birthday be the fust o' March. Name's Died o' Fright. She be with 'er pa and 'er'll come when 'er can. Got it?'

'With her pa,' repeated Simon. 'Where is she now?'

'I dunno.'

'Where do you come from?'

'Pimlico, I got the missidge. But it came a long way afore then. Lotsa bringers atwixt here and there. Whitechapel way, maybe. Or Spitalfields. All rosy?' said the boy, and slipped away, shaking his head as Sophie offered to reward him. They saw him dash through the gate and disappear into the traffic of the King's Road.

The brother and sister remained staring at one another in the doorway.

Then Sophie asked in a low voice, 'Is Dido's birthday the first of March, would you know?'

He frowned, and rubbed his brow.

'The first of March? How can I possibly remember?'

'The first of March is St David's Day,' offered Sophie helpfully.

'So it is! And – you are right – that *is* Dido's birthday. I remember her saying something about leeks, once – ' His voice trailed away, he stood gazing across the courtyard.

'Whitechapel. You don't think it would be any use searching for her, or telling the Bow Street Runners?' suggested Sophie.

Simon shook his head. 'It would be looking for a grain of sand in the desert. And the boy only said *maybe* Whitechapel. But at least she said she will come when she can. Dido is certain to keep her promise.'

Sophie gently took the rusty apple-core from her brother.

'At least,' she said, 'we know that she is safe.'

When Dido next woke up, it was with an aching head, and a mouth that tasted, she thought with disgust, just like that musty, fusty room in the basement where all the kids spent the night, dangling in nooses. What had Mrs Bloodvessel called them? The lollpoops. And she charged them a farthing a night. Eighty-three of them she had counted out the door . . . so that meant she made over one shilling and eight pence a night – enough to buy three or four pounds of meat or five pots of beer. She's a right shrewd one, that Mrs B., thought Dido, raising herself up on one elbow – which caused another sharp scrunch of pain to run through her head. Massy me, what's up with me? Could it be that yellow jossop she gave me. It did taste mighty spicy. Maybe she put a hocus in it.

Doing her best to ignore the hammer blows inside her skull, Dido struggled up into a sitting position. To her surprise, she found that she was not in the place where she had fallen asleep. Great fish swallow us, I *must* have been deep under, not to know about it when they carried me here.

The room in which she now lay seemed to be an attic, judging from the steep slant of the ceilings and the triangular dormer windows. Scrambling to her feet – she had been curled up on a straw pallet on the floor – Dido pattered over to one of the windows and looked out. Sure enough, she was high up – she could see dozens of distant steeples, the huge black dome of St Paul's, with its cross and ball of gold gleaming through a thin snow that fell like a curtain; closer at hand there were cranes and ships' masts and the grimy bulk of warehouses. Peering out to her left, Dido saw the wide Thames, running swift and black, snatching away the white snow as it fell, turning it to frothy dark water; one or two ships were ploughing up-river against the tide with ruffles of dirty foam against their noses. Pushing open – with some trouble – the cracked and grimy window, Dido took several deep sniffs of rusty-smelling sharp air into her lungs and felt a little better. She looked down, but could not see the street below; the window opened on to a ledge of roof, with a railed parapet along the edge, which was already beginning to be outlined in snow.

I could use a drink o' water, thought Dido, looking at the river, and turned back into the attic. Its door was shut and, she found when she tried it, locked; she rattled it vigorously, and yelled, 'Hey! Lemme outa here! Lemme out!' several times, but nobody came and nobody answered.

Reconsidering the room, Dido found a pint mug full of water and a chamber-pot. Apart from these articles, and the straw mattress, with its single worn blanket, the room was unfurnished, and quite cold. Philosophically, Dido drank the water, made use of the pot, and then, squatting down on the mattress again, wrapped the blanket round her shoulders while she meditated.

What's all this about? Some weaselly scheme o' Pa's; some of his Hanoverian dealings, that's for sure. Let's think, what was they a-talking about while I was drinking that mickey liquor? Something about B.P.G. What did Pa say? I know: he said B.P.G. has stuck his spoon in the wall. So who is B.P.G.? Was B.P.G. the one as Pa wanted me to look after?

After a moment or two of thought the solution came to her. Love a duck! It's Bonnie Prince Georgie! He's hopped the twig! He's kicked the bucket! That's it for a certainty! Now I remember Mrs B. saying, 'You can't have a party without a prince,' just afore I passed out.

Bonnie Prince Georgie has took and died on them.

So what'll Pa and his cullies do now? They'll just have to pipe down and make the best o' King Dick.

But no, Dido recollected, her father had said something else. Someone – she could not remember the name – 'has other fish to fry.'

Fish, thought Dido; wish to goodness I had a few fish to fry. A sudden pang of hunger made her get up and rattle the door again. She yelled, 'Hey! I'm starving in here. What's the idea?' Still there came no answer.

No use staying in here if I can find some way to get out, Dido decided. If it can't be the door, then it'll hatta be the window.

Pushing the casement wider open, she hoisted herself up, got a knee over the sill, and scrambled out on to the ledge, which ran along the edge of the roof outside. The parapet was only six inches high; kneeling against it, Dido squinted down through small, stinging snowflakes, and found there was a sheer drop to the street a long way below; the house must be four, perhaps five storeys high. Can't let meself down by the blanket, thought Dido; firstly it ain't big enough, even if I could tear it into strips; and secondly I wouldn't trust it above half, so moth-eaten as it is. Let's see what's round the corner.

On hands and knees, proceeding carefully, for the narrow ledge was aswim with wet snow, she crawled leftwards, towards the river end of the house. Humph! There's those timbers a-slanting down to the river. Could slide down one o' those, maybe . . .

Not over enthusiastic about this possibility – for the bulky piles were very steeply slanted, and slimy-looking with age and weather – Dido explored on around the other two sides of the roof. But she found that the sloping buttresses did, in fact, offer her only

chance of escape. She had hoped there might be a way of climbing across to the roof of another house, but a yard, bordered by a creek, lay at the back, and on the fourth side of the house a gully, three storeys deep and too wide to jump, separated her from the next house in the alley. And, even if she could clear the gully, the house on the far side had only a sloping slate roof to land on, white, now, with snow; I'd roll off there like an egg, Dido thought, that would be no manner o' use at all.

No: it's got to be a slither down one o' the joists, I reckon; like it or lump it. Resolving to lump it, she returned to the river end of the house and glumly surveyed the sloping piles once more. There were five of them, and they met the wall of the house some six feet below the parapet over which she peered. Slanting outwards, they went into the river about fifteen to twenty feet away from the ground floor of the house; twenty feet of swirling, frothing, freezing Thames water. But the end pile, the westward one, entered the water only a short distance from the iron fence, embellished with spikes, which ran out past the house and curved into the water.

If I can climb down that joist, thought Dido – and it'll be as quick as a monkey sliding down an organ grinder's stick – I ought to be able to reach across and grab the railing – if the beam ain't so slimy I shoot straight into the water. Thing is to try and go slow. Well: best get it over and done with, light's going fast, shan't be able to see in ten minutes.

The parapet had a stone rail, or coping, on top, supported by a row of fat little stone or plaster balusters, their fatness diminishing to thinness down below; wonder if they'll hold my weight, thought Dido carefully, shaking one of them. It joggled. She tried another, which seemed firm enough. Returning to the attic, she had one more go at yelling and thumping on the door. Nobody answered. Be blowed to 'em, thought Dido. She removed the blanket from the mattress and poked it through the casement, climbed out, crawled along the ledge with it, and doubled it around the baluster she had chosen, so that the ends hung down on either side; then, holding on to the blanket, she scrambled over the parapet and let herself down towards the end beam. Just as she felt the timber with her feet, the baluster pulled away from its rotten foundation and crashed past her, cleaving the water far below. Dido fell too, but was able to grab the beam when she hit it, and hung on tightly, wrapping her arms and legs round it. She began to slide down backwards, much faster than she liked, unable to get a proper hold of the slimy, slippery, massive timber. Luckily it was not regular in shape, but just a tree-trunk, propped against the end of the house; soon various lumps and bumps on it slowed down Dido's progress. They also bruised her and banged her. Never mind – she had not been stunned or knocked into the water by the falling baluster, which might easily have happened.

If this were a fair, thought Dido, they'd charge you a penny and call it the Jungle Glide; and I'll be tarnal lucky if I don't get a sousing at the bottom.

But no: she managed to reach over and grab the rusty fence as she neared the bottom, and then swing across to it, scraping her hands rather badly and getting her trousers soaked in the process. Her feet trailed in the water, and at first, kicking about, she could find no purchase for them; gritting her teeth, she hoisted and dragged herself up by her arms, edged a knee on to the bottom rung of the railing, and so managed to work herself along the fence to its street end.

'Not bad!' said Dido, very pleased with herself; and she stepped ashore on the green-weedy, cobbled ramp that formed the end of the alley, running down to the river. Her knees felt weak and trembly; she waited for a minute or two, holding on to the fence, until her legs were stronger and her head stopped banging, then set off resolutely, but quietly, towards the landward end of the alley. Passing the steps which she had gone down that morning with her father and Mrs Bloodvessel – was it only that morning? it seemed a very long time ago – she noticed a green and tarnished sign on the rail that said *Bart's Building* in barely readable letters. Probably once upon a time the place had been a warehouse.

She was just tiptoeing, with great caution, past the front door when, to her utter dismay and annoyance, it opened, and her father stepped out.

'There now!' he said gaily. 'Now isn't that a quincidence! Sink – sink – sinkro – nicity. Why, we might have – hic – arranged to meet on this spot by apple-pointment – hic – I never experienced anything so simmle – simmle – simmle-taneoglous. Lily had just said to me, "Denzil, what was that splash in the river? I do show – so hope," says she, "that wasn't your dear daughter, our divine Dido, a-falling to her death." "No, no, my angel," says I in reply, "our canny little Dido would never do anything so – hic – harumscarum and headstrong, not to say – hic – so downright ungiggle-grateful as to climb out the window. But," said I, " 'tis an excellent thing, my love, you reminded me of our dear little sprite, for 'tis high time I took her along to meet our friend and bigglebenefactor. I'll step out the door a moment," says I, "to see if it snows, and then rouse up our little Angle from her slumbers." And out I steps. And, who should I see, a-coming along the lane, but her own self – all a-ready for our outing, and frisky as a lamprey.'

Dido could see that her father was the better – or worse – for a good many mugs of Organ Grinder's Oil. He grasped her tightly by the arm and marched her along the lane at a smart pace, sometimes singing to himself:

> 'Oh, tooral-aye-ooral-aye-ingle
> Oh tangle and tingle and tea
> A man will live longer if single
> Or that's what it looks like to me . . .'

Sometimes he shook Dido's arm and mumbled, 'You wasn't trying to *run away*, was you, daughter? Not from your own dear diddle-dad as loves you so? No, no, you'd never do a thing like that, stap me, you wouldn't be so ungiggle-grateful.'

Dido, angry and thwarted, said nothing; if only,

she kept thinking, if *only* I hadn't waited a minute by that fence, if only I'd run off directly, I'd have got clear away before Pa ever came out. What a clunch I was! Another time I'll know better . . .

At the corner, Mr Twite stopped. There was a man standing on the pavement, under a street-lamp. His face, shaded by the wide brim of his three-cornered hat, was not visible, but he and Mr Twite evidently knew one another. They nodded.

'See that cove, daughter?' said Mr Twite, as they walked on.

'What of him?' growled Dido.

'He's the Margrave's watchman. He's set there to keep – to keep an eye on the neighbourhood. Once he sets eyes on you, you'd get no farther than you could throw a cushion – not unless you was with me.'

To this, Dido made no reply.

At the next corner – where there was another watching man in black cloak and hat – Mr Twite stopped, hiccuped several times, and said, 'Daughter!'

'Well, what, Pa? Where are we going?'

'To visit our friend and protector. Our champion, guardian, patron, supporter, de – hic – liverer and libbler-ator.'

'What's his name?'

'Eisengrim. He's the Margrave – '

'What's a Margrave?'

' – The Margrave of Bad Nordmarck.'

Dido could not decide whether her father was frightened or angry. He had become rather quiet, stopped singing, and frowned a good deal. Holding Dido's arm in a punishing grip, he said, after a few more minutes' walking, 'Now listen to me, my chickadee!'

'Yes, Pa, what?'

'Where was you a-running to, just now?'

'That's my business, Pa.'

'Were you a-running to that friend Simon of yours? Because – you take my word for it, my blossom, you better *not*. I told you that was my friend the Margrave's man back there. You'll see a-plenty of 'em around here. And they'll see *you*. Wherever you go, it'll be known. You go to your friend Simon, he'll be eels' meat afore he's a day older. You know what happened to King Dick's friends – Fo'castle and Tipstaff and the Dean? They're a-floating down the river to Gravesend at this very minute on their backs, nibbled by dace. And there'll be others to follow 'em. Lord Raven's next on the list. And your friend Simon'll be the one after, sure as you're alive, if you go scampering off to him. See? If you want to keep him walking about and eating bread-and-butter – if you know what's good for him – you'll stay with me. Comprenny?'

Dido was silent.

'There's a job for you to do here,' Mr Twite went on. 'When that's done, *then* we'll see.'

'What'll we see, Pa?'

'Why, we'll see whether it'll be safe for you to go and visit your friend Simon.

Simple, simple Simon,'

sang Mr Twite,

> 'Met an apple pieman
> Bought a pair and et them there and – '

'Pa?'

'Yes, my diggle-duckling?'

'What *is* this job? How long will it take?'

'Isn't that just why I'm *taking* you to our benefactor? That's where you will hear *all* about it. *All* about it,' repeated Mr Twite, walking much faster now, practically dragging Dido behind him round several corners, almost all of them guarded by the Margrave's watchmen.

As they went along, Mr Twite embarked on what seemed to be a rehearsal of his intended conversation with his patron, muttering different phrases over to himself experimentally.

'This is my little chick-child, excellency. Look at her with wonder – use her with tact and tenderness. You will not find her like in the whole of – Margravia. Or even in Belgravia. Not this side of Habakkuk Corner. She is a veritable chip off the old block – an unbidden, unchidden spirit – '

'Unchidden, Pa?'

'Hold your hush, will you!' snapped Mr Twite, and dragged Dido still faster.

He was a most awkward person to walk along the street with, as he moved neither to the right nor left, choosing a way for himself, but taking no account of whether Dido was obliged to hop over obstacles, or round people coming in the other direction, or over holes, or through puddles.

The ways they passed along, at first narrow, black, and murky, gradually became wider and more respectable. But this part of London was notably quiet. Perhaps it was the unseasonably early snow, or the time of day, but hardly a soul was to be met in the street, not a passer-by, not a chaise, not a wagon, not a tumbrel. A few of the Margrave's cloaked and hatted guards stood in their places or went about their business, whatever that was. There were no women to be seen, no children. Where did all the lollpoops go, Dido wondered, who lodged nightly in Mrs Bloodvessel's basement? Did they take themselves off to livelier parts of the town, to make their living in the streets?

'Who is the Margrave of Bad Thingummy, Pa?'

'He's a Great Man, daughter – that's what he is. His anciggle-hiç-ancestors go all the way back through history – all the way back to Adam. He's an Aristocrat. And – what's more to the purpose – he's a Musician. He values music as he ought. Got more of it in his little finger than old King Jamie had in his whole corpus. And if – and if matters fall out as hoped,' said Mr Twite, hesitating for a moment and then going on rapidly, 'if ciggle-circumstances fall out prosperously for us, *then* your old da will be conducting the Phiggle-harmonic Orchestra, and will be appointed Musician to the Royal Bedchamber and Master of the King's Music. How about *that*, my chickabiddy? Us'll have a mansion in the Strand, a carriage-and-four, and twenty footmen to open the door when you come in outa the street. And a page in buttons for your very own.'

Dido found and held the brass button in the pocket of her sheepskin coat.

Did that boy carry my message? she wondered. And then felt an icy chill of fear as she recalled her father's warning. Even if I do manage to scarper off, I better not go near Simon. Pa really meant what he said, I'm sure of that.

Reckon I'd better stay with Pa, and do this job, whatever it is?

At the end of a fairly wide street, Mr Twite and his daughter stopped in front of a handsome brick mansion, approached by a noble curving flight of brick steps. A porter, who stood in a box by its impressive pair of iron gates, stepped out, inspected a card that Mr Twite showed him, then nodded and gestured them in. Another man, at the double front doors, inquired, 'Name?'

'You know me, Fred!'

'Name?' repeated the man impassively.

'Bredalbane, for Habakkuk's sake! And this is my little chick-child.'

'Name?'

'Dido – I told you that I dunnamany times!'

'Mr Bredalbane and Miss Dido Bredalbane!' bawled the doorman, and they ascended another flight of stairs. Rows of pages, dressed in black velvet suits, stood on either side, looking at nothing. Boring for 'em, thought Dido. The house was very grand, with crystal chandeliers, gilt chairs, marble statues, and thick velvet carpets. Dido, cold and dripping in her wet midshipman's trousers, began to feel out of place. Still, it's warm here, she thought; that's one blessing.

They turned off the main staircase and Mr Twite led the way along a gallery, down more marble steps, and into a little black and white music room. It was circular, with a white marble floor and columns, and two rings of grey-velvet-covered benches. Four musicians sat waiting for Mr Twite. From their patient look, they had been waiting for a long time. One sat ready at a harpsichord, two held hoboys, and the last one had a fagott. Mr Twite nodded briefly at them, picked up another hoboy which was lying ready on a music stand, gestured with it, and they all began to play.

Dido glanced about her. Wet as she was, she did not think it right to sit on one of the grey velvet seats, so she settled herself crosslegged on the white marble steps that led down to the musicians' plinth in the middle.

Wisht I had a bite to eat, she thought, sighing – for she knew full well how long her father and his mates were capable of going on, once they all got to playing together.

After a few minutes, though, the sheer beauty of the music made Dido forget her need for solid nourishment. Pa really can toss it out, she thought happily and dreamily. She was interested, though not at all surprised, to see that, as soon as he began to conduct, the last traces of alcoholic fuddlement dropped away from Mr Twite, and he became wholly intent on the matter in hand. Dido felt certain that the music the group were playing was his own, for she recognized several themes in it – the one she had once used to call 'Calico Alley'; and 'Black Cat Coming Down Stairs', and another one which she remembered without a name; it was very sad . . . They were all cleverly knit together, like strands in a piece of woven material, so that first you heard one of them, then another, then they twined round each other to make a new strand, then that crossed over yet another and showed itself in a different character, cheerful instead of gloomy, or dark instead of bright. It's like that thing you look through, with mirrors, and the pieces all slide about, thought Dido, remembering a peep-show at the Battersea Fair. If this Margrave of Bad What'shisname can get Pa made Master of the King's Music, then it's no more than he deserves. Pa's music is the best I ever heard; and I reckon he *ought* to have a house in the Strand with twenty footmen . . .

She sat rapt, with her elbows on her knees and her chin propped on her doubled fists; almost an hour had passed before a slight noise behind caused her to turn her head. She saw that a large, rather fat man, grandly dressed in a velvet suit, had come in and sat himself down in a gilded chair with silk cushions that stood on a small marble platform by itself. Mr Twite continued conducting the music, regardless of the new arrival, but the other four players hesitated a moment, and the rhythm was lost. The Margrave – for Dido guessed that it was he – gestured them to go on playing, so they stopped, went back a few bars, started again, and finished the piece.

'Bravo, gentlemen,' said the Margrave. 'That was most pleasing. I am obliged to you.'

He had a light, high voice.

Pleasing, thought Dido, it was a lot more than *pleasing*. A *whole* lot more.

'Now you – ' the Margrave nodded imperiously at the harpsichordist, the hoboy and fagott players – 'all of you retire. I wish to speak to Bredalbane.'

The players bowed and retired with silent speed.

'No doubt, Bredalbane, this is your daughter?'

The Margrave's eye rested coldly on Dido.

'Dido!' hissed her father. 'Make your curtsy to his excellency!'

How's a person going to curtsy when they're wearing sopping-wet middy's breeks? thought Dido crossly. Instead she got up and ducked her head politely at the nobleman, then sat down again, despite her father's reproving scowl and warning gesture.

'Yes, my lord – this is my little Dido – the neatest little craft as ever sailed along Battersea Reach.'

Pa's allus silliest when he's scared, thought Dido; what is there in this fat fellow to scare him so? Why don't Pa stand up to the Margrave of Thingembob?

She lifted her eyes and met those of the Margrave. *Blimey*, she thought – *now* I see what has got Pa so rattled. This man is like – what is he like? He's like summat I've seen somewhere not so long ago . . .

Chasing the memory, which slipped away from her like a fish in dark water, she studied her father's patron. The Margrave of Nordmarck was tall, and fat, but not immensely so; his black hair appeared to be dyed, but there was quite a lot of it; his colour was high – maybe from rouge – and his skin was shiny; he carried himself with a kind of carefree dignity, as if everything he had ever tried turned out successfully. He wore stays: Dido could hear them creak, just a little, when he breathed. His velvet suit was of deep, dark blue, and his snow-white shirt had ruffles at throat and wrist; diamonds flashed on his fingers and in his ears and ruffles and the buckles of his shoes.

He's wicked, thought Dido; wicked clean through and through.

Then she remembered what his cold, unmoving eye had recalled to her: once, when she was aboard a whaling vessel, she had been allowed to go out in a rowing-boat and a huge shark had followed and rubbed its great spine along the keel of the dory, observing the crew of the boat with a chill, passionless, round eye, showing its rows of ghastly teeth as it rolled; this man is like that shark, Dido thought. He'd swallow you and never notice he'd done it.

'Your daughter appears to be wet,' said the Margrave gently.

'She fell in the river, my lord . . .'

'She had best change her attire,' the Margrave continued, observing with distaste how Dido was dripping on the white marble steps. 'My steward will find her something – '

He nodded towards the door where a man in black jacket and striped trousers waited.

'Go with Boletus, my love,' said Mr Twite hastily. 'His excellency is so kind as to – '

Dido went with the steward and was swiftly fitted out with a page's uniform of black velvet, muslin collar, and gilt buttons.

'Not bad at all,' she said, regarding herself carefully in the glass.

'His lordship does not care to be kept waiting.'

'All right, I'm a-going – '

Indeed Mr Twite was anxiously pacing about the entrance to the music room, while his master remained seated in the gilded chair.

'Now, my angel, tell his excellency how you met the Pre – how you met King Richard.'

'There ain't a lot to tell,' said Dido, surprised. 'It was on account o' the Georgians a-fixing to knock down St Paul's at the crowning. Me and my mates had got inside the church to warn the king afore he was crowned. He ain't a bad cove – quite a deal of sense, he has. He was up in the top o' the church, chewing the rag with the old Dean, playing cards. We had a bit of a parley. And then he got the folk down in the church a-singing hymns while the constables went round, looking for the Georgian coves and sorting them out. He sure knows a sight of hymns, King Dick do. And then – arter that – he said me and another gal and a couple o' boys should carry his train at the crowning . . . That's all there is to it, really.'

'So you were talking with the – with the king for an hour or two before his coronation. And then carried his train. Would you know him again?'

'O' *course* I would,' said Dido testily. 'I'm not thick!'

'Dido!' hissed her father.

'Beg pardon, yer lordship.'

'And you would recognize his voice? You remember the way he speaks?'

'Sartin sure I would; he speaks rather quick and short, like a Scotsfeller. That's what he is.'

'Look at these pictures and tell me which is his likeness.'

Boletus the steward laid out twenty or so portraits on the velvet benches. They were all very similar – slight, active-looking men in their thirties with long noses, weatherbeaten skin, bright grey eyes, and reddish hair. Some were smiling, some serious, Dido considered them all, slowly, once, then again. Then she put her finger on one and said, 'That's him.'

Mr Twite looked up anxiously at the Margrave, who nodded.

'Yes, she knows him. But has she the ear for a voice?'

'She has *my* ear,' said Mr Twite with much more assurance.

The Margrave nodded again, slowly.

'Very well. She may – for the time – instruct the replacement. We shall see if he makes good progress. If not – '

Mr Twite, already rather pale, became paler at that *if not*.

'My daughter is a very clever girl, your excellency – '

'We shall see,' repeated the Margrave impassively. His expressionless eyes moved from Dido to her father. 'Have you completed the Tunnel Music?' he asked.

'V-very nearly, your worship. The last movement must be a Coro. That is not quite com –'

'It is of no moment. I do not at present see how it can be used at the Tunnel Opening. The Pretender is not yet – ah – displaced. Your music must be held over for a subsequent occasion – a Firework Progress, perhaps.'

'Fireworks?' muttered Mr Twite, sounding anything but pleased.

'You. What about the other two who carried the royal train at the coronation – the two boys and the girl?' suddenly demanded the Margrave of Dido. 'Where are they?'

'One of 'em's gone off to Wales with his dad, sir; Owen Hughes, that is; and the other two has gone back to Sussex where they lives.'

'Very well – they are out of the way,' murmured the Margrave. 'You may leave me, Bredalbane. Leave the child here, in Cinnamon Court.'

Mr Twite seemed utterly dismayed at this order. He stammered, 'B-beg pardon, your eminency – but wouldn't it be better – don't you reckon – if Dido was to teach the cove round at our place? At Bart's Building? It'd be quieter there. She – she'd not feel easy in – in your lordship's house; 'tis much too grand, she's not accustomed – '

'Oh? Very well. Mijnheer X shall be escorted to Bart's Building later this evening. Now leave me, if you please.'

'Your lordship don't want any therapeutical music this evening – ?'

'No. I am well. Leave me.'

Mr Twite scuttled away, dragging Dido after him.

'Hey! Wait a bit, Pa! I want my own cloes and sheepskin jacket back,' she protested, as he was about to whisk her out through the front entrance. 'Look – there's that Boletus chap – I'll ask him for them – '

'Oh, never mind them, my sparrow – I'll get you others – '

But Dido, knowing the nature of her father's promises, disengaged herself from his nervous clutch and asked the steward for her clothes.

'I'll make sure this rig is sent back to you soon's my breeks are dry,' she said politely.

Boletus curtly instucted a page to find the clothes – 'if they have not already been burned,' he added.

Dido's mouth and eyes opened wide at this, but fortunately, before she could speak her mind about people who burned up other people's trousers, a red-headed page was able to produce the damp bundle. He looked a little downcast as he handed it to Dido; she wondered if he had planned to sell her clothes to a rag-man. 'Thanks, cully, much obliged,' she said to him gruffly. 'I sets store by that-there jacket; a pal gave it to me.' Hoping to soften his disappointment, and remembering the apple-boy, she added, 'My birthday's March the fust. When's yours?'

His face lit up. 'July second!' he whispered. 'In the days of Queen Dick!' and he gave Dido a quick, friendly grin before dashing away up the marble stair.

'Who's this cove I've got to teach, Pa?' Dido asked, as she and her father walked homewards.

Mr Twite seemed very preoccupied. '*Fireworks*,' he was muttering. 'Fireworks and promises – both made to be blown to blazes! Yet it is true matters are in a different train now that the Prince Over the Water is under the ground – '

'Is it true then, Pa – that Bonnie Prince Georgie has croaked?'

'*Hush*, child! Mind your tongue in the open street!' Mr Twite glanced round warily. But the streets of Wapping were even emptier than before; it snowed harder than ever. He added in a low tone, 'Yes, I fear that our gallant leader is no more. Alas! But –' brightening up, 'his excellency the Margrave is never at a loss. Such a mind! Such a sagacity! He has already found an alternative. But let me think now – let me think – how my Tunnel Music can be brought into play.'

'An alternative?' said Dido slowly. 'Oh, *now* I begin to twig. Was that what His Nabs meant by "the replacement"? The cove that I'm to teach? But what am I to teach him? Don't he speak English?'

'Why, as to that, my dove, I really cannot say,' her father answered hastily. 'But I am very sure that you will be able to instruct him in whatever is needful – and so I told his excellency – you are such a remarkably clever chick! And you had better do so, and quickly – mind that!' he added. 'It was only because I persuaded the Margrave as to – as to your special knowledge – that he agreed to give you a trial. Otherwise, believe me, you would by now be floating in the Pool of London along with Lord Forecastle and the others. – And *that* would be a hem waste,' he added to himself, 'if what the costermonger said is right.'

Dido stared frowningly at her father; then walked along beside him in silence, deep in thought. The Margrave is arranging for all the king's friends to be killed off, she thought; or anyone who knows him to speak to. There aren't many of those. Why's he doing that? So as no one will cut up rough when this other cove is fetched in? But who is the other cove – the one I'm to teach? Bonnie Prince Georgie's son? His brother? – And *that's* why Simon is in danger, she thought – because he knows the king, he said so. Croopus, things around here are in a rabshackle way. I ought to warn Simon; but if I sent a message it might just make more danger for him.

One thing's for certain, she thought; that Margrave is a right spooky devil. I sure don't go for him above half. And here's Pa, a-readied to lick a path for the guy, all the way down the stairs and out into the street, do he only say the word. It's fair disgusting.

'Pa,' she said after a while, 'that was a ripsmashing piece that you and the others was a-playing on your fagotts and hoboys.'

'Naturally it was,' her father replied absently. 'I am the greatest composer of these times.'

'What's it called?'

'It is my Eisengrim Concerto number three. I am writing a set of seven in honour of the Margrave.'

'*Must* you work for that pesky fellow, Pa? I don't like him.'

'My sylph, he is the only one who appreciates me.

Furthermore, if King Richard's officers were aware of my presence in London, I would be hanged up directly, like a flitch of bacon. A musician of my calibre!'

But that ain't to do with your music, thought Dido, it's naught to do with music; it's on account of your havey-cavey Hanoverian dealings.

Oh, why can't people do just *one* thing, instead of being so muxed-up?

She sighed and said, 'I ain't half hungry, Pa.'

'I could peck a bit myself,' he said. 'we'll send the Slut round to the cooked-meat shop.'

The Slut, Dido wondered. And who may the Slut be?

They were now back in Farthing Fields, and soon turned into Farthing Court, the narrow alley in which Bart's Building stood. Dido had a momentary impulse to take to her heels and make a dash for it; she could easily outrun her father and would soon be clear away from him in the network of dark silent streets. She could ask her way to Chelsea . . . But there was the man in the three-cornered hat at the end of the street. 'Once he'd seen you, you'd get no farther,' her father had said.

And then Simon would be in horrible danger. Maybe things is best as they are, Dido thought. The way I'm fixed here, teaching this Mijnheer X, whoever he be, mayhap I can find out more about what old Margrave Eisengrim is up to, and put a spoke in his wheel. He's one as'll bear watching, that's certain. I reckon it'd be a good thing for King Dick if that one were under hatches.

Mr Twite had brought a key with him this time and used it to unlock the door. As they re-entered the black, silent, leaning house by the water's edge, Dido asked, 'Do this house belong to Mrs Bloodvessel, Pa?'

'She rents it from the Margrave, child,' he replied absently. 'The Margrave owns much property hereabouts.' He was paying little heed, for, as they passed through the door, loud hysterical sobs could be heard coming from the room where, that morning, Dido had been given the over-spiced eggnog.

When they entered the room – which was thick with blue cigar smoke – Dido found that the source of the noise was Mrs Bloodvessel, who seemed very afflicted, crying, wailing, and shrieking, throwing herself back and forth in an armchair until she nearly tipped it over, and exclaiming at the top of her lungs that savage ants were walking over her.

'Oh! they bite! Oh! they sting! They are drilling holes right through me! Yellow and creeping and biting and boring! Ants, ants, and devilish pinching crabs!'

'Mercy, what's amiss with her?' said Dido, startled and shaken. 'I don't see no ants.'

'Ah, it is a mere hysterical spasm. It will pass. I know what she needs,' said Mr T·wite, who did not seem surprised or perturbed. 'Fetch the Slut, will you, child? She can run round to the druggist and get us some supper as well, while she's out.'

'Who's this-here Slut?'

'Down the basement stair. First door on the left.' Mr Twite selected a key from the bunch at Mrs Bloodvessel's belt – not without some trouble, for she was writhing from side to side, screaming that a crocodile was gnawing a hole in her back.

'*Help* me, *help* me, why won't you *help* me?'

'We're a-going to help you, Lily, you'll be slap up to the echo in no time,' said Mr Twite, calmly passing the key to Dido, who ran down the basement stair and unlocked the designated door. The room beyond was pitch dark, and she would have been able to see nothing inside, had not one small window opened on to the river, and the rigging-lights from a passing barge, slowly battling its way against the tide, thrown a dim, sliding glimmer across the floor. In this half-light Dido could just make out a tiny huddled dark shape perched on something that was probably a box. The floor itself was shining with wet, and the room was icy cold.

'Hilloo?' called Dido softly and doubtfully. 'Is – is anyone here?'

She found it hard to believe that a live person could emerge from such a dank and freezing lair.

'Who're *you*?' breathed a voice.

'Dido Twite. My dad's upstairs. He wants you to go for a bite o' supper. And some medicine for Mrs Bloodvessel.'

'Yes, miss,' whispered the voice meekly, and the small shape removed itself from the box and limped slowly across the floor. Dido and whoever it was returned up the stairs, and in the light of the room above, where Mr Twite had kindled several lamps, the Slut was revealed as a tiny girl, wearing a grubby apron over a skimpy dress, and a bunchy calico cap bound round her head with a bit of string. She was the most mournful, wizened, shrunken little creature that Dido had ever laid eyes on; she might be nine or ten, perhaps; but her size was that of a six-year-old, and her face drawn and haggard as that of an old woman. Her limp was explained by the fact that on her feet she wore canvas shoes which were evidently several sizes too small, for her toes had pushed their way through the canvas and stuck out in two blue and battered rows.

Mr Twite greeted her with a sharp box on the ear.

'Took your time getting here, didn't you, you Slut! Here's your mistress sick and sorry. Remember, you *run* when she needs you.'

'Yes, sir,' whispered the child.

'Now you run to the druggist's in Wapping High

Street, and buy your mistress six-pennorth of laudanum – here's sixpence; and on the way back stop at the cookshop in Dyke Street and buy three hot faggots – here's threepence for them – and a jug of gravy – there's a halfpenny for the gravy – and a quartern loaf – there's another fourpence. Mind you don't nibble the bread on the way back, for I shall see directly if you have. And I shall give you *such* a beating! There, now, make haste – you'll get a thump for every minute over ten that you take. Here's the bottle for the laudanum.'

The child nodded, took bottle and money, which she counted carefully, then hobbled off as fast as her tight, broken shoes would allow.

Dido, looking after the Slut, recollected that in the past her father used to thump *her* on the ear, quite often, if she annoyed him or failed to obey his orders. Reckon he wouldn't try it now, she thought, and realized how much she had grown during the years she had been away from home. He knows I'd give him as good as I got. It's a hem shame the way he clobbered that little 'un.

The child heeded Mr Twite's warning and despite her bad footwear made good speed; in six or seven minutes she was back, and this was just as well, for all the time she was out of the house Mrs Bloodvessel continued to shriek and writhe. Mr Twite seemed accustomed to this, and paid it little heed.

'She often gets seized this way of an evening,' he explained. He took the laudanum the Slut had bought – it was a red, syrupy liquid – poured a spoonful into a glass, added some spirits of Geneva

96

from a square bottle, and a teaspoonful of sugar, then administered the dose to Mrs Bloodvessel.

It soon calmed her; she drew a deep breath, smiled, looked at herself in the glass, and, muttering that she was a sight, withdrew and was heard going upstairs, but called down to ask that her faggot be set before the fire to keep hot, for she was sharp set and would be down to eat it directly.

Mr Twite sliced up the loaf of bread – having first inspected it narrowly to make sure that the crust had not been nibbled. Then he gave Dido her faggot. This was quite different from the instruments played upon by Mr Twite's companions. It consisted of a lump of chopped liver and lights, rolled into a ball and cooked inside a pig's caul. It was served on a slice of bread, with gravy poured over.

Being ravenous, Dido was about to take a bite when Mr Twite said to the Slut, 'What are *you* hanging about for? Get back to the basement.'

'Don't *she* get no supper?' demanded Dido, surprised; and the Slut humbly whispered, 'Oh, please, sir, mayn't I have a bit o' bread?'

'*Fresh bread?* D'you think we are aldermen?' growled Mr Twite. 'Wait till your mistress comes down.'

The shuffling steps of Mrs Bloodvessel were now heard descending. When she came in, with her hair newly dressed in corkscrew curls and some rouge dabbed about her cheeks, Mr Twite said, 'Here's the Slut asking for dinner.'

'Ho, she is, is she?'

Mrs Bloodvessel unlocked a small cupboard with

a zinc mesh across the front, and took from it a tin plate on which lay some stale crusts and half a cold potato.

'There, then, take that and go back below,' she said shortly, pushing it at the servant.

'Don't she get no faggot?' said Dido.

The Slut gaped at Dido, as if she had said something in Portuguese.

'Meat? For her? Are you daft, girl?' said Mrs Bloodvessel. 'Give us another dram of loddy, Desmond.'

While Mr Twite was mixing the drink, Dido quickly broke her own faggot in half – by no means an easy operation, for it was soft, hot, and greasy – and put the larger portion on the child's plate, gesturing with a nod that she had better make off with it before anybody noticed. The Slut's eyes and mouth opened so wide that there was nothing left of her face; staring at the plate as if it held a ruby-studded crown, she slip-slopped out of the room at top speed.

'Best lock her in, Desmond,' said Mrs Bloodvessel, sipping her ruby drink. 'Or there's no saying what she'll be up to.'

'Dido will do that,' said Mr Twite. 'Take the key, Dido.'

A candle on the hall table was guttering toward its end in a pool of wax. Dido blew out the candle, scooped it and the hot wax together into a lump, and then pressed the key, hard, into the side of the lump. She wrapped this among her bundle of jacket and trousers, which had been left on the stairs, then ran softly down to the basement room.

'You got any bedclothes in here?' she asked.

'What, miss?' mumbled the Slut, who was eating as fast as she could.

'Bedding, covers?'

'No, miss.'

'I'll only make believe to lock up. Then later I'll see if I can bring you summat.'

'All right, miss.'

The Slut sounded doubtful; probably she did not believe Dido meant what she said.

'What's your name?'

'I dunno, miss; sometimes 'e calls me Is.'

'Is? Is that a name? When's your birthday? Mine's March first.'

'I don't think as I've got a birthday, miss; what is a birthday?'

'Oh, never mind,' said Dido. 'I'll be back soon.'

She left the door unlocked and went back up the stairs rather slowly.

Mr Twite and Mrs Bloodvessel, having finished their meal and taken several more drams, he of Geneva, she of laudanum, became cheerful and talkative over pipe and cigar.

'If what the costermonger said is true, Dido will be a gold mine to us, my amaranth,' said Mr Twite, looking fondly at Dido. '"A gold crown in her hand," he said – sure as I stand here.'

'Maybe he meant a crown piece,' said the lady, yawning and swaying tipsily, dropping a great worm of cigar ash down her muslin frills.

'You are as shrewd as you are beautiful, my dove, but no: I am convinced he didn't. A *royal* crown was what he meant. Hooraluyah! Think what that must mean!'

'Hark,' said Mrs Bloodvessel, 'I hear St Paul's strike. The lollpoops'll be along, you go down, Twite, and take their fardens; I feel nohowish. If any of 'em want to lie flat, it's a ha'penny. Remember that. And don't forget to lock both doors when they're all in.'

'Couldn't Dido do it?' suggested Mr Twite hopefully.

Mrs Bloodvessel shot a sharp glance at Dido. Though her face was jollier looking now, being flushed with food and spirits, the three-cornered eyes were keen as flint arrow-heads; there was something in their survey which reminded Dido of the Margrave.

'*Her* take the money? Not on your Oliphant. We'd not see her for dust.'

'Oh, very well,' said Mr Twite discontentedly; he selected another pair of keys from the bunch, and departed for the basement, swaying rather as he walked.

He had not been gone a couple of minutes when there came a sharp peal at the front doorbell.

'*Now* what?' grumbled Mrs Bloodvessel. 'Don't tell me as how those little monsters expects to be let in at the front door now, like quality? Go answer it, you, what'syername, and send 'em down smartly to the area. With a flea in their ear. Here's the front door key.'

On the way to answer the front door, Dido took the opportunity of pressing the key into the other side of her lump of wax. Come, we're making progress, she thought; all we want now's a locksmith.

'Who is it?' called Mrs Bloodvessel from the inner room. 'Is it a lollpoop?'

'No it ain't,' called back Dido. 'It's three men.'

They stood in a silent row on the doorstep. Two of them wore long caped black coats and three-cornered hats, like the watchers at the street corners. The third one, who stood between them, had his head entirely wrapped in bandages, with two small holes cut for eyes.

4

The new king had dropped in to take a cup of after-dinner tea with Simon and Sophie. He was in very low spirits.

'Och!' he sighed. 'Three o' my dearest freends drooned in one fell plunge! Yon was a dooms crushing blow. And then, late this e'en, what do I hear? Lord Raven, anither o' my cullies, crushed to death under a falling wall, puir mon. Whit gar'd him walk past a building that was aboot tae fall doon? Aweel, aweel, we'll never ken. I speer I am the unluckiest mon in London this nicht.'

Sophie could not help thinking that Lord Forecastle, Sir Percy Tipstaff, the Dean of St Paul's and Lord Raven were unluckier still, but she was too kind-hearted to utter this thought aloud.

'If it were not for you, my dear Battersea,' said the king, drinking another large jorum of tea, his fourth, 'and bonnie Lady Sophie here, I'd have nae freend tae my name in this weary city.'

'Never mind, sir. We'll soon introduce you to plenty of people that you can't help liking,' said Simon comfortingly. 'I know a coach-maker called Cobb – he and his wife are the best people in the world; and there's Dr Furneaux, the President of the Chelsea Art Academy – he's a great gun – and some of the students are real good fellows too – '

Sophie, looking out of the window, said, 'Indeed, I see one of them now, crossing the forecourt. But perhaps your majesty would rather not meet any strangers just at present? I can send Fidd to say that we are engaged.'

'Na, na,' said the king. 'Dinna deny your goodselves on my account. I'll be fain to meet anybody recommendit by such a pair of fine, trustable friends as I know ye to be. Let your friend be admitted.'

'Thank you, sir,' said Simon, and walked to the door, putting his head out to call, 'Tarrant! Tell Fidd that his majesty would like to meet Mr Greenaway. Bring him into the library, will you? And bring a few nuts, too, and a bottle of wine, there's a good fellow.'

In consequence of which, after a moment or two's startled silence outside, just enough time for somebody to run a quick comb through their hair and hurriedly re-tie their neckerchief, the elderly Tarrant limped in, lurched to one side, and announced, 'Mr David Greenaway!'

The person who followed Tarrant was about twice his size, in all directions: a tall, plump, quick-moving, light-brown-haired young man, with a round, good-tempered face and shabby, paint-stained clothes. Just now he looked startled to death, quite round-eyed with wonder, at suddenly finding himself in the presence of the king, and he made so deep and long a bow that Sophie began to wonder anxiously if he would ever manage to get himself

vertical again; certainly he was somewhat red in the face when he did so.

'Your majesty,' said Simon, 'allow me to present to you my friend Mr David Greenaway.'

'Any friend of yours, my dear Battersea, I'm blythe to meet,' said the king 'Let alane one who bears my ain name – for myself I'm Davie Jamie Charlie Neddie Georgie Harry Dick Tudor-Stuart.'

'As a matter of fact, your majesty,' said Sophie, smiling, 'his close friends have all somehow fallen into the habit of calling Mr Greenaway *Podge* – I do not quite know how it comes about – '

'Och weel,' said the king, 'in that case he shall be Podge for me as well. I am happy to make your acquaintance, Mr Podge. And whit manner o' trade or profession do ye follow?'

Sophie felt that it was very polite of the king to ask this, for anybody might have guessed the answer from the condition of Podge's clothes.

'Faith, sir, I was a fellow student of Simon, here, at the Chelsea Art Academy,' said Podge, grinning and blushing. 'But, as folk didn't run too fast to buy my paintings when I left the school, I thought it best to go out and look for my own customers; so I travel around London painting inn-signs. I have just come from painting the sign of the Wig and Fetter in Chancery Lane.'

'Have ye so?' said the king. 'Now there's a fine, practical trade. Even during my short stay in this city I hae seen many a tavern that could use your services – auld signs, foul signs, fadit signs – ye have a life's work ahead of ye, Mr Podge.'

'Just like your majesty,' said Podge, who, once his first surprise and confusion had abated, was settling down for a comfortable chat just as he might with any landlady in an ale-house.

'Aye, that's so,' agreed the king laughing heartily. 'And did your dad, like mine, follow the same calling afore ye, Mr Podge?'

'No sir, my father (who is still alive I'm glad to say), is a foreteller. That's his gift. But by profession he is a coster-monger.'

'An apple-seller. 'Deed, and there's a trade even more ancient than mine; it goes, I dare swear, all the way back to Adam! In fact, now I come tae think aboot it, the word *costard*, signifying an apple, proceeds from the word *coste*, meaning a rib; nae doot of it, there is some connection with Adam's rib.'

105

'You have me there, sir,' said Podge. I'm not educated. I know nothing of those clever propositions. I leave that kind of thing to Simon and Sophie here – they are the ones for riddles and acrostics and book-learning. Or my brother Wally – he's another sharp one.'

'And in whit trade is your brither Wally employed?'

'Nay, he's only a nipper, your kingship – only ten. Still, he does have a trade; he has a coffee-stall. And he mixes coffee.'

'A blender? He blends different kinds of coffee?'

'Not different kinds, no, sir; he mixes coffee with all manner o' different mash – beans, peas, broken corn, potatoes, acorns, horse-chestnuts, lupin seed, earth, brickdust, sawdust, dog-biscuit, tan – why, in your common pound of coffee, your majesty, you'll be lucky if you ever come across two ounces o' the regular bean; the rest's makeweight. Otherwise, you see, the poor folk couldn't afford it.'

'Thank my stars I prefer tea,' said the king, shuddering and drinking another cup that Sophie had just poured for him. 'But 'tis a black peety the puir folk should be obleeged tae drink sic a clamjamfry of adulterated nasty stuff, and this mun be seen to; aye indeed, and afore I'm a month older.'

'Then my brother Wally will be out of a job, sir.'

The king sighed.

'Fill one pitcher, ye empty anither,' he said. 'Government is no' sic a simple affair, I'm finding.'

'But, sir,' said Podge, 'and indeed I'm happy to come across you like this at Simon's house, for you might say that in a way it's an errand of government I've come here on – '

'Och, maircy, an arrant o' government? Weel, tell me yer mind, my mannie, speak on!'

'Well, sir,' said Podge, settling himself comfortably, hands on knees. 'You've been crowned such a short time, you'll likely not yet have heard of the Birthday League.'

'Nay, I havena.'

'The Birthday League,' said Simon, 'I never heard tell of it either, Podge. What is it for?'

'I have heard of it,' put in Sophie.

Podge beamed at her. 'I'll lay you have, Sophie dear! There's not much passes you by as concerns the kinchins – the children, that is, sir,' he explained, noticing the king's look of puzzlement. 'The Birthday League is a kind – a kind of a union, ye see, sir; a union of homeless children, or those with parents missing.'

'Eh, puir bairns,' sighed the king.

'There's more than ten thousand of them, they say, here in London – '

'Man, ye canna mean it!'

'But I do mean it,' said Podge. 'For all I know, it's more. And, as times are so hard, they're fair bothered, most of 'em, to get a bit of bread; so they formed this league to help one another, not to fight for what takings there are.'

'Losh,' said the king admiringly. 'Oot o' the mouths o' bairns – And whit connection do ye have with this league, Mr Podge?'

'Why,' said Podge modestly, ' 'tis not I, your

worship, but my young brother Wally; he's the Conductor of the League. 'Twas his idea, in the first place; he's a clever one. And the reason why I dropped over this night to see Simon and Sophie – '

At this moment a shriek from the courtyard distracted Sophie from what Podge was saying.

'Oh – if you will excuse me, your majesty – I see one of the children has fallen from the fountain – he seems to be bleeding rather badly.'

She picked up a basket full of bandages, scissors, ointments, lotions, and court plasters; it was plain that she was accustomed to dealing with such emergencies. With a nod to Podge she slipped from the room.

'Yes, Mr Podge,' said the king. 'Ye were saying – '

But now, to Simon's great surprise, a very grand carriage rolled to a stop outside the main door of Bakerloo House. It was drawn by four white horses and had a crest with a fist and a hammer emblazoned on the door, which a footman jumped down to open.

'Good lord!' exclaimed Simon. 'What a lot of company we are having this evening. Who in the world can it be this time? Forgive me, your majesty!'

He went into the ante-room of the library, where Tarrant told him in an undertone: ' 'Tis the Margrave of Bad Scrannery, him as calls hisself the Hanoverian Ambassador.'

'Humph,' said Simon thoughtfully. 'I am sure that man is no friend to his majesty. I wonder what we had best do?'

'Let King Dick decide for himself; there's a cove as

108

don't lack for sense,' said Tarrant with rusty approval.

'Yes, you are right.' Simon returned to the library and said, 'Your majesty, it seems that the Hanoverian Ambassador has come to call on us. I cannot imagine why! He has never been to this house, and is no acquaintance of ours. Is it your pleasure that – that he should be invited in?'

'What's your mind on this, Battersea?' the king asked Simon. 'Shall we see the man? Although he's a cousin – of a sort – he's no freend of mine; he's aye been hand-in-glove with my cousin George of Hanover, that dee'd this week. Maybe now puir Georgie is nae mair, the Margrave has decidit tae cut his losses and make friends with the conquering side.'

'I think it would be sensible to see him, sir,' Simon agreed. 'Then perhaps we can discover what is in his mind.'

This, though, he thought a few minutes later, would be no easy task. He had never met a person whose mind was so wholly concealed from other people as the smiling Margrave. He professed unbounded delight and amazement at finding the king in Bakerloo House.

'What a joyfully fortunate chance. What a surpassing pleasure! What an enchanting surprise! You might think I had been inspired! Why not drop in on those charming Batterseas, thought I, for I happened to be driving through Chelsea, and I have so long wished to make your acquaintance, my dear duke – I heard so much about you from that delightful Sir

Percy Tipstaff, now – alas! – drowned beneath the gliding tide of the Thames – '

'Will you take tea, your excellency?' suggested Simon.

'Why, thank you, my dear duke – perhaps, if you had anything a touch stronger – a mouthful of Canary – cognac – aquavit – or any such thing – '

While Simon gave orders to Tarrant, the king very civilly condoled with the Margrave on the death of Prince George of Hanover; and Eisengrim, quite as politely and very much more effusively, expressed sympathy with his majesty on the loss of his four friends.

'Well, well, we must support one another, my dear sir, that is all we can do!' he sighed. 'Perhaps a memorial service for all of them together in St Paul's Cathedral, would that be a good scheme, what do you think?'

But the king said, in a rather constrained tone that the cathedral was not, after the regrettable mishap at the coronation, when it had tilted sideways, yet in a fit state for large public services; he did not think this would be a possibility.

'No, no, of course you are right, my dear sir,' exclaimed the Margrave. 'Our grief must be a private affair, we must shed our tears in seclusion. I stand corrected.' And he pulled out a large white handkerchief, embroidered with a gold hammer, and delicately dabbed at the corners of his eyes.

Simon found himself uncomfortable in the presence of this large, self-possessed, genial person. – He could not like the Margrave. And he wondered why the man kept watching the king, all the time, so very closely and attentively, listened so extremely hard whenever the king said anything. He paid little attention to Simon, none at all to Podge, who had withdrawn, bashfully, to a distant corner of the room. For some reason he reminded Simon of a cat, head thrust forward, alertly keeping watch by the entrance to a mouse hole.

'I am cognisant that in the past,' went on the Margrave, after a good deal more eye-dabbing and sighing, 'in the past our beloved Prince George did not always – his interests were not quite identical with those of your majesty – or your majesty's father before you.'

'Ye could say so,' agreed the king. 'Indeed the callant was forever plotting to hist my dad off the throne of England, and set himself upon it.'

'But now, he and his plans alike are laid to rest! And it is my devout hope, your grace, that all such small past differences shall be forgotten in the happy, happy sunshine of your majesty's new administration?'

'Tush!' said his majesty. 'For my part, 'tis all water under the bridge. *De mortuis*, and so forth, since the puir deil is dead and gone, I'll not be girning against him, providit his followers will be content to hold their peace and rest quiet in their homes from this day on.'

And he gave the Margrave a fairly sharp look which the latter parried with one of smiling, bland amiability.

'My dear sir, that's of course! Of *course* Prince George's erstwhile followers know on which side their bread is buttered — and honeyed too! I am quite certain that not one of them has the least intention of taking arms against your majesty.'

'Aweel, aweel,' said the king. 'I am blythe tae hear that news. And now my dear Battersea, I believe I'll be taking maself off to my ain palace and bed, for I've a lang day tomorrow and a wheen tasks tae perform. I will wish you gude e'en, and thank ye kindly for the fine drap of tea; 'tis a muckle sight better than they make in St James's Palace. Pray give my regards to Lady Sophie when she returns from her ministrations. I shall be here to take anither cup very soon, I warn ye!'

'Your majesty cannot call too often for us,' Simon told him. 'You are welcome to drop in whenever the fancy takes you.'

'There was just one trifling matter — ' put in the Margrave, 'before your majesty leaves — not that I was in any expectation of finding your majesty in this house, no indeed! It was the most felicitous of coincidences that brought me under this charming roof at the same moment as your good grace. But since we *are* together, I cannot forbear to mention — '

'Aye, aye, come awa' then,' said the king, a little impatiently. 'Speak yer mind, man, let us hear whit ye have to say.'

'I believe, sir,' said the Margrave, 'that your majesty's father, your royal and much loved father — '

Except by the Hanoverians, thought Simon.

'I believe your majesty's father had arranged for some kind of triumphal procession at the opening of the new tunnel under the Thames between Shadwell and Rotherhithe, which is to take place in the not too distant future?'

'Aye, faith, that's so,' said the king. 'The auld boy was gey set on his tunnel jollifications; he had laid plans for junketing and marching, regimental bands playing, and a' sic whigmaleeries. I've half a mind to revoke the whole business, I've no great stomach for such ploys maself; the less so since the puir auld dad is no so lang in his grave; yet Battersea here tells me the people are looking forward to the merrymaking and it wad be a peety tae disappoint 'em. I wadnae wish them tae think their new monarch is a kill-joy and a mar-sport.'

'I am *certain* your majesty is in the right,' purred the Margrave. 'And I am happy to hear that plans are still going forward for this happy affair. In my employ, sir, I have a musician – a most talented musician, I may say – and his talent is only exceeded by his zeal and patriotism. What has he taken it into his head to do, but to write a suite of music designed expressly for this tunnel opening, and he solicited me to ask your majesty's permission to dedicate it to your gracious self and ask if it might be played on the occasion, while the procession is marching through the tunnel. Dare I ask your majesty's acceptance of this small offering?'

'Ech. Ach. Humph,' said the king, evidently taken aback by this request and not quite certain how to respond. 'I am not in the musical way maself, and nor was my dad,' he confessed, 'I can tell a reel from a strathspey, that's aboot all; – ye say this man is very talented?'

113

'Oh, very *very*, your majesty; to tell the truth, I believe him to be the most talented composer alive at this time. Moreover he is thought to have the power of healing illness by his music; indeed I believe that myself. He has done me great good.'

'What is his name?'

'Boris Bredalbane.'

'Have ye e'er heard of the fellow, Battersea?'

Simon had looked up, half expecting to hear the name *Twite*; he shook his head.

'How does this offer jump with you?' the king asked him. 'Would it fit in with your arrangements? – I have placed the duke here in charge of the festivities,' he told the Margrave.

'And a fine choice, I've no doubt,' said that gentleman, giving Simon a brief glance. 'Let me assure you, my dear Battersea, that my Chapelmaster's music can only add a brilliant lustre to your no doubt superlative dispositions. My good, simple fellow will be quite out of his mind with joy when I tell him of the gracious acceptance of his tribute.'

'Aweel,' said the king, who had not yet said yes.

'Your majesty's name will resound over the world as a patron of the arts!' continued the Margrave. 'The Tunnel Music will be remembered long after our poor names are forgotten – our descendants will be playing it three hundred years from now, I daresay – '

'Aye, aye, verra weel, let it be so,' said King Richard. 'If it will give the chiel such pleasure. For me, one tune is the same as anither, to tell truth. But Battersea here will look to the matter – will ye no' Battersea? – and tell the mon what's needed.'

'Certainly, sir,' said Simon, who had taken a strong dislike to the Margrave and was not at all pleased at being obliged to have dealings with him. 'Pray command me in whatever way you think necessary.'

'I will come and see you tomorrow,' said the Margrave, all smiles now his purpose had been achieved. 'It is but to make a small re-arrangement of the procession. I shall be happy to explain it to you at your better convenience. And I shall, of course, be happy to supply musicians; my own household players are highly trained and talented far beyond what is commonly met with.'

'That's settled, then,' said the king, and called for his carriage. The Margrave taking his departure immediately after, Simon and Podge were left to explain the matter to Sophie, who came in just then with her basket of first-aid equipment.

'Wicked little things!' she said cheerfully. 'They had been fighting; I had to stitch up his head; but he did not mean to push him off the fountain . . . Now, what was that man's purpose in coming here?'

'It's a thundering nuisance!' exclaimed Simon. 'I don't care for that fellow, I don't trust him. I hope this offer is not the cloak for some piece of devilment. I wish I had not got to deal with him.'

'Still,' pointed out Sophie, 'Bonnie Prince George is dead and they do not have any other person to put at the head of their party – so I do not really see what they can do – '

'But what about the Margrave himself? Isn't he a

cousin of Prince George — so he must be the king's cousin also? And an heir to the throne.'

'No, he ain't,' said Podge, who read the papers every day and knew much about public matters. 'The Margrave's parents weren't married. His father was Prince Rupert of Hanover, but his mother was only a dairymaid. So he ain't eligible. But anyhow it seems to me, Simon, that if they *are* hatching something connected with this procession, it is better if he comes and consults you — then at least you have a chance to find out what he is up to — '

'Oh well, I suppose so,' said Simon crossly. I wish Dido were here, he thought. She's as quick as a needle; she'd soon spot anything shravey in the business. He went over to the window and stood looking out at the snow-covered yard. The children who played there had gone, to whatever cellars and hovels they huddled into at night time.

'Sophie,' began Podge shyly, and then stood tongue-tied.

'Yes, Podge?' said Sophie, smiling at him encouragingly. His diffidence in retiring to the back of the room while the grand folks were talking had not escaped her notice. (This had not prevented him, however, from watching the other three very heedfully; and he had come to several conclusions, which he kept to himself.)

'I brought you a little token to mark St Gothold's Day,' he now explained bashfully, 'but I didn't like to give it you while those gentry were here.' And he pulled out from his pocket a small twist of silver paper. 'It's to keep your needles bright — '

'Oh, Podge, how pretty! Sophie cried in delight, undoing the paper, which contained a tiny velvet apple, green on one side, red on the other. 'An emery ball! It is exactly what I need. Podge, you give nicer and more useful presents than anybody else in the world.'

This was true. Podge had a very low opinion of his own ability to make friends, or keep them, because he was so plain and plump, and not clever; because of this, he thought a great deal about the people he loved, and knew exactly the kind of thing that would please them. He had given Sophie a number of gifts, mostly small and inexpensive, but just what she liked best, and could use: a box with compartments to keep her embroidery silks in, a pair of scissors like a bird, a book about the language of flowers, a white dove which sat on her shoulder and ate peas from her hand, a pair of small pink-and-silver Turkish slippers with turned-up toes which he had bought from a sailor.

'I know'd they'd just exactly fit your tiny feet,' he had said proudly. Podge's own feet were enormous, and he was rather ashamed of them. – He had also learned Japanese wrestling because he hated his own clumsiness; and had then taught the art to Simon.

'Podge, just before the Margrave came in, you were starting to tell something to his majesty, and then you never said any more about it. Did you forget?' asked Sophie, when the velvet apple had been put in a place of honour in her work-basket.

'No, I didn't. But I could see the king wanted to leave; and I didn't reckon on blabbing out a lot o' business in front of that Margrave. He's got his finger in too many pies as it is; he owns a deal o' property round our way and is up to a deal o' mischief. I wouldn't wonder if this trouble's his brewing – '

'What is it then?' asked Simon, returning to the fire-place and throwing another log to crackle on the fire.

'Why, it's the hot cockle-sellers.'

'The cockle-sellers, Podge?'

'Mostways, like I was saying before, the young 'uns all helps each other. The ones as sells cresses, or walnuts, or whatever it is, they agrees among themselves about who's to have which pitch, in which street; and the buskers and street singers the same. But now there's this new lot of hot cockle-sellers, the Bowmen, they call themselves . . .'

5

'We are here from his excellency the Margrave,' said one of the two men in black hats. 'We have brought the gentleman who is to lodge with Mr Bredalbane.'

'Lodge?' said Dido, startled. 'I didn't reckon as he was to lodge here? I thought he was just to step round for a bit o' conversation once in a while. You'd best talk to my pa.' And she called, 'Pa? Pa? There's a cove here from His Nabs – '

'Hush, hush, my canary,' exclaimed Mr Twite, hurrying up the basement stair and jingling a fistful of farthings as he came. 'Bricks have ears and cobbles have eyes. Now then, what's all this, pray?'

'We've brought the chap as is to lodge with you. Here's his traps – ' and the black-hatted man produced a carpetbag and a portmanteau. The bandaged stranger, meanwhile, stood silent in his line wrappings; Dido, somewhat awestruck and mystified, wondered if he were able to speak; his mouth was all covered over by white strapping.

Mr Twite reacted just as his daughter had done.

'Lodge here? No one said anything about his *lodging* here.' He scowled at the stranger.

'His excellency thought it best,' said one of the two

escorts stolidly. 'Dr Finster will be round to see the gentleman in the morning. He will call twice a day.'

And with that the two men in black turned smartly on their heels and marched off into the darkness.

'Canker it!' muttered Mr Twite, evidently much discomposed. 'I never reckoned as the plaguy fellow was going to be *bedded* on us; that's the outside of enough, that is!'

He looked indecisively at the two bags on the floor, and the bandaged man standing helpless in the doorway.

'Blest if *I* know what to do about it,' grumbled Mr Twite.

Without making the least effort to welcome the unexpected caller, or even address him, Mr Twite returned to the back room, calling over his shoulder, 'Shut the door, daughter, do; we don't want half Wapping gleering in at us; and it sets up a freezing draught, furthermore.'

From sounds within the room, Dido gathered that her father was helping himself to another jorum of Organ Grinder's Oil.

Dido felt sorry for the visitor, standing there abandoned by his escorts and blinded by bandages.

'Shall I take the cove – shall I take the gentleman to a room, Pa?' she suggested, putting her head round the door. 'Or would Mrs Bloodvessel rather – '.

She stopped, for it was plainly no use expecting any instructions from Mrs Bloodvessel, who was snoring loudly on the tousled couch. Her head dangled upside down over the side, above a glass which had rolled across the dusty floor, leaving a trail of red syrup. A half-smoked cigar still dangled from her fingers. Dido removed it and dropped it into the dying fire.

'A room, a room,' mumbled Mr Twite. 'A room, a-rum, a-rum, a-riddle-me-ree! What'll we do with the bandaged stranger? Feed him in the stable, bed him in the manger . . .' and he gave a great wrenching yawn, looking fondly at the couch·where Mrs Bloodvessel lay, where there was just room for a second person, provided that person were thin.

'We haven't *got* a manger, Pa,' said Dido impatiently. 'Let alone a stable.'

She felt dog-tired herself; the ill-effects of Mrs Bloodvessel's potion had by no means worn off, and she too longed to lie down somewhere peaceful and sleep for hours together. Dunno when I last slept in a proper bed, she thought; and it won't be for a fair stretch yet, I reckon.

But there the stranger stood, blinded, powerless, and dependent on the inhabitants of Bart's Building for some sort of hospitality. If there was a tiresome job to be done, Dido preferred to do it at once and get it out of the way.

'I'll put him somewhere, then, Pa; he shouldn't be left standing about like a hitching post, poor devil. Here, where's those keys?'

With distaste, she knelt by the unconscious Mrs Bloodvessel and managed to untie the whole bunch of keys that dangled from her belt. The woman snored and rolled over but took no other notice of Dido's action.

'That's the ticket, my aphasia,' yawned Mr Twite. 'Give him – hic! – one o' the best rooms, wi' panelling and bedcurtains. Nothing too good for His Nabs's candi-hic-candi-diggle. Any friend of Eisengrim is a friend of Desmond Twite – hic! – ipso hicso facto. Let him lay his head on a goosefeather bed . . . and rest his feet on a silken sheet. Hickety-cup!'

Dido picked up a straightbacked chair and carried it into the hall. It would not, she thought, be at all possible to lead the blind visitor through the total muddle of that back room.

'Would you please to sit there a minute, sir,' she said, and guided him to the chair. 'I'll just step upstairs and find a room for you, and I'll be down again directly.'

Carrying a lighted candle and the heavy bunch of keys, she made her way upstairs.

The house called Bart's Building proved to have three upper storeys, including the attics. Starting at the top, Dido unlocked and flung open all the doors in turn. Nobody was in any of the rooms; the house appeared to be unused, apart from Mr Twite and Mrs Bloodvessel on the ground floor, and the Slut and the lollpoops in the basement.

All the doors were locked, though there seemed little purpose in this, as many of the cold, high-ceilinged rooms were unfurnished. One was piled high with clothes, very gorgeous clothes, Mrs Blood-vessel's perhaps, from some earlier period of her life. One of the three attics, as Dido had expected, was the room she had been shut up in. The attics were approached by a ladder.

Pa and Mrs B. must have had the dickens of a job hoisting me up there, thought Dido with a grin.

The stairs to the upper floors were so steep that a ship's rope ran up beside them instead of a rail.

In a room on the third floor Dido found some articles which she recognized as belonging to her father: several hoboys, a dusty spinet with one key missing, some shoes, some books, lying on the floor, and a bundle of music. There was also a rather nice bag of her own, with blue flowers on it, which a fagott-playing friend of her father's had once given her; it had vanished long ago, when she was seven or eight. It held a comb and a razor. Fancy it being here all that time, Dido thought; wonder how many years Pa has been coming to this house?

If Pa had to pick a lady friend, she thought, walking into another room and inspecting it with her candle, wouldn't you think he'd pick one with a bit better looks and better temper? Mrs B. seems just as disagreeable as Ma, there's naught to choose between 'em.

Of course, it's true that Mrs B. has a house of her own; leastways one she rents from the Margrave, recalled Dido, descending the stairs to the first floor.

The rooms here were even higher. What a lot o' locked rooms, thought Dido, going from one to another. What a lot o' keys. Suppose I were to collect all the keys from all the houses in the street; suppose I were to pile up all the keys in London. What a pile that 'ud be. High as a church tower, very likely. All made so folk can keep themselves private. Wonder who first made a key and stuck it in a lock? Pa ought to write a bit o' music about keys and locks . . . You'd have one part for the lock – with a kind of space in it, a-waiting – and then the other part for the key, long and thin . . .

Blimey, I ain't *half* tired, thought Dido.

She was now in a room which contained a four-poster bed, a three-legged stool, and a sailor's chest; it was the most fully furnished apartment she had yet come across, and she decided that it would have to do for the bandaged gentleman. There were no sheets or blankets, but she recalled piles of such coverings in the all-purpose room where her father and Mrs Bloodvessel spent their time. Slipping back there, she helped herself to an armful of bedding, also some other comforts: a candle, lucifer matches, a plate and mug and a tin basin.

124

'That's the dandy, my serviceable sprite,' murmured her father, who neither helped nor hindered these activities, but drowsily reclined on the bed by Mrs Bloodvessel, occasionally picking out a pattern of notes on his hoboy.

'Dido Twite, a serviceable sprite,' he warbled, and as Dido climbed the stairs a second time with her load she heard him begin to set those words to a slippery, catchy little tune which he repeated in several different keys.

Just fancy! thought Dido, Pa's gone and made up a tune about me! and she could not help feeling rather proud, with part of her mind, though the other half wished impatiently that her father would do something more helpful about the bandaged guest.

When the upstairs room had been rendered as comfortable as seemed possible, she returned to the hall and laid her hand upon the bandaged man's arm.

'Will you please to follow me up the stairs, mister?' she said, and took his hand to lead him. He came after her biddably, and seemed quite content with the room, what he could see of it through his eye-holes, though, thought Dido, it must seem poor and bare compared with any chamber in the Margrave's establishment.

'D'you want any supper, mister?' inquired Dido, wondering what she would do if he said yes. But luckily he shook his head. Maybe he can't eat, with his mouth all bandaged up, she thought, but then, to her great surprise, he carefully unwound the bandage from around the upper and lower parts of his face and head, leaving only the portion covering his nose. There seemed nothing wrong with the expanse of skin thus uncovered.

'Croopus! What was the point of all them bandages then?' Dido exclaimed

'His excellency thought it best – ' said the man, after clearing his throat. 'So I should not be recognized in the street; or tempted to speak, you know – '

Dido stared at him, really puzzled now, studying what she could see of his face.

'Great fish, sir, ain't you the king?' He shook his head.

'Well you're as like him as one pin to another. Did you know that? Are you his brother?'

He shook his head again.

'No, there is no kinship. And I was not so like him before – my nose was a different shape from his – but his excellency's doctor has changed that – ' He touched the bandaged nose delicately – 'and now *you*, it seems, have to teach me to speak exactly like his majesty.'

'Yus; and I can see I'm a-going to have my work cut out,' said Dido bluntly. 'You ain't even English, are you?'

'No, I am Dutch. But I speak the English very well. My name is Henk van Doon.'

'But what's the point? Why should the king have a ringer?'

'?'

'A double, a lookalike.'

'Oh, it is not at all uncommon. To take the king's place if he feels ill – or for boring business, you

126

know, opening hospitals, cutting ribbons, talking to burgomasters – '

'Mayors,' corrected Dido. 'And you should say it burgo*mass*ter – that's the way the king does – short, like that – '

'Mayors, I thank you. Masster. Many royal persons have such a double-goer to save them trouble. I am – I am to be a gift from his excellency the Margrave to his cousin the king.'

'Well, *I* think it's right rum. And you must have to keep it mighty dark. Once folk get to know, they'd everlastingly be a-wondering whether they'd got the real 'un, the real king, or only the ringer.'

'Oh yes, I shall have to live very private. People must not know.'

'But do you *want* to do it?' Dido stared at him. 'Ain't you got anything else you'd *rather* be doing? Seems a shravey kind of life. What did you do before?'

'I am an actor – a comic actor, a clown.'

'Well?' demanded Dido. 'Ain't *that* better than letting-on to be a king, allus cutting ribbons? What's the point? Making jokes, making folk laugh is better. I know which *I'd* rather!'

Henk van Doon suddenly looked desperately sad.

'My child, you do not understand. The jokes left me. They flew away.'

'Why.'

'I had a hard loss. My dear wife, my little daughter of six years, they caught the cholera. They died. How can I make jokes then?'

'Send your voice *up*, at the end,' absently corrected Dido. 'Make jokes *then*?'

127

'Then. I thank you. How can I make jokes then?'

'So what did you do?'

'The heart went out of me. I was starving in the streets of Leyden. And a man from his excellency's household saw me — I was brought to him at his house in Bad Wald — he said he would pay me well to play this part of king, all I need is a new nose, and to learn to speak like King Richard — '

'If you could go and live with the king, in his house, that would be best — and study the way he talks — '

'But then, too many people would know that there are two of us.'

'Humph. No, it ain't easy, I see,' pondered Dido.

A flight of joyful notes rose from below, like birds circling upward on an evening wind, and steps were heard on the stairs.

'Here comes Pa. Have you all you want, mister?'

'Yes, I thank you, my good child.'

'See you in the morning, then, mister, and we'll talk some more.'

'Oh, tooral eye ooral eye agony,'

sang Mr Twite ascending the stairs,

'Oh, pickle a pocket of rye,
If a man can't find cheer in a flagon, he
Might as well lie down and die.

'That's well, that's good, my fairy. Time you betook yourself to the downy. Time all juvenile

128

females was abed. *I'll* take care of the visitor,' said Mr Twite loftily. And he lurched past his daughter, who began climbing the ladder towards her own attic, greatly relieved at the prospect of being able, at last, to lie down and sleep. Halfway up, though, she remembered her promise to take down some bedding to the Slut. Poor little devil, huddling alone there in that damp cellar hole without a scrap of cloth to cover her; it's not to be borne, thought Dido angrily, and she turned round and went downstairs again. Her father, in the Dutchman's room, seemed to be singing the visitor to sleep. Dido wondered if van Doon was glad of this attention.

Mrs Bloodvessel still snored in the lower room by the last glow of the fire. Taking a tattered, but ample quilt, Dido made off with it to the basement, past the locked door of the lollpoops' room (inside which she could hear a faint murmuring and shuffling like a flock of starlings settling to sleep). There's *another* lot of poor devils, but croopus, I can't find quilts for all of 'ęm, and anyways I reckon they must all keep each other warm, packed together like pickles in a jar; and anyhow Pa's got the key . . .

Thinking about keys, she slipped into the Slut's room and heard a faint gasp of fright.

'It's all rug – it's only me, Dido. I brung you a comforter, like I said. Don't make a row, or Pa'll hear.'

Mr Twite's music had returned to the ground floor; apparently the Dutch gentleman had not welcomed his lullabies.

'Ain't that a ripsmashing tune, though,' sighed

129

Dido, as the notes of the hoboy scribbled a silvery pattern above their heads.

'It makes me want to spew!' croaked the Slut suddenly from her dark corner. 'Gives me a pain in me belly. Makes me want to lob me groats.'

'*Pa's music* does? My blessed stars! Why?' demanded Dido, really amazed – though, after a moment, she thought she began to guess the answer.

'I *hates* that cove. She treated me a bit better before he come to live here. I just wisht he was dead.'

It was astonishing that such a tiny, bony creature, crouched in such a damp, dark cellar, could speak with such ferocious force.

'Well – dunno as I blame you,' murmured Dido. 'Still – you know – it don't do no *good* to think that way. Here – have a warm-up – ' and she felt her way across the room and wrapped a capacious fold of the quilt around the Slut, who, however, shook it off fiercely.

'I don't want his mucky quilt. Or hers! *They* don't give me one. She don't! He don't! You swiped it.'

'Well, blister me, girl,' remonstrated Dido. 'You'll freeze to *death* down here, one o' these nights. You wants to stay alive, don't you?'

'Yus,' agreed the Slut, after some thought about this. 'And give 'im and Mrs B. a taste o' their own!'

'Well, then. Wrap up.'

'*No*, I tell 'ee. I don't *want* her slummocky quilt.'

The Slut was crying with rage now. Dido's gift of half a faggot seemed to have fortified her with a fiery spirit and sense of her grievances.

'All right; suit yourself,' said Dido crossly, and

started for the door. But she trod in a puddle on the way, and heard something scuttle along beside the wall. She stopped again.

'I can't leave you in this nook-shotten place with nowt – was that a rat?'

'There's plenty rats,' sobbed the Slut indifferently. 'Ten rats for every 'uman, they say. Rats don't bother me. I got a cat. Hain't I Figgin?'

A sound between a waul and a snarl answered her.

'Figgin had a bite o' faggot too,' said the Slut with pride. 'We looks arter each other.'

'I reckon Figgin wouldn't say no to a bit of quilt to curl up in,' suggested Dido shrewdly. 'You oughta think of him as well as yourself.'

There was a silence. Then –

'Would you stay too?'

Dido's mind filled with longing for the attic.

Shut up in it, this morning, she had found little in its favour. But now, how peaceful, airy, and clean it seemed – far cleaner, at least, than this dank den.

'Guess I will, if you want me,' she said reluctantly.

'If 'e finds you here in the morning, mebbe 'e won't give me the stick. Or not so much. 'E thinks a deal o' you.'

'How do you know that?' said Dido doubtfully.

' 'Eard 'em talk. "That Dido'll make all our fortunes yet," he say to 'er.'

'What the pize could he mean by that?' wondered Dido, arranging herself and the Slut in the driest corner – which she could by now make out, tolerably well, by the light of passing barges. It was much harder to see Figgin, who seemed to be pure black, but by the feel of him he must be the scrawniest, boniest cat in Wapping, with coat as bristly as a doormat and a tendency to bite. 'You keep Figgin on your side,' Dido recommended.

'Now: tell me summat,' said Is.

'What? Tell you what?' yawned Dido, who was dying to go to sleep.

'*I* don't care. Anything! You musta seen lotsa things. I never had no one to keep me company afore.'

'How long have you been here?'

'Dunno. Since I can remember.'

'Is Mrs B. your ma?'

'Dunno. She never say. Tell me summat!'

In her mind's eye, Dido could dimly see all the adventures of her life, like a huge tapestry covered with tangled pictures – trees and rivers, ships and horses, people, good, bad, or wicked – mountains bursting into flames, St Paul's Cathedral sliding into the Thames, rough seas filled with whales, men firing guns, cats carrying messages in the collars round their necks. There seemed far too much to put into words.

Instead, she remembered the pile of keys she had imagined as she climbed the stairs.

'Once there was a king as lost the key to his money-box,' began Dido dreamily. 'So he made a law that everyone in the whole country hadda bring all their keys and lay 'em in a heap in front of St Jim's Palace. So he could find if any of 'em fitted. All the folk brought their keys – church keys, stable keys, desk keys, strongbox keys, door keys, watch keys, clock keys – '

'Did any of 'em fit?' croaked the Slut.

'The heap was so huge that it filled the whole square, higher than the palace. And when the sun shone, didn't those keys half glitter! Then – the king said – '

'Said what?' demanded Is, but her voice trailed away in a yawn.

Dido was already asleep.

Just before she drifted off, she had a quick thought about the Dutchman, van Doon, training himself to look and sound exactly like the king. That's a right rum business – can it be all hunky dory? Or is the Margrave up to summat?

Anything that my pa's in *must* be crooked, thought Dido.

Then she floated into dreams.

6

Simon and Sophie were taking breakfast in the morning room of Bakerloo House. Grey light from the east window fell across the table with its white cloth, bowls of fruit, rolls, and pots of honey, but the morning was not a bright one; purple-black snow-clouds were piling across the sky, and the children out in the yard played their games under a thin flurry of flakes.

Simon was still worried about Dido.

'If she were with anybody but her father! He is such an out-and-out rascal. He might get her mixed up in all manner of wrongdoing – and then leave her without scruple – '

'Don't you think she can look after herself?' suggested Sophie. 'After all she managed to find her own way home from – Nantucket, did you say? The Galapagos Islands?'

'She is such a little scrap of a thing.'

Mrs Buckle came curtseying in with a letter.

'From his majesty, your grace.'

'Oh, dear, so early in the day?' said Sophie, as Simon broke the large red-and-gold-seal. 'The poor man depends on you so. What does he want now?'

'He is asking if I will take on Lord Raven's job.'

'The Office of Home Affairs? *That* won't leave you much time for painting,' sighed Sophie. 'Of *course* you'll say yes?'

She knew her brother far too well to suppose that he would disoblige the unfortunate new king in his difficulties.

'I'll do it just for the time,' said Simon. 'Until he can find a better person. And he also wishes to consult me about wolves in Kent. Mogg!' he shouted. 'Can you fetch my boots and coat, please? And tell Sam and Sim to get out the curricle; I have to go to St James's.'

'Wolves in Kent? Are there so many?'

'A number of reports have been coming in. The wolves in Europe are migrating westwards, because of the early winter. Belgium and France are already overrun; now they have begun finding their way to Dover, by night, along the undersea road from Calais. South-east Kent – Ashford, Dymchurch and Romney Marsh,' said Simon, studying the notes that accompanied the king's letter, 'are infested by packs of wolves which are moving daily closer to London. The king asks me to make a plan. Armed wolf patrols, perhaps.'

'What fun! We can all go out on horseback, with muskets.' Sophie's eyes sparkled at the idea.

Mrs Buckle reappeared with another letter.

'From that mirksy Hanoverian fellow.'

She managed to convey disapproval in her curtsey.

'See what he wants, Sophie, there's a kind sister,' said Simon, who was pulling on his boots.

'He says he is indisposed; asks you to go round to Cinnamon Court this morning to discuss the Rotherhithe tunnel opening celebrations.'

'Oh, curse the man! What a nuisance he is. Anyway I can't go this morning – I suppose I'll have to write a note and tell him so.'

'He'll be offended.'

'Can't be helped. Unless – I say, Sophie – I don't suppose you'd like to be a good sort and go for me, would you? It's only to hear his plans. You may borrow my plum velvet suit – you said yourself you look well in that.'

Sophie dimpled.

'Wretch! You did say that you wouldn't ask me to play that trick any more – '

'Just this last time. You know that you really enjoy it. And since I have to see the king – and it's important not to offend the Margrave – '

'But suppose he sees that it's me, not you? After all he was here at the house, he saw both of us, so lately – '

'I do not think he will. You were out with the children, he never met you face to face. And he hardly looked at me; he kept his eyes fixed, all the time, on the king.'

'Oh well,' sighed Sophie, 'I suppose I must oblige you.'

'You *are* a prime gun,' said Simon, giving her a hug. 'And I tell you what – you shall drive the curricle – even Mogg says you drive it better than I do – and I'll take the big carriage. You can have my caped coat, too.'

Seen side by side the brother and sister were, indeed, so remarkably alike – black-eyed, with dark curly hair, wide mouths, and resolute noses – that, dressed for riding, they were often mistaken for each other. Sophie went off now to put on Simon's plum velvet suit, while Mrs Buckle muttered something severe about 'harum-scarum ways'.

Simon had already left for St James's Palace when Sophie drove off in the curricle, looking extremely smart in her brother's caped greatcoat and beaver hat, with her curls tied severely back in a grosgrain ribbon.

The Margrave received her graciously.

'Many, *many* apologies – my dear duke – for my discourtesy in not waiting on you myself – but a touch of my old malady – it is *most* kind of you to oblige me in this way? A drop of sherry wine? Or Bohea? Or Canary?'

The Margrave was decidely pale. He did look unwell, Sophie thought. His eyes were deep-sunken, his cheeks waxen.

She politely declined the offered refreshments, glancing with frank interest around the salon they were sitting in, which was very gorgeous, with Chinese carpets, and bronze furniture, and pictures of bygone Hanoverian nobilities on the walls.

'To our task, then. It is the most trifling affair, after all! I need not detain you, I am sure, above ten minutes. Morel, fetch the Chapelmaster, will you?'

Mr Twite arrived in his kilt and red wig. At the sight of Sophie he started and turned a little green; he took pains to remain at a considerable distance

from her, eyeing her, meanwhile, with great attention. Sophie, who had never seen him before, could not imagine what ailed him but thought perhaps he was afraid of his master.

'Now!' said the Margrave. 'This is my Chapel-master's plan. It is really most ingenious! But first let me ask you, my dear duke, what are your principal feelings about watching a procession – your main emotion on such an occasion?'

'Why,' said Sophie, after thinking about it for a moment, 'I suppose the dreadful boredom. You have to go there hours before, to secure a good place, you wait and wait, the procession passes, and then you are in the middle of such a crowd that you can't get away, so you wait and wait again.'

'Precisely!' said the Margrave in triumph. 'Exactly so! You wait and wait. The procession passes, and all your waiting has been for just a few minutes of spectacle. But how would it be if there were *two* processions, travelling in opposite directions?'

'Well,' said Sophie, 'I suppose that might be – '

'Of course!' said the Margrave, without waiting for her to finish. 'You are right! It is far, far better. It is fairer. And in this way Herr Bredalbane, my clever Chapelmaster, has planned it all. To be accompanied by his superb music! *Two* processions – one commencing in London, marching under the Thames, out into Rotherhithe, ending in the fields of Kent – at Greenwich, perhaps; the other commencing in Kent, proceeding under the Thames, and so into the city of London to end at St James's. It is sublime! In from the country: yeomen, local militia, farm wagons garlanded with flowers – '

'Flowers in January, your excellency?'

'Tush!' said the Margrave. 'Well – holly, mistletoe, greenstuff, I know not – milkmaids tripping, shepherds dancing, morris men. Music of pipes and tabors – joyful rustic music, suitable for such an assembly. – And then *out*, from the city: the king's own household regiments, guards in full regalia, aldermen, city dignitaries, peers, lords, barons, and so forth. And their music will be of a more dignified nature – yet joyous too – music suitable for city regiments, for the royal retinue – '

'Yes, I see,' said Sophie, nodding. 'And, when the two processions meet – '

'Ah then!' cried the Margrave, in heights of ecstasy. 'You have hit on the nub of the matter, my dear duke. Where the two processions meet – that

139

is the crown, the crest, the culminating point of the affair! Then the music blends, the city themes with the country themes, they are combined, are harmonized, are extended into a surmounting climax of beauty!'

'Gracious me. How clever,' said Sophie – who did think it sounded a most ingenious plan, really quite out of the common. 'And where will this happen? One procession, you say, comes in from Greenwich, one goes out from London – where will they meet?'

She glanced at a large map of London and its environs which the Margrave had spread out on a gold-and-onyx table.

'Why, where should they meet but in the middle of the tunnel – the reason, the object of the whole affair? Where could they possibly meet but under the River Thames?'

Sophie at once perceived several objections to this plan, but she judged it best to be tactful, and only said, with caution, 'Will the tunnel be illuminated?'

'Who should know that better than yourself, my dear duke?' the Margrave replied in slight surprise. 'But yes, it will be lit by gas flares. The scene will be brilliant – magnificent!'

'And the tunnel is wide enough to contain two processions, passing in opposite directions?'

'So I am informed. There will be sufficient width.'

'For spectators also?'

'Spectators? Now there, my dear duke, you ask the impossible! The spectators must content themselves with assembling outside, at each end of the tunnel.'

To Sophie it seemed more than a little odd that the

most significant moment of the whole occasion should take place underground, in a tunnel, where no one could see what was happening, except the people who were marching, or riding. Yet – the tunnel *was* the object of the festivities – and the crowds on each side of the river would have the excitement of seeing one procession march into the cavity and then, two minutes later, a different one march out. With appropriate music, as the Margrave said.

'It really is clever,' she said. 'How long will it take?'

'For the two processions to reach the Thames from their starting points, say half an hour. To pass through the tunnel – ten minutes. And then another half hour to reach their final destination.'

'And in which procession will the king be?'

'Aha! My dear duke – as before – you dive straight to the heart of the matter.'

The Margrave seemed more and more delighted with Sophie; he beamed at her enthusiastically, though she noticed that he had become even paler, and now carried a bright red spot on either cheekbone. His hands shook. His brow was bedewed with beads of perspiration. In spite of his vivacity, Sophie thought, he looked like a seriously ill man.

'Which procession?' he repeated. 'Which indeed? Shall I leave you to guess – like the public!'

'Well, sir,' said Sophie cheerfully, 'you have me entirely puzzled and all agog. And I assume that is your intention.'

The Margrave turned, and directed his wide smile (*could* those teeth be real? wondered Sophie) like a lighthouse beam at Mr Bredalbane, who, all this

time, had been seated nervously at the spinet, sometimes lifting his hands as if about to play a few notes,
but never daring to do so.

'Can you believe it, my dear Chapelmaster? What
luck for me that the duke, here, is a young man of
parts, of rare discernment. He is a jewel. He can
appreciate our scheme. And I am not surprised that
he should be so sympathetic – have you taken note
of his voice, Chapelmaster? It is so musical, so fine-
toned – I cannot recall when I was last charmed by
such a voice!

This remark caused Sophie more than a little
alarm. She had been forgetting, in her interest, to
pitch her voice as deep as Simon's. She said, quickly
and gruffly, 'I conclude that the king's whereabouts
in the procession will be kept a secret until the last
moment? Is that it? Pray, your excellency, may I hear
a little of the music that you offer to accompany this
scheme?'

'With the greatest of pleasure,' the Margrave purred. 'Bredalbane – play the duke your themes; let
him have some idea of the grandeur of our concept.'

'Y-yes, your excel-cellency, c-certainly, your
excellency. You s-see, your griddle-grace, it will be
– it will be after this fashion – ' stammered the
musician. He gave Sophie a quick, slanting look,
then began rapidly fingering the keys. 'This will be
the theme for the Household Regiments – and this
for the city dignitaries; this for the yeomen – ' all
the while he was rattling out different tunes, some
stately, some rousing, some light-hearted, some
grand – 'then, for his majesty, this – ' he played a

142

noble, simple, haunting air – 'then there will be country dances for the farmers, milk-maids, and shepherds coming in to town – ' and he changed to a series of such lively airs that it was all Sophie could do to stop her feet from tapping on the marble floor.

'Why, they are beautiful!' she exclaimed, much impressed. 'They are truly beautiful.'

Bredalbane glanced at her again, a rapid, needle-like look.

'And th-then, you s-see, the themes all mix and combine as the two processions begin to pass one another – ' He gave a demonstration of this, combining several themes together.

'Really,' said Sophie, 'it is the greatest pity that Mr Bredalbane's music could not have been used at his majesty's coronation; it is by far superior to what was played on that occasion.'

'My dear duke – I could embrace you!' said the Margrave. 'Such judgement! Such perception!'

Sophie had to control an impulse to back away in case he meant his words literally; but luckily he did not. She noticed with interest that Bredalbane's music seemed to have had as beneficial an effect on the Margrave as if he had swallowed brandy or sniffed a bottle of smelling-salts; his pallor had been replaced by a warm flush, his eyes were brighter, the beads of sweat had dried off his brow.

'So you approve our scheme, my dear duke?'

'Oh, it is not for me to approve,' said Sophie. 'His majesty has already done so. For myself I think it is tremendous – superb. All I need now is to take a memorandum of times and places where the parties will need to assemble and in which order. I will transmit these to the king for his final assent.'

She pulled out a small ivory writing tablet and began taking notes. 'There! I believe I have it all recorded now – the household cavalry, the guards, knights, barons, aldermen – and the farmers, milkmaids, shepherds, yeomen – his majesty will have cause for infinite gratitude to you, your excellency! And now I shall take my leave – '

She stood up, anxious to be gone.

The Margrave seemed really disappointed. 'Must you indeed go? Can you not remain and hear more of Bredalbane's music, played at greater length – those were but extracts – '

'I wish I might. But the preparation for this – ' Sophie tapped her notes – 'must be put in hand at once.'

'Could you not send a messenger?'

Wondering why the Margrave was so anxious to keep her, Sophie said, 'No, your excellency. An affair of this kind, so complicated, deserves to have careful attention. I should give these instructions in person.'

Really, she wished to tell Simon all about it as quickly as possible.

'Well – if it must be so – ' sighed the Margrave.

As a red-headed page brought Sophie's greatcoat and helped her into it, the Margrave turned to his Chapelmaster and said, 'But a rare spirit such as the dukes's must not be wasted. We must persuade him to take some part in our future music-making – eh, Chapelmaster?'

Bredalbane looked quite sick with alarm, but

ducked his head over the spinet and stammered, 'Yes, s-s-s-sir, my l-l-lord – ' making a variety of strange grimaces at his master as he shuffled a few sheets of music together.

'I'll bid you goodbye, then, excellency,' said Sophie, and turned to go, receiving, to her surprise, a wink from the red-headed page as he handed her Simon's Russia-leather driving gloves.

Sophie never wore gloves for driving; bare fingers, she found, gave more sensitive contact with the reins and the horses' mouths; so it was not until she reached Bakerloo House and handed the gloves over to Mogg that the chewed apple-core was discovered, lodged in one of the fingers.

When Simon returned home, Sophie told him all about the Margrave's plan.

'Simon, he is such a strange man! I cannot like him! And yet this scheme of his seems truly – truly – ' She hunted for a word.

'Well-intended?'

'Yes. And – and remarkable! He seems most sincere in his love of music – quite unselfish in wishing the work of his Chapelmaster to be heard.'

'What does he look like, this Chapelmaster?'

At Sophie's description of the red hair, the kilt, the moustache, Simon shook his head.

'I thought it might be Twite – but no . . .' He frowned. 'Just the same, I do not put any trust in that Margrave. Let me see those notes again.'

They both studied Sophie's outline of the tunnel programme.

'It *seems* innocent enough,' Simon was forced to admit. 'Yet I wonder – ? Could he – for instance – be planning to blow up the tunnel as the king passes through?'

'Oh Simon! What a shocking notion! Surely he could not have such a monstrous scheme in mind?'

'I'd not put it past him. After all, the Georgians blew up Battersea Castle. And it was a near thing with St Paul's. Yet – now Bonnie Prince Georgie is dead, where would be the advantage? Still,' Simon said thoughtfully, 'I shall make sure that a vigilant watch is kept over the tunnel from now until the day of the opening. The gates can be kept locked until the very last moment; that will have the advantage of keeping wolves out of London also.'

'Mercy! Have they come so close?'

'As far as Greenwich and Blackheath. The weather favours them,' said Simon, looking out at the falling snow, in which few citizens were about. 'They can slink along by-ways without being observed.'

Sophie was still anxious about the possibility of the Margrave's dynamiting the new Thames tunnel while the king and two processions were passing through.

'I suppose a barge – or a ship floating down the river – could hold explosive – ?'

'I will see that none are permitted on the day,' said Simon, making a note. 'What a head you have, Soph! Mind, they say that the river is likely to freeze if this cold weather keeps up. Ice is forming on the banks already. In which case no ships will be making passage on the river.'

'No, but if it is frozen,' said Sophie, wrinkling her

forehead, 'people might be able to *walk* on the ice, over the tunnel – '

'That will have to be forbidden also.' Simon made another note. 'Mogg! See that all these notes are taken round to the Comptroller of the King's Household at dawn tomorrow. I have to go out again at sun-up,' he told Sophie. 'We have to try and clear the wolves out of Blackheath and Rotherhithe. Otherwise, as soon as the tunnel is thrown open, they will all come pouring through into London. I shall probably be gone all day.'

'Suppose the Margrave wishes another interview with you?'

'I'm afraid you will have to go again. In any case if I went now, he would be sure to notice the difference, as he has taken such a liking to you! But why should he trouble us again? His plan is being used – he must be content with that.'

At this moment the Margrave was saying to his trembling Chapelmaster, 'Come on! Out with it, man! What is making your teeth chatter so?'

'Oh, s-s-s-sir! I kept trying to signal to you while he was here!'

'You looked like a Barbary ape with lockjaw. What was all that about? Why could you not speak up then?'

'S-s-sir! That young fellow – whoever he was – he was not the Duke of Battersea!'

The Margrave, who had been pacing nervously to and fro, stopped abruptly and stared at his musician. His former pallor had returned.

'How do you know?'

'W-w-why, s-s-sir – at one time I had the duke lodging with me, as a student, for some months – I could not mistake. That young man was very like him – a young brother, a relation perhaps – but it was not the duke. It was a s-s-substitute.'

Mr Twite suddenly gave a lugubrious giggle.

'When you think about it,' he said, 'it is rather droll . . . is it not?'

The Margrave did not reply, apart from a ferocious scowl, which made his Chapelmaster cower down, shivering, behind the spinet.

7

Dido was roused in the morning by angry shouts. Evidently the Slut's hope about Mr Twite had not been justified; he was furious to find the basement room unlocked and his daughter sharing the servant's accommodation.

'Using one of our best quilts, too! How dare you? No breakfast or dinner for *you* today.' And he aimed a blow at Is with the bunch of keys he held, which, if it had struck her, would certainly have cracked her skull. But Dido, shocked out of sleep, stumbled to her feet and knocked up his arm.

'Blister it, Pa! Leave the girl alone! Pick on someone your own size!'

She glared at him, skinny and tousled, looking, though she was not aware of it, very like the cat Figgin, likewise crouched snarling and spitting in a corner.

He glared back. 'What in Ticklepenny's name are you doing down here, daughter? Get upstairs where you belong. And don't let me catch you down here again. And you,' he said to Is, 'make haste, let out the lollpoops and scrub the floor in there, then run out and get us some breakfast.'

'Yessir,' snuffled the Slut, ducking to avoid another blow.

'*I'll* go for the breakfast,' said Dido. 'And I'll sleep where I please, Pa; so you put that in your pipe and blow it! If I choose to sleep with Is, I will. And if you don't lay off lambasting her, I won't teach that Dutchman – or I'll teach him naught but a load o' wallop, and then you'll be in trouble with your precious Margrave.'

Mr Twite's jaw dropped. He gaped at her in horror.

'A present for the king from His Nabs,' said Dido. 'Hah! A likely tale, I don't think! Find a better one! You must reckon I'm addlepated to swallow that. And if that was one o' the best quilts, preserve us from the worst! It's got holes big enough for a buffalo to fall through.'

Defeated, and speechless for once, Mr Twite retired upstairs.

Dido crossed the passage and peered into the fusty room where, shock-headed, blear-eyed, and yawning, the last of the lollpoops were taking their departure, while the Slut hurriedly swept about with her birch-broom and sprinkled vinegar.

'Hey!' whispered a voice in Dido's ear. 'Hey, Died o' Fright! I been a-laying for you! My brother wants a word with 'e.'

'Your brother? Who's he? And who are you – no, don't say, don't say –' as she recognized his crossed eyes steadily regarding her, 'I knows who you are. You're the apple-monger's boy – Wally. I owe your dad a farden.'

'Right, Died o' Fright! And never mind the farden. You don't know my bro', yet, but he wants to meet ye, wants to ask you summat, and tell you summat. When can you come out and have a barney with him?'

'Where is he?'

'Painting a pub sign. The Feathers, in Wapping High Street.'

'I'll try and come along in ten minutes, tell him.'

The cross-eyed Wally nodded, and ran off, whistling.

To the Slut, Dido said, 'Don't you fash yourself with what Pa said about breakfast, young 'un. I'll see you get fed.'

'*I* ain't a-worrying,' the Slut said with scorn. 'Figgin fetches me breakfast, often as not.'

'Figgin does?' Dido eyed the scrawny, ill-favoured cat, rubbing and winding against his mistress's ankles. 'He don't look as if he could find breakfast for a ghost. Where does he get it?'

'Down chimbleys!' said Is, unexpectedly. " 'E used to be a chimbley-sweeper's mog. 'E goes down chimbleys all over Wapping – pubs, folk's houses, all sorts – and fetches me prog. Mostly it's fried herrings – stuff what he fancies hisself. Then we shares. Onct in a way he's brung me real posh grub – from His Nabs's palace I reckon – chicking, and galangting, and mutting, and pudding. That were prime!' Her eyes shone at the memory.

'Love a duck! Well – I'll find summat for you today,' said Dido. 'And don't fret either if Pa or old hag Bloodsucker locks you in – I'll soon have you unbuckled.'

She ran upstairs, thinking it's a mercy someone looks out for the poor little article. Just the same, I'd not reckon on that skinny beast fetching her more than half a herring once in a way – judging from the size of her.

Upstairs she found Mrs Bloodvessel still snoring and her father happily and dreamily extracting soft, yearning notes from his hoboy. He had two salt-cellars on the bamboo table, and from time to time he would tip all the salt from one vessel into the other, and then gaze at the result with his head on one side.

'Gimme the mish, Pa,' said Dido. 'I'll go and shop for breakfast. I ast the foreign gent last night what he fancies in the morning, he said coffee and toasted cheese.'

Relieved at having this responsibility taken off his hands, Mr Twite handed over a couple of shillings and instructed his daughter to bring back a gill of milk, bread, and a few slices of ham as well as the coffee and cheese. Dido found a basket and let herself out into the wintry morning.

'You will not do anything *foolish*, will you, my sarsaparilla?' Mr Twite called after her. 'Remember the fate of your friend depends on you.'

'No, Pa,' she answered shortly, and slammed the door. The hour was still early, and the smoke-blackened buildings and dingy streets of Wapping were silent under the falling snow. A barge hooted mournfully on its way up-river.

'Which way to Wapping High Street, mister?' said Dido pertly to the black-coated man on guard at the street corner. She wondered if he were the same who had been there last night − his hat was pulled so low, his muffler so high, that only two sharp eyes could be seen. He made no answer but pointed to the right.

'Don't strain yourself!' recommended Dido, and turned in the direction he pointed. When she reached the end of the street, he whistled shrilly on his fingers. She saw another black-coated man turn to watch her from the next corner.

Guess that old Margrave keeps tabs on the whole neighbourhood, thought Dido. Why? Don't he trust Pa? Or is it to keep an eye on the Dutchman? It can't be just to stop me from scarpering.

She walked by a whole series of silent boat-basins. The tide was low, the black, weed-coated piles were veiled by flying snow-flurries. A few anchored ships lay on the mud, waiting to be loaded or unloaded.

At the corner of Wapping High Street, yet another black-coated watcher was stationed. Dido saw that it would be extremely difficult to run off unobserved − unless she jumped into the river and swam across the Pool of London.

In the High Street there were small shops, many stalls, and more people about, buying provisions. The stalls, Dido noticed, were almost all minded by children.

She virtuously bought bread, cheese, milk, and ham; she also slipped into a locksmith's shop, left her wax moulds, and was told to come back for the new keys in five minutes; she found the Feathers pub and saw a tall plump boy up a ladder, busy painting the

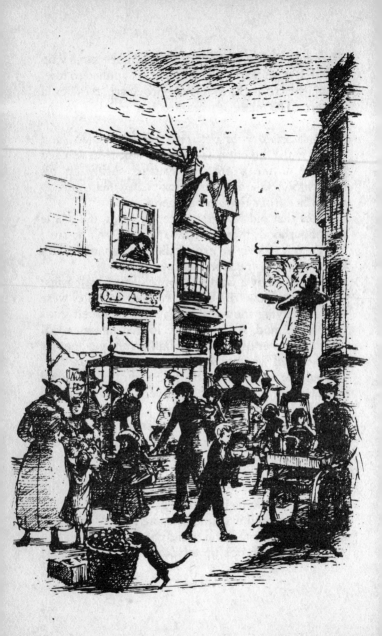

new sign; but how to attract his notice without being spotted by the Margrave's men?

Dido strolled on along the pavement, looking casually about her.

The stalls along by the edge of the footway sold rhubarb, spices, combs, nutmeg graters, crockery, dog-collars, pies, pictures in frames, lucifer matches, shrimps, boiled puddings, razor-paste, pea-soup – almost anything a person might need. The stall-keepers, or younger boys and girls employed by them, were calling their wares: '*Orang* – *es,* two a penny! Cut *flo* – *wers,* penny a bunch! *Dom* – *.in* – *oes*, tanner a box. Hot taties, all hot! Hot murphies only a ha'penny!'

Halfway along the street, very conveniently, Dido found a coffee-stall, which sold, as well as mugs of steaming brown liquid, sandwiches, packets of coffee-beans, and ready-ground coffee.

'Just what I needs,' said Dido grinning at the cross-eyed boy behind the stall. 'Give us a quarter o' your best Jamaica, ground up, matey – and make sure there ain't too perishing much grated carrot in it. And my birthday's still March the first!'

'The Java's better than the Jamaica, miss; you'd best have that,' said the boy seriously. 'And I'll mix it up for you special.'

'Ta, chum. I'm just a-going in over there to pick up a pair o' keys,' Dido said, nodding towards the locksmith's shop diagonally across the street. 'Shan't be more'n a couple o' minutes, then I'll be back.'

She rolled an eye significantly, as she said this, towards the Margrave's black-coated watcher, and then slipped across to the locksmith's shop. Wally, behind the coffee-stall, proved, as she had hoped, lightning quick to pick up her hint; not more than a moment or two later the tall boy who had been painting the pub sign also dropped into the locksmith's establishment.

'Pleased to meet you, young 'un,' he murmured, joining Dido at the back of the shop, where she was gazing with awestruck admiration at an elaborate warehouse lock, advertised 'Safe & Proof Against the Most Malignant & Experienced Cracksman'.

'I mustn't stop too long in here,' said Dido, 'or I've a notion that one o' them sooty-jackets'll smell a rat and come fossicking arter me. What's the row? Are you Wally's brother?'

'That's right, love. My name's Podge. And I'm a friend of Simon and Sophie.'

'You are? Oh, that's *prime*.' Dido's face broke into a joyful smile. 'Oh, I *wisht* I could see them. But – here, stoop down, wallses have earses and you're such a beanpole –' She whispered in his ear: 'My pa said as – as Simon might get drownded – same as old Lord Fo'castle – did I try to see him. So I just dassn't! It'd be too dangerous!'

'Aha!' Podge nodded. His bright grey eyes were very intelligent. 'I reckoned it might be summat o' that sort. So did Sophie. She's as shrewd as she can hold together, Sophie is!'

'I wisht I could see Sophie,' Dido said wistfully. 'She was real decent to me, when I were younger.'

'Heart of gold, Sophie has.' A fond, tender look spread over Podge's kind, plain face. 'Anyhow she

156

sends a message; they both do; hope to see you as soon as it's safe for you.'

'It ain't *me* I'm feared for, Mr Podge, it's *them*,' Dido said earnestly. 'I'll come when I can, sartin sure. But what was it you wanted to axe me?'

'It's all to do with the same kettle of fish,' whispered Podge. 'You went to see His Nabs, t'other day, didn't you?'

'How the pize did you know that?' demanded Dido, astonished. Then she recalled the red-headed page. 'Aye, I did; why?'

'He's up to a power of mischief round here. Folk's mortal feared of him – 'specially the barrow boys and the small shopkeepers. It's the Cover Game, you see. If we could only find out what his main lay is – bring him to book, or get him sent back to Hanover – '

'He's a – hey!' said Dido. '*Lurk!*' She had caught sight of the black shape of a watchman standing in the street doorway looking into the dark interior of the shop.

Podge, who seemed well acquainted with the place, nodded, slipped away along an aisle all lined with keys, and vanished out of some rear entrance. Dido walked over to the counter and was given her two keys. She paid for them out of her own dwindling store of cash. When she turned to leave, she found that the watcher had moved away from the door and was now farther along the street.

Dido returned to the coffee-stall where Wally had her blue paper bag of coffee ready for her. 'Like a mug o' hot, miss?' he said blandly. 'It's on the house – or I'll toss you for it!'

'I can't stop now, cully — got to get a foreign gent's breakfast,' said Dido. 'But I'll take you up on that some rainy day — and then I'll tell you all I can,' she added in a low voice, with a meaning nod. Wally nodded back; then his crossed eyes, looking over her shoulder in different directions, narrowed, and he added under his breath, 'Best mizzle, now, love! I see trouble coming this way!'

Dido moved on carelessly along the street, glancing at an interesting display of Royal Love Letters and another, less interesting, of Religious Tracts. Then, quickly turning her head, she saw a gang of half a dozen large, burly boys, dressed in black leather, with leggings, slouch hats, and metal caps on their boots, surround and overturn Wally's neatly kept stall with its gleaming tin urns, brass taps, oilcloth canopy and dangling mugs. They smashed the mugs and flung the loose coffee about. Wally stood aside, with arms folded, and face impassive; he could not possibly have taken on all the attackers, there were far too many of them, all twice his size. But his brother Podge, with several companions, carrying brickbats, and staves, came tearing along the street to his rescue. Podge was shouting, 'Costers! Costers! Come and help smash the Bowmen!' A few other stall-holders joined them; but more, Dido noticed, stood undecided, or looked in the other direction. Farther along the street she saw that several other stalls had been knocked down and their contents scattered.

In another hasty look, Dido saw Podge tackle the leader of the black gang and hurl him to the cobbles, using a very neat hip-throw; but then she saw a metal-tipped boot connect with Podge's shin, and he, too, fell, his feet knocked from under him. If that haven't broke his leg he's lucky, thought Dido angrily. It's a shame such scaff and raff can come and spoil those poor chaps' trade like that. And then she wondered: is that what Podge meant when he talked about the Cover Game? Those peevy coves don't come and just do that out o' the blue, someone has told 'em which stalls to wreck, and pays 'em, too, I'll lay; dibs to dumplings it's the Margrave behind it.

She noticed more of the leather-clad boys, carrying mugs filched from Wally's coffee-stall, walking arrogantly along the street, calling out, 'Bowmen's dues! Bowmen's dues!' The stallholders, reluctantly, with looks of fear and anger, were dropping silver money, crowns and half-crowns, even gold half sovereigns, into the mugs.

It's a right wicked game, thought Dido indignantly. And I'll bet every penny of that money goes into His Nabs's fat purse, and that's how he can afford all them velvet carpets and that glittery furniture.

I better get outa here afore somebody drops on me.

She made her way quickly through the crowd, looking busy and preoccupied with her basket of provisions, and so back into the less crowded ways through which she had come. Nobody followed her. The watchmen were still guarding their corners.

That Margrave must have a packet o' money already to afford all these watch coves and bully boys, Dido thought. So now what does he want? Podge wants to know what his main lay is. I wisht

I knew. One thing's for sure; whatever it is, Pa's muxed up in it too.

Back at Bart's Building she banged on the knocker, not wishing to advertise the fact that she now possessed a front door key of her own. Mr Twite let her in.

'Took your time,' he said peevishly. 'Lil's woken up and reckoned she'd hardly get her breakfast before dinner time.'

'Tough turkey!' retorted Dido. 'There was trouble in the street – some rapscallions breaking up poor devils' barrows and stalls. The beaks oughta be told about them; they oughta be locked up in the Pongo.'

'That is no affair of ours,' said Mr Twite quickly. 'I – I trust you did not – did not t-take part in any f-fracas, daughter?'

'Nope,' snapped Dido. She dumped the food on the mantelpiece; Mrs Bloodvessel was out of sight behind a Chinese screen, washing, by the sound of it.

'Did you tell that gal to bring me some laudanum?' she called.

'No, my dilly.'

'You'll have to go out later, then.'

Mr Twite muttered something vexed under his breath.

Dido slipped a piece of bread and ham to the Slut, who was sweeping the front hall, and said, 'You might come and give a rub-over to the foreign gent's room when you've done that. Or lend me the broom. The dust's thick as sheepses' wool up there.'

'Yes, miss,' mumbled Is through the bread and ham.

'And you doesn't have to call me *miss*! Dido's my name.'

The Slut looked as if she had never heard of such a word, and could no more use it than she could play a bass viol.

Dido ran up the stairs to the Dutch gentleman's room and tapped on his door, which he had locked, but he came and opened it. She had brought kindling to light his fire, but was interested to see that, from his portmanteau, he had a small traveller's fire-pot, which was already alight, with a brass kettle steaming on it comfortably. While Dido lit the fire in the grate, and toasted the cheese, Mr van Doon made a pot of powerful black coffee, cupfuls of which he administered to himself with a dram of schnapps, and to Dido who took it without the firewater; even so it was stingo stuff.

Meanwhile they talked.

'Mister,' said Dido, 'are you sure that His Nabs – '

'Whom do you speak of thus, child?'

'*Up* at the end, don't forget, mister – *child* – so – '

'*Child*; I thank you – '

'D'you really reckon the Margrave means well by King Dick?'

'Means well by him?'

'Don't mean to hurt him?'

As the Dutch gentleman still seemed bewildered, Dido burst out impatiently, 'Well, blimey, he's fixing you up to be the exact copy of the king. Don't it ever come into your brain-box that maybe he plans to do a swap – a switch, a dicker,' she explained, as he still seemed perplexed. 'Put you in the king's place. Then what'd you do? You couldn't hardly cry rope — they'd think you was mad. Or it'd be *your* head they took and chopped off.'

Scowling to emphasize her point, she stared hard at van Doon. It was not easy to read his expression, because of the bandage across the middle part of his face, but his brow was furrowed, as if with difficult thought.

After a moment or two he said, 'His excellency the Margrave has told me the king may be tired; may wish for a holiday, to go and stay in peace on an island for a short time — then I would take his place and his excellency would instruct me — '

'Mister,' said Dido with pity, 'you must come from Greenland if you believe a tale like that. He's had you for a flat. Don't you see?'

It took some time for van Doon to understand her. Then he said in a troubled voice, 'But his excellency the Margrave is a good man. He has rescued me from starvation — he has been most kind to me — ' He looked shaken, but obstinate.

This Dutch cove really must be a simpleton if he truly reckons the Margrave to be kind, thought Dido. Any six-year-old would know better. How the dickens can I shift that notion he's got so fixed in his silly noddle?

There came a timid tap at the door, and the Slut edged her way into the room, carrying the birch-broom and a handful of dirty cleaning-rags. There were two new bruises on her face, and a cut, which bled.

'Who done that?' demanded Dido fiercely. 'Did my pa do it?'

'No, it were her. For taking the cover. 'E didn't stop her, mind. She's allus twitchy in the mornings. But I didn't care about it,' said the Slut stoutly, 'not wi' that great bit o' ham in me belly.' She wiped away a trail of tear, snuffle and blood with her elbow and got down to sweeping.

The Dutchman was staring at the Slut as if petrified.

'*You see!*' Dido was beginning angrily. 'What kind o' – ' when there came a ring at the doorbell.

'Oh, blister it, now what? I'd best go and see who that can be, you stay here, Is, with the Dutch gent – give her a dram of your coffee, mister, why don't you?' said Dido, and ran downstairs.

Mr Twite was nowhere about. Perhaps he had gone out for more laudanum. Mrs Bloodvessel reclined on her sofa gazing dreamily at the cracks on the high ceiling. She did not trouble to bring her eyes down when Dido addressed her.

'Listen, missus. It was me as took that quilt! And if you knock that young 'un about any more, I'll tell the beaks, and they'll put her in an orphanage.'

'She is not an orphan,' replied Mrs Bloodvessel coldly, still studying the ceiling. 'Nobody can take her. I have a perfect right to punish her. And *you* best watch out, miss!' she added, suddenly staring at Dido with venom. 'I am a very old friend of his excellency. I can settle *your* hash, if you don't stop meddling in what don't concern you – he'd have you dropped in the Pool like a tiddler – '

The doorbell rang again, peremptorily.

'Go answer that,' ordered Mrs Bloodvessel, turning on her side. 'And don't bother me.'

Angry, nonplussed, Dido went to open the front door. Outside stood a youngish pink-faced, fair-haired young man, respectably dressed in top hat and frock coat, carrying a black doctor's bag with – most unexpectedly – a grey monkey sitting on his shoulder.

'Dr Finster,' he announced himself briskly – she could see he was not pleased at being kept waiting. 'Where is my patient?'

'Your pa – ?' Dido had been gaping at the monkey. 'Oh – the Dutch feller? He's upstairs.'

Without waiting to be shown the way, Dr Finster brushed past her and ran up the stairs while Dido shut the door, observing that a grand coach, with a coat-of-arms (a black fist with a hammer on a gold shield), on the door, waited outside, the coachman walking the horses to and fro to keep them warm. The doctor must be sent by His Nabs, Dido thought, following Dr Finster up the stairs. As she reached the landing, a second slam of the front door and a flurry of hoboy notes announced the return of her father.

'Who came in the carriage, daughter?' he called up the stairs, with sharp alarm in his voice.

'The Crocus,' Dido replied.

'Oh, him,' Mr Twite said in evident relief. 'I'll just give this to Lil – tell Finster I'll be up in a trice.'

By the time Dido entered the Dutchman's room, Dr Finster had removed the facial bandage from his patient, studied the inflamed area that lay below, applied cooling lotion, and was now preparing to put on a new dressing.

'That goes on well,' he said, approving his own handiwork. 'In two days more the bandage may come off. I shall inform his excellency.'

All the while he had attended to his patient, the monkey had remained on Dr Finster's shoulder, clinging to his velvet collar with its fingers and toes. The Slut watched from a distant corner, astounded, halfway through her cleaning operations.

Now the air of 'Calico Alley', growing louder, preceded Mr Twite up the stairs. Is turned pale and looked as if she would have liked to escape, but there was no way she could do so. Whereas, at the sound of the hoboy music, the monkey became filled with energy and joy; he bounded from the doctor's shoulder and began to spring and caper about the floor, waving his arms, leaping high in the air, sweeping his long tail from side to side, and chattering shrilly in time to the music. The Slut shut her eyes and covered her ears with her fingers.

'The monkey remembers well what cured him, you see,' observed Dr Finster to Mr Twite, as the latter entered the room, still playing. Indeed the monkey, with evident recognition and delight, darted across the floor, ran up Mr Twite as if he were a tree, and sat chattering on his head.

'It is a most interesting case and demonstrates to the full the truth of my theory on the medicinal powers of music – especially yours,' pronounced the doctor, studying the monkey with great self-satisfaction. 'Do not neglect to play to Mijnheer van

Doon, also, for at least two hours a day; that will assist the healing process better than my lotion.'

'Sartin sure, I'll – I'll play to the poor sufferer,' replied Mr Twite, who appeared to have been dosing himself downstairs along with Mrs Bloodvessel. 'Now, if you'd be so ob – obliggleous as to remove this little monster off of my noddle – '

He began to sing:

'Dr Finster met a monster,
In the merry month of May –
First he rinsed her, then he minced her
All for half a guinea pay – '

'Did Pa's music really cure that monkey of summat?' Dido asked the doctor, who was now replacing his instruments in the black bag. He gave her a cool glance.

'Yes, miss, most certainly it did; the animal was at death's door with Mishkin's disease – weighed only five ounces, and all its fur had fallen out. I had your father playing to it for twelve hours a day. I hope that information will encourage you to behave towards your father with proper respect; which he certainly deserves!' Finster gave Dido another quelling look, then reclaimed his monkey from the head of Mr Twite (who was not looking particularly respect-worthy) and remarked to the latter in a low tone: 'Do not neglect to continue the treatment with his excellency, *whether he asks for it or not*! It is most necessary. At least three hours a day. I cannot over-stress the importance of this.'

'Aye, aye, aye, I'll not forget,' replied Mr Twite, nodding so many times that his wig, already knocked awry by the monkey, fell off completely. He put it on again back to front. The doctor frowned, stuck out his lower lip, looked as if he thought of saying something more, then sighed, shrugged, and ran downstairs.

Dido had a sudden idea and scurried after him.

'Hey, mister!' she called.

Dr Finster, in the act of stepping into the coach, paused and looked at her impatiently.

'Well? What?'

'Could you go and look arter a boy called Podge Greenaway who's been painting the sign of the Feathers pub, down Wapping High Street? He had his leg kicked by a mobster – could a broke the

bone, easy. Anyone'll tell you where to find him –
his dad is blind and keeps the apple-stall.'

'Have you taken leave of your wits, child? Such
people are not the affair of a physician such as
myself. Let him find himself an apothecary. Good
day.'

A footman slammed the carriage door and the
horses broke into a trot.

And slumguzzle to *you*, thought Dido, looking
after him; then she turned back into the house, shut
the door, and began walking slowly back up the
stairs.

Maybe I oughta write to the king, she thought. I
could write a note, give it to Wally, he'd give it to
Podge – if his leg ain't broke he could get it to Simon
who'd pass it along to King Dick – but would he
ever believe it? It's bezants to barleycorns he'd take
no heed . . . Or he'd fetch in his dear cousin the
Margrave and ask him about it all; and the Margrave
'ud deny everything. 'How could you listen to such
wicked tales about me?' And then the fat 'ud really
be in the fire.

I've got to think of some plan.

But what?

Mr Twite had retired once again to the frowzy nest
he shared with Mrs Bloodvessel; the exquisite notes
of 'Three Herrings for a Ha'penny' floated up the
stairs. Too bad the monkey ain't in the house still,
that'd make his fur grow twice as fast, ruminated
Dido, continuing to climb the stairs. It's right rum
that Pa's music does the monkey so much good, while
that poor little morsel Is can't stand it . . . What was

168

the doctor saying to Pa, just afore he left? Something about His Nabs?

Dido came to the door of the Dutchman's room and stood still in wonder.

Van Doon had produced a little set of travellers' dominoes from his baggage and laid them out on top of his smaller valise. Across this improvised board he faced the Slut, who, cap laid aside, hair combed, face washed, and cheeks pink with interest, squatted like a gargoyle, chin on elbows, studying the pieces. After a moment or two, very slowly and hesitantly, she brought a piece up from the floor and laid it at the end of the pattern.

But it was the Dutch gentleman's face which really riveted Dido's attention. And his attitude. He was watching the little Slut as if she were some long-lost, long-loved book that he had had not a hope of ever reading again.

When she laid down her domino and looked up at him, half proud, half doubtful, he gave her a little smiling nod. Then very gently he leaned across and patted her small head.

8

The street children were flocking earlier and earlier to the forecourt of Bakerloo House as the days went by. This morning they had come well before daylight, and were playing their games by the light of the gas flares that blazed outside in the King's Road.

It was a freezing, foggy morning, and the snow, by now several inches deep, glowed like dusty gold as the children kicked and pranced and sang their rhymes.

'Mingle, mangle, mingle,' they sang, running and crissing and crossing, catching and swinging round one another if they met, then loosing and running on again.

> 'Mingle, mangle, mingle.
> Poor King Dick is single –
> Not a chick, not a wife
> To cheer his lonely life,
> Not a sweetheart, not a friend
> To cheer his latter end!'

Then they all turned and raced for the plane tree that grew by the porter's lodge. The last one to reach

it was given the part of King Dick, and sat sorrow-
fully on the fountain in the middle of the court.

'Let us choose, let us pick,'

sang the others

'Pick a wife for lonely Dick
Is she nimble, is she quick
Can she jump over a walking stick?'

Then they began setting each other a series of
trials, leapfrogging, jumping over sticks held higher
and higher, balancing along the rails of the fence, turning cartwheels, handstands and somersaults, until
one could be judged the best, suitable to marry the
bachelor king. But then, just as one was finally
chosen, an outsider arrived, singing,

'I'm the queen from over the sea –
Before you wed him you'll have to fight me!'

The two 'queens' fought until one of them gave in,
and the other was married to the 'king' in a mock
ceremony. Then it all began again.

One of the children, seeing Sophie at the window,
waved vigorously and held up a hand with something
white in it. Sophie ran down to the front door and
met the child, a round-faced, cheerful little girl of not
more than seven or eight, with untidily braided
tawny hair and a great many freckles.

''Tis a letter for the lady Sophie – from Podge.
When's your birthday? Mine's some time in June.'

'Thank you, my love. I'm the lady Sophie and my birthday's in April. The tenth. Have you no father nor mother, my poor child?'

'Nary a one! But I manages! In summer I sells cresses, and in winter pincushions.'

'Bring a pincushion next time you come and I'll buy it,' Sophie promised as the small creature raced back to her companions.

'My dear Sophie,' said the letter from Podge. 'I am sorry not to come and see you myself, as the sight of your pretty face is like a Tonic. But wished to lose no time in telling you that I have seen your friend Dido & she is well & living with her dad in Wapping. She said she feared she could not vist you as it wd be too Dangerous (as you & I thought). Her father is working for You know who (also as we thought). Hope to see you in a Day or two, but have a bad leg just at present. Yr very affct friend,
                              D. Greenaway.'

Sophie ran upstairs with this epistle to find Simon pulling on his boots. He was already dressed in riding costume. Mogg was greasing his flintlock.

'Oh, no!' said Sophie in dismay. 'Must you go out after wolves again?'

'I fear I must, love. The king has asked me to most particularly. Blackheath and Dulwich are quite over-run; poor old ladies are being pulled out of their beds and children devoured on the way to school.'

172

'Then can't I come too?' eagerly demanded Sophie.

He said reluctantly, 'I don't think you ought. What about the poor king? One of us should stay at hand to cheer him up, don't you think?'

Sophie made a face at her brother.

'Besides, it is quite dangerous,' he went on apologetically. 'I got this gash on the arm, and one of the brutes bit clean through my boot yesterday – you are safer here in Chelsea. But, of course, if you really insist on coming – '

She sighed.

'No, you are right. Just do me a favour, and don't get eaten!'

'I'll be home late again – probably long after you have gone to bed.'

'I daresay you will . . . Simon, Podge writes that he has seen Dido. Is not that good news?'

'Oh, famous!' he said, his face brightening wonderfully. 'Where?'

'In Wapping.'

'I will find some way of getting to see her,' he said. 'In disguise, perhaps. The very minute that we have these wolves under control – '

Half an hour after Simon had gone, another note arrived from the Margrave.

'My dear Battersea: I am reluctant to make a second call upon your time, knowing how busy you are; but I have a small point regarding the Royal Route that needs confirming. I am wondering if I can tempt you to a recital of Tea Music by my excellent

173

Chapelmaster this evening, at eight? We could have our small chat, and then I can promise you a rare musical treat. Dare I hope to see you?

Your friend, Eisengrim.'

'Oh, drat the man,' muttered Sophie, chewing the end of her quill pen as she considered what her answer should be. 'I wish Simon had not gone off. Or that Podge didn't have a bad leg; then I could get him to escort me.'

She decided that she must accept, and penned a polite note to that effect.

Simon and his companions rode across Chelsea Bridge, east through Lambeth village, and so on up to the wooded hills of Kent – Streatham Hill, Sydenham Hill, Forest Hill, Hilly Fields, Blackheath, Shooters Hill. All these forested summits were now infested by wolves, which, singly, might not have been dangerous, but they ranged in large packs and, ten or twenty together, could easily bring down a horse.

The weather made hunting them more difficult. Snow fell continually, blinding the huntsmen and their mounts, giving good cover for the wolves to slip away among ancient oaks and thickset hazel and thorn coppices.

Towards mid-afternoon, somewhere in the region of Blackheath Edge, when the light was already beginning to fail, Simon became separated from his companions. His horse had strained a fetlock, stumbling on a concealed rabbit hole that was masked by snow; it limped badly and could not keep up with the others. Soon Simon was alone, among great barricades of thorn trees.

Plague on it, he thought. I had best turn for home. At this pace, Lochinvar won't get me back to Chelsea before dark. Where can the others have got to? Will they have the sense to know that is what I have done?

It was a desolate, silent region where he found himself. The gnarled ancient thorn trees grew close together. He had not passed a house for miles. London seemed far away, though he knew that the villages of Greenwich and Deptford must lie somewhere in the valley below and to the north.

'Hold up, poor old fellow!' he said, as Lochinvar stumbled again. 'I'd better lead you through all these tangled thorn trees. It's lucky there aren't any wolves about.'

During the day, the hunters had accounted for several hundred of the creatures, and their mates, limping, bleeding and cowed, had been driven southwards and eastwards.

Simon had no sooner dismounted, however, than he heard a faint scream ahead of him, and the familiar, ominous sound of snarls, growls and high-pitched howls.

Cursing the flutter of snow that obscured his view, he struggled on, tugging the reluctant Lochinvar after him, and came out into a small clearing where there was a wooden cabin. In front of the building he could see the black, ragged shapes of six or seven wolves, leaping, crouching, and darting as they attacked a human figure that tried to defend itself with no weapon but a metal pail.

The faint cry came again: a thin, despairing sound.

'Hold on! I'm coming!' Simon shouted. 'Get away, you brutes!' he yelled at the wolves, who took no notice.

Simon did not dare discharge his loaded gun, for fear of accidentally wounding the wolves' victim, so he flung Lochinvar's bridle over a thorn bough, and crept closer, until one wolf spotted him and turned; then he was able to shoot it at almost point-blank range. The rest, frightened by the report, reluctantly retreated; Simon was able to kill two more of them, one with his second musket, the next with the short sword, called a Save-All, which every hunter carried.

Then he turned to assist the person he had rescued who, all this time, was crouched trembling in the snow. She seemed to be an elderly woman.

'Have they hurt you badly?' Simon asked her. 'Can you walk? If so you had best get inside. I'll just chase away the last of those beasts.'

But the woman seemed unable to walk, whether from fright or injuries, so he picked her up and carried her into the hut. This proved to be a roomy place, as big as a barn. Indeed, a donkey was stabled at one end. Simon deposited the woman in a hammock, which was slung across a corner.

'I'll just fetch in my horse, too, by your leave,' Simon said. 'Else the wolves are likely to attack him, tethered as he is.'

The woman made some faint sounds of agreement. 'Were you fetching water?' Simon asked, remembering the bucket. 'I'll get you some.' He had noticed a well-head and stone trough outside.

Several of the wolves, which had gone no farther than the edge of the cleared space, were now on the attack again, creeping back towards the terrified Lochinvar. Simon, who had reloaded his guns, was able to dispatch another two wolves; the others, giving up, loped away into the wood.

Returning with the horse and pail of water, Simon discovered that the woman had managed to pull herself together, get out of the hammock, put brushwood on a fire that smouldered in a brick hearth, and light a lamp.

'Do you live here all alone, ma'am?' he asked.

'I'm obliged to,' she replied shortly. 'I've got nobody.'

As the light burned brighter, Simon observed two things with surprise. One was the enormous number of toy animals, arranged on shelves, which covered one entire wall of the cabin. They were of all sizes; some of them had plaster heads, some china, some waxen, some papier mâché; the bodies were mostly made of cloth, or fur, standing, sitting, or lying; there were foxes, bears, rabbits, leopards, dogs, cats, sheep – besides more exotic creatures, lions, tigers, crocodiles, polar bears, some of them very fancifully shaped, but all made with great skill. Their glass eyes gleamed in the firelight; the whole wall seemed to be looking at Simon.

The other thing that surprised him, surveying the woman he had rescued, was the discovery that she was by no means as old as he had first thought her;

she was skinny, her face was lined and weather-beaten, and she walked with a limp, but after a minute or two he began to think that she was hardly out of her thirties, and then, as she went on talking, he decided that she must be younger still.

'It was a bit o' luck for me that you come along when you did,' she remarked briefly; and then, after a moment or two, in a more doubtful tone, '*maybe*,' as if, reconsidering, she was not so certain about the luck. This was all the thanks she gave Simon, but she filled a kettle from the pail of water he had brought in, and offered, 'You'd best have a dram of tea. It's only mint. I can't afford the real.'

'Thank you. I'd like that. Did the wolves maul you at all? Were you hurt?'

'No; they only tore my dress.' She sniffed. 'It warn't much before. Anyhow it'll tear up for stuffing.' She gave a sour smile. She was sharp-faced, with a bad scar over one cheekbone; her hair, which might once have been pale yellow, was now a yellowish grey, pulled back in a knot.

'Did you make all those?' Simon asked, sitting down on a tree-stump that did duty for a stool and looking at the display of toy animals.

'Who else?' she snapped. 'You see any factory hands round here?'

He shook his head.

'O' course I made 'em. Winters I works on 'em; the heads are fashioned in Hamburg and I buys 'em from Whites, in Houndsditch; and the wax and pappy mashy in Barbican; then I moulds and stuffs the bodies myself; I've a book with pictures – ' she nodded towards an old, tattered natural history book on a shelf; 'and in the summer I sells 'em around Knightsbridge or Stuart Park. I used to hire a feller to do so, but he was a cheat and robbed me of a whole summer's takings; so now I do it myself.'

She poured hot water on to a bundle of crushed mint leaves. Then, with an acute glance at Simon's handsome silver-mounted muskets, well polished boots, and well-fed horse, she added wheedlingly, 'Have you any young ones, sir? I've some real fancy toys in stock – poodle dogs, lambs with real wool. Think how their little eyes would light up if you brought 'em home one o' those.'

And she waved a hand towards the wall glittering with eyes.

'No, I haven't any children. I'm not married,' said

Simon hastily, taking the cup of mint tea she handed him. 'Do you never make dolls?' he asked.

'No,' she snapped. 'I don't care for people. Animals are better.'

Her scowl at his reply was so very familiar that he cried out in astonishment, '*I* know who you are! You're Penelope Twite! I *thought* I recognized your voice! Aren't you Penny? Dido's elder sister? Don't you remember me? Simon, who used to lodge with your father in Rose Alley?'

She was so taken aback that she dropped her own cup of mint tea and it smashed on the cobbled floor.

'There!' she said crossly. 'Now look what you made me do.'

'But aren't you Mr Twite's elder daughter Penny? Dido's sister?'

'What if I am?' she said dourly. '*That* ain't going to put any diamond rings on my fingers.'

'Do you never see your father?'

She shook her head.

'Not since I left home.'

Simon then vaguely recollected that she had run off with a buttonhook salesman.

'I heard tell as how Ma died,' Penelope added, without any display of grief. 'Is Pa still alive, then?'

'So far as I know; your sister Dido said she had seen him recently.'

'I guess he'll be up to his usual goings-on in that case,' she said indifferently. 'What's Dido doing?'

'She – she has been travelling. She is staying with your father in Wapping.'

'*Travelling?*' Penelope said bitterly. 'Some folk have all the luck.'

'What happened to—? Were you not married?'

'Oh! Him! He left me flat. Years ago. Took all my savings. I had a baby – but it died,' Penelope said in a toneless voice. She fetched a brush and swept up the fragments of broken crockery. 'You won't be wanting to spend the night here,' she said. 'Luckily you won't have to – which is just as well, for I've no extra grub. Some chaps'll be coming past about midnight. Surveyors.'

'Surveyors?'

'Summat to do with that new Thames tunnel and the procession,' she explained without interest. 'They been planning the way it's to go, and working out how long it takes. They said they'd be by tonight, and one of 'em agreed to bring me a parcel o' piece-goods from Chislehurst. The carrier leaves 'em for me there. Mostly I walks over – but with the wolves it's getting too dangerous.'

'I should think so,' said Simon. 'It's lucky I came along when I did, or you'd not be needing that parcel.'

He could not avoid a feeling of relief that he need not spend the night with this crabbed creature. Still, he felt sorry for her.

'Wouldn't you be better living in a – in a place that wasn't so lonely?'

'Why?' said Penny. 'I don't like folk. I do well enough here – if the wolves hadn't grown so pesky. I ain't keen on being bothered. This procession coming past here is going to be a blame nuisance.'

'Maybe you can sell some of your animals?'

181

'Hah! Not on your oliphant! In town's the place to sell toys. Coves in processions don't want 'em.'

'No, I suppose not.'

Penelope sat down and began sewing the whiskers on a stuffed kitten with small fierce stitches.

'Shall I – would you like me to send a message to your father – or to Dido – telling them where you are?' suggested Simon uncertainly.

'Why?'

'You might like to see them? They might be glad to see you?'

'Fish! Why'd they want to see me? Anyhow, I don't want to see *them*.' She snapped a thread, re-threaded her needle, then added, 'You'd best have a nap. Talking's tiring. And there's no point in it. You can doss down in my hammock till the men come.'

Simon saw that it would be kinder to do this than to sit asking questions. He lay in the hammock and thought that he would never fall asleep, but, in fact, he did drift off after a while.

He was roused by Penelope shaking him, quite sharply.

'Hark! There's horses coming.'

'Your ears are quicker than mine,' Simon said, getting out of the hammock.

'Comes of living alone,' she said. 'Weeks go by when I hear nowt but my own voice.'

A few minutes later there were shouts beyond the door; with trampling and jingling of bridles and snorts and whinnies a party of horsemen drew up outside. Someone banged on the door, calling, 'Passel o' dry goods for Missus Curd – anyone in?'

182

'There's a chap here wants to ride to Rotherhithe with you,' Penelope said, opening the door and receiving the parcel.

'And welcome. He can ride the chain horse.'

Stepping out, Simon explained that he had a horse of his own, but it was lame and could only go at a slow pace. He was assured that he might use the cob which carried their tools and measuring equipment; without a rider his own mount would probably be able to keep up well enough.

Simon said goodbye to Penelope. He bought a stuffed mouse from her, thinking that Sophie would be able to find some child to give it to. Penelope stuck out her lower lip but accepted his money.

'There's nothing I can do for you – send you?'

She sniffed. 'Not as I can think on.'

'No message for your father? Your sister?'

'I never cared for Pa. And that Dido used to be a right plague. They don't care if I'm alive or dead.'

'I wonder! Well, goodbye. And thank you for the tea.' He remembered the cup she had dropped, and added, 'I'll bring another cup, next time I come by.'

'*You* won't be coming here again.'

Abruptly she turned her back on Simon and paid the man who had brought her parcel. Simon led out Lochinvar and mounted the survey troop's chain horse.

'What the deuce was the Duke o' Battersea doing in this nook-shotten spot?' asked the man who had brought Penelope's parcel, biting her sixpence to make sure it was a good one.

'Him? *He* ain't no duke,' said Penelope scornfully.

'Then that's all *you* know!'

Whistling, the man swung on to his horse and kicked it to make it catch up with the others. Penelope stared after the group, her usual sour look replaced by one of real amazement, before stepping back inside and bolting the door.

The survey group rode down Blackheath Hill and through Deptford.

'Come through the new tunnel if you wish, sir, we have the key of the gate,' said the leader of the troop, a burly, cheerful, red-headed man with a feather in his hat. 'You may ride to Chelsea as well north of the Thames as south of it.'

The route south of the river was more direct, but Simon, curious to see the new tunnel, accepted the offer. After all, he thought, I am going to be home so late that an hour or two won't make all that difference. Sophie will be long in bed.

The approach to the new Rotherhithe tunnel began among docks and warehouses half a mile away from the river itself, and plunged steeply downhill between massive walls built from great granite blocks.

'It's a grand piece of work,' said Simon, greatly impressed. 'Pity the old king didn't live long enough to see it completed and join in the celebrations.'

'All this junketing – bands, flag-waving, processions – that's a waste o' public money if you ask me,' grumbled the surveyor. 'Foolish, too. Suppose the river floods into the tunnel?'

'Is that likely?' asked Simon, startled.

'Not to say *likely*,' the man admitted. 'But there were a great flood in my granda's granfer's day – a

184

mort o' folk drowned in Deptford and Rotherhithe. If there were a sudden flood coming down-river – from rain at Henley, say – and that were to meet with a high tide coming up—'

'Well let us hope there is not,' said Simon with a shiver, as, pulling out a bunch of large keys, the surveyor unlocked the massive iron gates which barred the entrance to the tunnel. The gates slid back in a track, the party passed through, and then the leader closed up and locked the gates again behind them.

'That way no wolves can get through to Shadwell,' he remarked, striking a phosphorous match and lighting a tar-soaked torch, which he held above his head. The rest of the troop did likewise.

'The gas lighting don't come on till next week, day before the opening,' he explained. 'But these do well enough.'

The tunnel's high arched dome was lined with brilliant white tiles, which reflected the orange light of the torches and threw back eerie echoes as the horses clattered nervously along the paved footway; the Margrave's idea, of two processions moving in opposite directions, would be, Simon saw, perfectly possible, for the road was wide enough to accommodate two coaches driving abreast. Yet now that he was down here the scheme had lost its appeal for Simon: this was such a terribly gloomy place in which to have a public event take place. It is just like that creepy Margrave, thought Simon, to plan that the most important action should happen underground where no one could see it.

185

Except the people taking part, of course.

The surveyor unlocked the Shadwell gate and led his troop out into the snowy night.

'We have our depot and stables in Tower Hill, sir,' he told Simon. 'Can you manage to get home from there? Or would you like to borrow our horse for the night?'

'Oh, I can get a hackney carriage from Tower Hill, thank you. I'm much obliged to you for your help.'

'Gloomy, doomy sort o' place, that tunnel, though, ain't it?' said the surveyor, echoing Simon's thought, as they rode up the enclosed slope from the northern entrance. 'Useful enough, I don't deny – not that there ain't enough bridges, if you go westwards; myself, I'd sooner take a ferry. I'd enough o' tunnels when I were a lad; trap-opener in a Kentish colliery half a mile underground – ugh! I'll stay above ground for the rest of my life, thank you.'

'I quite agree with you,' said Simon, as they rode along Wapping High Street. 'Good heavens, what a lot of carriages – some of them very handsome – where can they be coming from in these parts, so late?'

'Oh, it's that feller as calls himself the Margrave of Bad Thingemajig. He was holding a big assembly tonight, what he called a musical swarry. My boy Alf is a page at Cinnamon Court, the Margrave's place; he told me there were a lot of nobs coming. There was going to be music and refreshments, everything very *à la*.'

I wonder if he sent an invitation to Sophie and me? thought Simon as coach after glittering coach passed their weary, mud-splashed troop. Perhaps Sophie is there now? Perhaps I ought to call in and offer to escort her home? But it would hardly do for me to present myself at such a gathering in my torn breeches and powder-grimed jacket.

He rode on his way.

9

'Daughter, his excellency is giving a musical soirée this evening, at which two of my Eisengrim Concertos are to be played,' remarked Mr Twite, strolling into the lodger's room, where Dido was teaching van Doon how to say, 'Och havers' and 'Aweel, aweel' while the Dutchman, in his turn, taught Is how to play noughts and crosses. Mr Twite scowled at this latter activity, and demanded, 'Has that little wretch nothing better to do than scribble on a bit of paper? Why is she not at work, pray?'

'She's being useful, Pa,' said Dido briefly. 'She keeps Mr van Doon from scratching his nose.'

'It tickles at me dreadfully,' sighed the patient.

'*Sair*, mister; you should say, "it itches me sair." '

'It itches me sair,' he repeated dutifully.

Mr Twite gave a nod of approval.

'Not bad; not bad at all! You sound just like one of those haggis-eaters. – Daughter, I wish you to accompany me to the recital at his excellency's residence.'

'Me, Pa? Why?'

Dido was not in the least enchanted at what her father plainly considered a great honour.

'Highty tighty! Don't take that tone with me, miss! You should be grateful.'

'Why?' asked Dido again.

'I wish – Ahem! That is to say – If his excellency should take a liking to you – as he has to our friend here – '

'But that's in the way of business. Ain't it?' said Dido bluntly. 'Mister van Doon is useful to His Nabs.'

'And so could you be, daughter – if you chose. And then your fortune would be made.'

'I'd as soon be useful to a crocodile. And a crocodile'd have just about the same use for me, I reckon,' said Dido.

'Don't be impertinent, child.'

'Anyways, how could I come to a grand party! I ain't got any grand clothes. I'd look as out of place as a herring in a harp factory.'

'Fiddlestick,' said her father. 'You can put on that page's uniform again, then you will sink into the background like a – like – ' He sought in vain for the right word.

By this time Dido had thought again. She said, 'Oh – very well. Tol-lol. I'll come.' It had occurred to her that, by going to the Margrave's palace, during a musical party when the host, no doubt, would be busy entertaining his guests, she might be able to fulfil her promise to Podge Greenaway and acquire some useful knowledge about his excellency.

'Just you keep on making Mr van Doon say "Och, havers" and "gudesakes",' she instructed Is. 'And whatever you do, don't let him scratch his nose – even if you have to tie his hands behind his back.'

Is nodded solemnly.

Dido ran up to the attic and put on the black velvet page's uniform, which had not been returned to Cinnamon Court. Returning to the ground floor, she heard sounds of angry disputation coming through the open door of Mrs Bloodvessel's frowsty parlour.

'You won't take *me*; oh no; but you take along that finical, mopsy little drab! *I'm* not good enough any more – though it was I introduced you to his excel – hich! – excellency, but no, I'm not fine enough to appear at his party now. Time was when I was – when I was his Matron of Honour – when I'd have been there, receiving the guests, sitting in the front row in pink velvet and pearls. How do you know Eisengrim wouldn't be *pleased* to see me there, enjoying meself – you pig, you!'

'Take a look in the glass, you miserable old canker-moll! Do you think Eisengrim wants to see *that*, gleering at him among the duchesses and viscountesses? Think yourself lucky he don't turn you out of this house! And now *will* you stop badgering on at me? Yes, yes, I'll see you right – I've promised to, haven't I? – when I'm Master of the King's Music. But, blister me, if you go on like this, I won't, I'll cut loose – Oh, stuff a belcher in it!' Mr Twite cried in exasperation as she let out a wail. 'Here, take a dram of loddy – do; take several drams; only *don't* obfuscate me, just when I'm wondering if I ought to speed up the tempo in the second movement before the fiddle comes in – '

'I'm ready, Pa,' Dido said, walking through the door. Mrs Bloodvessel threw her a venomous look. She reclined on her sofa as usual, with a large glass of her laudanum mixture in one hand, and a half smoked cigar in the other. At her elbow stood a bottle of port and a plate of bread and butter. She was much flushed.

'Have you let in the lollpoops?' Mr Twite asked Dido.

'Yes.'

'Where's the keys?'

'Here.'

'Put them on the mantel.'

'Little vixen!' Mrs Bloodvessel shook her cigar angrily as Dido did so, and a large lump of burning ash fell on to the bedspread. She rubbed it away with the hand that held the glass. 'You think yourself so nim, in your black velvet suit – don't you?'

'No, I don't, said Dido. 'Not partickle. Pa told me to put it on.'

'Oh yes – he favours *you* – so he does – because you can be useful to him. He favours you,' repeated Mrs Bloodvessel. 'But what about me? What about poor little Is, down in the cellar? He got no time for us, any more than if we was lollpoops.'

Dido was about to point out that Mrs Bloodvessel herself had not appeared to set any value on little Is – except as a slave – when her father exclaimed, 'Hold your row, Lily, do! I shall be late if we don't go at once. Drink up your dram – there – and I'll pour you another.' He did so, tipping in, Dido noticed, an extra quantity of liquor from a small bottle he pulled out of his hoboy case. 'Now then, read a book, why don't you,' he advised. 'Or – or do some embroidery. Or mend one o' my shirts – they all need it, lud knows! Come on Dido. – I will say for Ella Twite,' he continued loudly as they went through the door, 'she could keep a man mended up and cook a meal, even if it was mostly fish porridge.'

As he slammed and locked the front door another wail from Mrs Bloodvessel showed that this shaft had struck home.

'Pa,' said Dido as they hurried along over the snow-covered cobbles. 'You said just now that you'd see Mrs Bloodvessel right when you was Master o' the King's Music. Is the Margrave going to put in a word for you with the king, then? I thought you said the king would be sure to throw you in the Tower for – for Hanoverian jiggery-pokery?'

'Hush!' snapped her father. It was plain that, unlike Mrs Bloodvessel, he had had nothing to drink and was as nervous and jumpy as a barrel of weasels. 'I'll – I'll explain all that later. Just you keep your mouth shut now and pay attention to what's going on. What *you* have to remember is that his excellency sets a proper value on *me*. He knows there's no one writing music like mine.'

I reckon that's true, thought Dido. And ain't it queer?

She wondered what the real reason was for her father's taking her to this party. Guess I'll find out soon enough. Hope there's summat to eat. I'm hollow.

Fare in Bart's Building was scanty, except that

provided for Mijnheer van Doon; and little Is was so evidently half starved that Dido generally gave the child most of her own share of whatever was going.

From several streets away it was plain that a tremendous fête was taking place at Cinnamon Court. Dozens of carriages rolled past them, and when they came in view of the building they saw that it was a blaze of light with doors open and red carpet running, not just down the steps, but half the length of the street. Glittering conveyances were setting down their passengers, while others waited; knee-breeched, white-wigged footmen were kept busy opening carriage doors and handing down gorgeously dressed ladies and gentlemen. Flaring lights at the gates and on the stone stairway made the scene brighter than day and turned the falling snow to a spangle of gold.

Dido felt shy and out of place, climbing the steps in her page's uniform at the side of her father – who, for once, was tidily dressed in black, though he still wore his red wig and moustache. But the porter bowed respectfully to him and it was plain to Dido that he and his music were an important part of the evening's programme.

This time they did not turn into the small music room, but made their way up a double flight of stairs to a huge salon, already more than half filled with guests, who strolled or chatted or sat on groups of gilt chairs. Along one side of the room a row of huge windows gave on to the river. On a platform at the far end a small orchestra was assembling; the string players were quietly tuning their instruments, the

spinet player had opened the lid of his and was peering inside it, the flautists were softly comparing notes.

Mr Twite started towards the platform at a purposeful pace, evidently forgetting all about Dido.

'Where shall I go, Pa?' she asked urgently, before she had lost him for good.

'Ah – humph – ah – just mingle with the guests, why don't you my chickadee, until it is time for us to start playing.'

'Don't be silly, Pa – that won't do at all. *Look* at the guests! Half of 'em are wearing crowns – they're all dukes and duchesses and noblenesses.'

It was true that the guests were all magnificently dressed – the ladies in flashing tiaras, or feather

195

headdresses, in crinolines with spangles and precious stones at every seam; while the men were almost as dazzling, in satin knee-breeches, with jewelled military orders pinned on their jackets, gold epaulettes on their shoulders, rings on their fingers and diamonds on their shoe-buckles.

'His Nabs certainly do know all of the top nobs,' said Dido, impressed

'They come because of my music,' said Mr Twite with certainty.

He flipped a white-and-gold programme out of the gilt basket of a passing page-boy and showed Dido its contents:

His Excellency the Margrave of Nordmarck,
Landgraf of Bad Wald,
Plenipotentiary in Ordinary from the
Court of Hanover
to His Majesty King Richard IV of England
presents
an evening of Healing and Harmony
with the Eisengrim Household Players
conducted by
Herr Boris von Bredalbane

Programme:

A Suite of Tea Music	*B. Bredalbane*
Eisengrim Concerto No. 1	*B. Bredalbane*
Eisengrim Concerto No. 2	*B. Bredalbane*

'Coo! Pa, what a lot of your music. Is that really what they've come for?'

'Of course. And to observe a demonstration of its healing power. But that is neither here nor there – Now I must wait no longer – be a good child – behave yourself – '

Dido saw that she would get no help or advice from her father as to how she should conduct herself. In fact he left her without more ado and made his way to the platform, where he conferred with the members of his group.

Glancing warily around her, Dido was pleased to see the red-headed page whose birthday was July the fourth. He, too, carried a basket of programmes, which he was offering to new arrivals.

'Hey – cully – gimme that basket – be a pal,' muttered Dido in his ear. 'Remember me – March the first? I feel like a busted back-stay without summat to do – '

He grinned, passed her his basket, and went off to collect a tray of brimming wine-glasses from the buffet that ran along the side of the room.

Strolling among the crowd, proffering her programmes, Dido felt much more comfortable, and was able to pick up a number of comments from the elegant guests.

'They say this musical feller – what'shisname – Bredalbane – is really something quite out of the common . . .'

'I prefer a good military march myself . . .'

'But does his music really have the power of healing?'

'Ha, ha! So Eisengrim asserts, but for my part I take that with a pinch of salt!'

'Poor Eisengrim! I see that, despite all his lures, the king has not come to his party.'

'No, and I hear the Margrave's monstrous put about at such a snub – face as long as a fiddle.'

'As long as a viol da gamba.'

'Oh, ha ha ha! Begad, your grace has such a wit!'

'Poor Eisengrim! They say that, since Prince George of Hanover died, he has been trying in every way to win King Richard's favour – with very small success.'

'He certainly sets a lavish table – '

Dido noticed that the other pages, having supplied every guest with a programme, were now carrying round trays of refreshments – bowls piled with gleaming caviare, lobster patties, crystallized grapes, ices – besides all kinds of delicacies she had never seen before; besides oceans of champagne in sparkling myriads of glasses. Maybe the people come for the nosh, not Pa's music, Dido thought; but no, they probably get just as good at home.

Following the example of the pages, Dido went to the buffet for a tray of glasses, wondering a little anxiously if she would be spotted as an intruder; but it seemed that extra staff must have been taken on for the occasion; nobody gave her a second look. Behind the buffet, busy opening bottles of wine, she noticed a couple of the black-leather-coated boys whom she had last seen bullying half-crowns and half sovereigns out of the poor traders in Wapping High Street. Now they were dressed up stiff and grand in white wigs and gold-laced white uniforms.

It sure is handy to be small and nohow-looking,

thought Dido, receiving a tray from one of these, whose glance passed over her indifferently. Wouldn't it be a joke if I saw somebody I know amongst the guests – Simon or Sophie maybe? Gliding about like a small black ghost in her page's uniform, she listened and watched, offered food and drink, ice creams and sorbets, tea and coffee, for upwards of an hour. Then the service of refreshments came to a stop, the guests began to settle themselves on the gilded chairs, and the musicians to tune their instruments more loudly, as a hint that they would shortly begin playing.

All this time, Dido had not once laid eyes on the Margrave; but now she noticed him walk in at the end of the room farthest from the platform; his face looked puffed and red, oddly so – from bad temper, because the king had not come to his party, or for some other reason? – He walked, too, with a slight limp, and sometimes pressed a hand against the small of his back as if he had a pain there. Snatching a glass of champagne from the tray of Dido, who happened to be nearest to him, he gulped it down without looking at her. He was as gorgeously dressed as any of his guests in white velvet with gold trimmings, which had the effect of making his face appear even redder and puffier.

'*Dear* excellency!' said a lady in a diamond coronet and amber satin gown. 'We are *so* much looking forward to your musical treat.'

'I am happy to think, Lady Maria, that you will not be disappointed.'

The Margrave was obviously making a strong effort to collect himself and behave as if nothing were amiss.

'Do, *do* tell me, Margrave, who is to be healed? I am so curious – '

'Why, you see that row of seats to the right of the platform – some ailing Chelsea Pensioners, some afflicted children from the Foundling Hospital are to be brought – indeed, there they are now – '

Half a dozen elderly men in pensioners' uniforms, limping on crutches, were followed by children who were wheeled in basket chairs.

'What a dismal sight!' whispered one lady. But others said, 'How touching! What quaint mites! How wonderful it will be if this evening's programme can really help them.'

Somebody clapped hands for silence and the Margrave walked to the front of the orchestra and said, 'My friends, I am happy to welcome you here. I need say no more. My personal physician and medical adviser, Doctor Willibald Finster, will explain to you about the use of Herr Bredalbane's music.'

Dr Finster, looking neat and brisk in black with a grey cravat, gave a short talk on the healing power of music; and that of Bredalbane in particular, with allusions to natural harmonies, waves of magnetism, currents of power, and other things that Dido did not understand. Croopus, she thought, does Pa's music really do all that? Or is it a load of boffle?

'Some people do say that the Margrave himself is only kept alive by the power of this fellow's music . . .'

'He is not much of a recommendation for it, then; he looks far from well.'

'Ah, but think how much worse he might be!'

'He is a strange fellow! What is he really after?'

Dido edged closer, hoping to learn something useful.

'Oh, power, undoubtedly,' said Lady Maria's companion. He inserted a quizzing-glass into his elderly eye, in order to study the Margrave more closely – but at this moment the group of musicians began to play, and, as always when she heard her father's music, Dido was swept away into another world, and a far more beautiful one, where everything was orderly and perfect, where no explanations were needed at all, because nothing could vary or be in any way better than it was.

The Tea Suite, played first, turned out to have many of her old favourite tunes in it – 'Tapioca Pudding', 'Galloping Mokes', 'The Lost Slipper', 'The Day Before the Day Before May Day', and 'Penny-lope's Peevy', the tune that always, for some reason, made Dido think of her sister in a bad temper. Wonder where old Penny has got to now, with that buttonhook fellow of hers, Dido mused, and then the music carried her on, through flowery fields, past rushing rivers, into a place of total content.

Too bad I ain't got a broken leg; this music'd fix it for me, she thought, and forgot to watch the audience.

She had positioned herself among the other pages, who were lined up against the long wall opposite the row of huge arched windows that looked out on to the river. The guests, glittering and plumed, randomly grouped on their gilt chairs, occupied the middle of the room, with the Margrave among them; the sick people and children, with their nurses or attendants, were assembled in a small crescent near the orchestra platform; and beyond the great row of arched windows the snow fell steadily, and the river lapped higher and higher, flowing westwards; then, as the tide came to its peak, the river began to eddy, the water waited, swung to and fro, and turned at last to flow in the reverse direction.

Dido wholly lost track of time while her father's music was playing. It might have lasted an hour, two hours or three; she could not have said.

'My: that was really, really prime,' she sighed to her neighbour, the red-headed page, when the final piece was finished, the last encore played, and her father, pale, sweating, dishevelled, his wig slightly askew, had taken his final bow.

'Wonderful! Truly wonderful!' fluted Lady Maria to the Margrave. 'Your Chapelmaster is a true genius, dear Eisengrim. May we not meet him – converse with him – ?' – as Mr Twite, with a last hasty bow, vanished through a door backstage, in pursuit of his musicians.

'Ah, no, dear lady – in most ways he is a rough diamond. It must be said that, apart from his music – which is everything – he has a rude, untrained mind, no culture, no breeding, no parts; in conversation with your ladyship he would be quite at a loss, unable to put two sentences together.'

Hearing this, Dido flushed with indignation; but a moment's thought obliged her to admit that what the Margrave said was mainly true; furthermore, Mr

Twite, carried away by his excitement and success, might easily have been capable of forgetting his false identity as Bredalbane and letting some terrible cat out of the bag.

The Margrave, Dido noticed, seemed to have derived considerable benefit from the music. His face was now a much more natural colour, less bloated and flushed; he moved more freely, smiled and spoke more easily. But what about the sick children and the pensioners? Dido craned on tiptoe; from where she stood she could not see them, since, now the music had come to an end, most of the noble guests had stood up and were moving about, strolling and conversing in groups that formed and re-formed.

'What's happened to the sick folk?' Dido asked her red-headed neighbour, who was taller.

'Dr Finster's looking at 'em and testing 'em,' he said. 'The little yaller-haired gal got up and walked.'

'Coo!' said Dido.

Murmurs of genteel wonder, polite oohs and ahs of amazement came from the elegant crowd.

'Can the music *really* have such sovereign virtue?' Lady Maria asked her elderly companion.

But suddenly – shocking and breaking the quiet, almost reverent atmosphere – a sharp little voice was heard, distinctly demanding, 'When does I get my orange?' and then, louder, 'That Dr Finster promised me an orange if I sat through the music and then walked six steps and said my legs was better. I want my blooming orange!'

There followed a moment's thunderstruck silence – then a ripple of amusement, polite but mocking laughter, which ran through the crowd, from front to back.

'I fear his excellency has done for himself!' said the man with the quizzing-glass to Lady Maria. 'Salting the mines, what?'

'My dear duke, what *can* you mean? What mines?'

Now the disillusioned audience began to drift away. Guests took their leave. With civil salutations, with courteous expressions of pleasure they said their farewells to the Margrave, admired his charming house, extended polished thanks for his delightful music, and walked away down the hall. And then – as soon as they were half a dozen paces from their furious host – the ridicule broke out: 'My dear, *did* you see? *Did* you hear – ? That absurd little creature gave the whole game away. Demanding payment! Depend upon it, they were all bribed to pretend that the music had cured them of desperate illnesses!'

'His poor excellency is wholly discredited.'

'Oh come, now, Maria, how the deuce could he bribe a Chelsea Pensioner?'

'I daresay they are all actors, you know, merely dressed up as pensioners.'

In five minutes the salon was empty – except for the pages, briskly collecting used plates and glasses, the small group of children and old men by the stage – who looked, most of them, utterly confused and bewildered – and the Margrave, who, pale with passion, was delivering a low-toned but savage reprimand to Dr Finster, furiously waving an empty champagne glass while he hissed his maledictions.

'Dolt! Idiot! Jackass! *Dummkopf!* Booby!

204

Blockhead! What in creation's name made you stoop to such a stupidity? How could you betray me so? How could you betray yourself so?'

'Oh – your highness – your excellency – forgive me! Forgive me! It was simply that – results are sometimes so unpredictable – I did so wish everybody to be certain – '

'And now you have ruined it all. No one will *ever* believe. What a fool you have made of me. I've a mind to dismiss you on the spot – send you packing back to Bad – '

'Oh, my lord – no! Think of your own health – I beg you – I beseech you – '

'Well, I won't do it at once; not yet. But you are in utter, utter disgrace – I do not wish to see your face – or only at consultation time – Well? What is it?' he snapped at Dido.

'Your glass, sir.'

'Bring me another – a full one,' he said, dropping the empty glass on her tray.

'Yessir.'

I wonder if Pa will be in disgrace too, Dido ruminated, filling a glass from one of the remaining bottles on the buffet.

'And have all those imposters locked up!' the Margrave was ordering, when she took him back his drink. 'In the cellars under the river! Immediately! I will not have it said that I let such an imposture go unpunished – '

'But, sir – but, my lord – most of them – '

'Be quiet! Don't argue with me, or – ' The Margrave added something in the German tongue which turned his physician ashen-white with horror; then he spun on his heel and walked out of the salon.

Poor devils, thought Dido, watching with anger and pity as the group of patients, or counterfeit patients, were swiftly hustled away by a dozen burly uniformed footmen. One of the children she recognized as a little creature who had been crying 'Sweet Lavender' the other day in Wapping High Street. Dido heard one of the old men, a Chelsea Pensioner, muttering, in total perplexity, 'But what did I do that was wrong? I *were* cured – sartin sure; no hocus-pocus – there's me crutch to prove it –' He looked back wistfully at his abandoned crutch leaning against the platform. 'So what the pize is 'e going on about?'

I'd best find Pa post-haste and get outa here, thought Dido, with the Margrave in this fratchety frame; there ain't a thing I can do for those poor souls on my own; I'd best tell somebody about them. But who?

'Where's Mr Twi – Mr Bredalbane?' she asked a page.

'Him? Oh, he went off ten minutes ago.'

'Plague take Pa,' muttered Dido, and made for the front entrance – passing, though she did not know it, by the door of the room where Sophie sat helplessly gagged, with her arms strapped together and her legs tethered to the legs of her chair.

'Hey, you,' said the porter, grabbing Dido, as she was about to run down the red-carpeted steps, 'where d'you think you're off too, my cocksparrer? Pages ain't allowed out after ten – '

'I'm no page. I came with my pa – Mr Bredalbane,' said Dido. Would he remember? Otherwise she would be in a fine fix.

But luckily he did remember.

'Very well, run along and let me close up. Brrrr! It's cold enough to freeze the sails off a brass windmill.'

It was. The snow had stopped falling, but a bitter wind blew, straight from the North Pole. The snow on the ground had frozen into a surface hard and slippery as marble. Dido shivered in her thin velvet, though she ran as fast as she could, hoping to overtake her father.

He had not hurried. In fact when she caught up with him he was drifting slowly along, veering from one side of the road to the other, hands in his pockets, head in the air, humming over the various themes from his suite and concertos.

'Pa, Pa! Wait for me!'

'Eh – ? Is that you, child? Why did you not meet me at the door?'

'How the blazes did I know when you was planning to leave?' Dido said crossly. 'I thought as you'd stay for the healing.'

'Pshaw! Mumbo jumbo! My music is the important thing – not all that pesky mystical nonsense of Finster's,' said Mr Twite. 'Oh, mystical nonsense of Finster's, he sang, 'it may affect dotards and spinsters . . . But was not my music magnificent, child? Was it not majestic, sublime, transcendent?'

'Oh yes, Pa, it was all those things,' Dido assured him sincerely. 'It was – it was naffy!'

'Now do you see why *no* position is good enough for me save Master of the King's Music!'

'Ye-es – but Pa, I *still* don't see – specially now His Nabs is in such a peck of trouble because of that clunch, Finster, going and rigging the cures – '

'*What*?' demanded Mr Twite, who had wandered out of Cinnamon Court, in dreamy, elevated spirits, quite unaware of the embarrassing scene that followed his concert.

When he heard about it he was almost as angry as the Margrave.

'That Finster is a complete clodpole! – Mind, His Nabs ain't easy to manage, I'll hand you that; he has to be humoured, he has to be wheedled; you need to pay heed to his whimsies:

> 'Just a little heed'll
> Save a deal of wheedle
> Skill and tact and speed'll
> Often win a way – '

sang Mr Twite. 'Well, now you see, my pippin, why there is such a need for you to marry the king – '

'*Marry the king?*' gasped Dido. 'Are you off your rocker? Have you gone clean out of your finical *wits*, Pa?'

'Stop acting skittish and silly and hysterical, child. What else do you suppose I ever had in mind? All you have to do is sit tight and play your cards cannily – as you would say to our Netherlandish friend up yonder – '

Mr Twite gestured with an airy hand towards the upper floors of Bart's Building which they were now approaching.

'But, Pa — Princess Adelaide of Thuringia is being fetched over to marry the king — everyone knows that.'

'Tush. I do not mean *that* king, child.'

'Sakes alive! *Pa!*' Dido interrupted him — in any case, what he was saying made no sense at all — 'Hey, Pa, look at the house. It's afire! There's smoke coming out!'

'Ahhhh — blessmysoul — ' muttered Mr Twite, slowly coming down from the lit-up, airy, fantastical regions where his mind had been floating. He stared at the house. 'Smoke. So there is. Coming from doors and windows. How very singular. Not to say unusual. I wonder, now, what could be occasioning such a phenomeniggle?'

He stood on the pavement outside Bart's Building, scratching his head slowly, staring vacantly. Dido stared too. The house looked like an old, black, whiskery cat. Smoke in plumes, in curls and tendrils, was finding a way through door and window cracks all over the downstairs part of the building.

'It's on fire!' said Dido again, horrified. 'With all those folk inside — Mrs Bloodvessel and little Is and Mr van Doon and the lollpoops — *quick*, Pa, we gotta get them out — give us the keys, quick, I'll go in and roust 'em out while you run for help — go and fetch the fire brigade — '

But Mr Twite did not seem inclined to hand her the keys, or to run for help. He still scratched his head. 'Well, now – ' he began ruminatively. 'Well, now we have to think about this – '

What he would have said was interrupted by Dr Finster, who arrived, in a curricle, at a gallop.

'Ah – Bredalbane – what a lucky chance – thank heaven you are here – ' he panted. 'Come back at once! His excellency has had a severe seizure – I have administred a strong opiate – but your music is more important still. Pray come directly –'

He reached down a hand, Mr Twite took it, and was swiftly hoisted into the carriage.

'But, *Pa*!' cried Dido. 'The keys – the fire – all those folk in there – you aren't just a-going to *leave* them – ?' She could hardly believe it, even of her father; she could hardly speak for horror.

But he said, 'Don't bother me now, my cherub – his lordship is more important. As for the fire – I daresay it will prove to be a trifle – '

His final words were blown back on the icy wind as Dr Finster, who had already turned the carriage, whipped his horses into a gallop.

'*Throw back the keys!*' screamed Dido, but Mr Twite took no notice.

She wasted no time in looking after the carriage. She had her own front door key, tucked into the page's cummerbund; she flung the front door open and raced up the stairs to van Doon's room before the hoofbeats had died away.

'Sir! Sir!' she called, beating on the door with both fists, 'come down quick! The house is afire! Make haste!'

The Dutchman was still awake; a light showed

under his door and he opened it directly. Little Is was there too; they had been playing dominoes; thank goodness for that, thought Dido.

'Quick!' she said to Is. 'You gotta help me get out the lollpoops – all those young 'uns locked in down there – the fire's downstairs, just smell the smoke!'

They came down none too soon; thick smoke was coiling up the stairs, and as they ran towards the front door a sudden fierce burst of flame shot out of Mrs Bloodvessel's door.

'Reckon that's where it begun – in there,' panted Dido. 'D'you think, mister, that she's – that she – ?'

Van Doon looked through the door at the raging flames and shook his head. 'If she is in there, child, she cannot be alive. But you say that there are others – there are children down below?'

'Yes, and I haven't a *key*!' Dido clenched her fists. 'Pa told me to put it on the mantel. We gotta bash open the door, else they'll all be kippered in there, poor brutes. Oh, if Pa hadn't gone off – '

The Dutchman displayed unexpected resource.

'We must take a post from the fence – I do not think it will be too difficult – so!' He dragged loose one of the rusty iron rails. 'Now we use it to knock down the door. You help me,' he ordered Dido. 'Not you, little one; you are too small.'

Five – six – seven – eight times he and Dido ran at the warped and paintless door and drove their improvised battering ram against it; at the ninth stroke the door gave way and they tumbled through into the smoke-filled room. Already from inside they had heard faint pitiful cries: 'Help, help!' and as soon as the door was down a mass of terrified, smoke-grimed children began to struggle and scramble out into the area and up the steps.

'Be careful!' called van Doon. 'Do not trample one another. There is time, we will help you all!'

Dido grabbed a grimy boy who seemed lively enough, not too choked or confused by fumes.

'Can you run and raise the alarm? If you get there quick enough, maybe the firemen can stop the whole house burning. I'll see that the rest of your mates get out safe.'

He nodded and ran off.

Dido and the Dutchman raced to and fro, lugging, dragging, hauling, tugging and pushing the rest of the lollpoops to safety. The ones near the street door had

been in better shape; the poor wretches who were packed together at the back – tight as cigars in a box, thought Dido – were, many of them, fainting or stupefied from breathing smoke, and had to be dragged or carried out and laid face-down on the cobbles.

The last two were fetched out only just in time; a whole section of the charred ceiling fell in, and a fear-some light from above was thrown across the dismal basement room where the ropes dangled, already beginning to burn.

'*Gott sei dank* – that is all of them,' said the Dutchman, rubbing his brow with his shirtsleeve. His face, like that of Dido, was black with smoke and grime. Just as well, she thought; all we need is somebody taking him for King Dick.

At this moment the fire wagon arrived with a clatter of sturdy horses and clank of brass pails.

'Any folk still inside?' the fire chief asked van Doon.

'We got out all the children from below – ' van Doon indicated the stupefied lollpoops, lying higgledy-piggledy on the pavement.

'Lucky for them,' the fire chief commented briefly. 'Always said that place were a death trap.'

'But there is the woman in that room there,' Van Doon pointed to the ground-floor room where flames sprouted like ferns from the front window.

'She's done for, then. No question. Still, I reckon we can save the house. Get going, lads!' he bellowed at his men, who had already formed a bucket chain to the river – where it was discovered that the ice had to be broken, for it had formed a rim, inches thick, along the edge, running out for several feet into the river.

While the full and empty buckets were passed to and fro at racing speed, Dido and van Doon worked hard at rousing the lollpoops – slapping their faces, shaking them, rubbing them with handfuls of snow and ice, and, as fast as they recovered, setting them to help their companions.

But all the time, while she worked, Dido's mind, spinning in a circle, chased one idea. Round and round, round and round.

How could Pa have gone off like that, with the front door key in his pocket, leaving the place to burn? Of course he was all lit up and excited after his concert – I know that – and upset, because of Finster's stupid trick – and worried, on account of His Nabs taking a bad turn – but, just the same – how could he?

He didn't know I'd got a front door key. That was just luck.

And what about that last dram he gave Mrs B? And what about the cigar she was smoking? When we left the house – was she still smoking it then? Holding it in her hand? When Pa said something spiteful about Ma – something that made Mrs B. give a kind of squawk – ?

How *can* somebody write such music – and act so?

At last the fire was quenched, and the half-choked lollpoops were all on the way to recovery. The fire wagon departed, taking with it the charred corpse of

Mrs Bloodvessel, decently wrapped in a counterpane. The room she and Mr Twite had occupied was the only one completely burned; it was gutted, with a hole through the floor to the basement below, which was now half full of water from the firemen's activities.

The upstairs part of the house was still habitable, though black as an oven with soot and grease, ice-cold from the night air, and soused with water which had already begun to freeze. And every room in the house was filled with the same stench – a rank, sharp, stifling smell of burnt timber.

'What'll we do now?' a girl lollpoop dismally asked Dido. 'Do us lie out all night in the street, us'll freeze to death. And he did take our fardens.'

Dido thought of those farthings, probably in her father's pocket.

'You'd best come back inside,' she said gruffly. 'Reckon it's safe enough. And there's plenty empty rooms upstairs. Find yourselves places.'

Silently they stumbled in, toiled up, and sank on the floors of the empty rooms. Is, her basement lair now flooded with six inches of half frozen water, went back to Mr van Doon's room, where Dido contrived her a bed from a folded mat and her own sheepskin jacket.

'Where's Figgin?' demanded the Slut suddenly. 'Where's my cat Figgin?'

Nobody had seen him. Is began to cry.

'Oh, if he's burned – if he's burned – I – I don't rightly know *what* I'll do!'

'Don't take on so! He'll turn up – that cat's got

a power of sense,' Dido reminded her. 'Anyhow he wouldn't be in Mrs B's room – he never went in there, she couldn't abide him.'

Leaving van Doon to comfort Is, if he could, Dido went, rather wearily, downstairs to shut the front door – though with the windows burned out, there seemed little point in such a precaution.

As she stood on the step, yawning, rubbing the smoke from her eyes, looking at the trampled, sooty snow, she saw Wally Greenaway approaching at a run.

10

Sophie had gone early to the Margrave's party, having dressed herself carefully in one of Simon's best evening suits – black satin knee-breeches, white ruffled cambric shirt, black velvet jacket, satin-lined cloak and tricorne hat.

Just as she was about to leave, her white dove fluttered down and perched on her shoulder. Nothing would persuade it to stay at home, or to travel back with Mogg in the carriage.

'I'll not be here long, Mogg, I don't intend to stay for the musical entertainment,' Sophie told the aged coachman. 'Can you come back for me in about an hour; though I am sorry to keep you tooling to and fro.'

'Never mind that, missie,' he grumbled. 'But I *am* sorry to see you dressed up so, like one o' them play-actors. And with that blessed bird! It ain't becoming. It'll lead to trouble, mark my words.'

'Fiddlestick, Mogg. *I* think it's *very* becoming,' said Sophie, looking admiringly at her black silk legs. 'Anyway, never mind that – you cross old man – but just come back for me at ten.'

'All rug, Missie Sophie; I'll be there.'

One of Sophie's reasons for intending to leave early was the possible awkwardness of meeting somebody she knew at the party, since she had herself announced as the Duke of Battersea. But, in fact, as soon as she gave her name to the major-domo, she was led away from the main salon, along a passage, down a stair, and into a small chamber, beautifully furnished with a dull greenish velvet carpet, grey satin walls, and all the furniture, to match the hearth, carved out of palest pink marble. A large bunch of pale pink roses stood in the empty grate; the room was rather cold. Evidently it was not in regular use. Sophie admired it very much.

Here, after a few minutes, the Margrave joined her. He was, Sophie noticed, extremely pale, and walked with a limp. When she bowed to him he gave her a cold, scrutinizing stare, then a chilly smile.

'Hmm, yes, I see . . . the likeness is really remarkable. Not anticipating anything of the kind I was, if only temporarily, deceived, last time we met. But you need not trouble to keep up the deception any longer, Lady Sophie. Pray be seated.'

Sophie gulped, but accepted his invitation to sit and managed to observe with tolerable calm, 'My brother was unable to come on either occasion, excellency, because he is out hunting wolves on the south side of the river – so as to render the area safe for your procession next week. He is in considerable danger. But we should not have practised the deception. Now: in what way can I be of service to you?'

She could not help blushing, felt a fool to have involved herself in the business, and, in her heart, blamed Simon a little; also herself; why *was* I such a fool, she thought, why didn't I just come as myself?

But the Margrave's next words blew all such vain repinings out of her mind.

'Originally, I must confess, I had forgotten your existence,' he said. 'You have complicated my arrangements. I planned that your brother should die, along with the rest of the king's friends – '

'*What* are you saying?' Sophie gasped.

' – And it may still be necessary,' the Margrave went on in a level tone. 'All depends at this point on you, my dear.'

He studied her again, carefully, then, with a sudden inarticulate sound of exasperation, stepped forward, snatched the dove from her shoulder, and wrung its neck. The bird was dead before Sophie could even open her mouth to protest.

'I cannot – *stand* – birds,' the Margrave said rather breathlessly. His pale face had become suffused with red. He put the dove on the pink marble mantelpiece.

Then he went on with what he was saying, as if nothing had happened.

'I will admit that I was greatly taken with your response, last week, to my Chapelmaster's music. I recognise that you have an intelligent spirit, that you are perceptive. You could be of great assistance to my design, if you could be persuaded to join me?'

Sophie could only gaze at him in silence, her eyes black as coals in a face perfectly bloodless from shock.

To hear of her brother's murder – to hear it alluded

to in that calm, matter-of-fact voice had made her ears ring and her throat close up. And then, the dove. She felt as if she would choke. She could not speak.

'I propose, you see, to replace the king with a substitute. One of my own selection, who will pay heed to *my* wishes,' the Margrave went on placidly. 'The substitution is to take place during the tunnel opening ceremony. The likeness is so exact that nobody – outside the king's close circle of intimates – can be aware of the change. Quite different from *your* little prank,' he said contemptuously. 'It is lucky,' he added, 'that the king was so seldom in London hitherto, and had so few friends.'

He paused, looking at Sophie for her response.

'I – I see,' she croaked, thinking the Margrave must be as mad as a hatter. Yet he *looked* sensible enough. Better humour him, anyway, until she could escape. 'What – pray – had you in – had you planned to do with – with the real king?' she asked in a shaking voice.

'Oh, nothing inhumane,' the Margrave replied airily. 'Nothing drastic, I assure you. There is a small island, Inchmore, off the coast of Scotland; it boasts a monastery, and the good monks also look after a number of persons whose wits have gone astray: I plan that the king shall be – shall be accomodated there, as a religious or as a lunatic; the choice is up to him.'

Sophie shivered at the thought; the poor king declaring, asserting, pleading that he was the real heir to the throne; who, in such a place, would pay the least attention?

220

'Now,' the Margrave went on in a mild persuasive tone, 'you can see, dear Lady Sophie, that the help of you and your brother would be of *sovereign* value in such an undertaking. Known, as you are, to be his intimate friends, who would doubt if you supported and countenanced my candidate? Who could doubt *him*? You know me – you esteem my musical taste – you must see the advantages of such a – '

'Oh, no,' Sophie interrupted hoarsely. 'Oh, no: that is quite, *quite* out of the question. I could not – we could not – be party to any such – it is a *wicked* plan – '

'Why?' The Margrave's face flushed even redder. 'To replace one honest dull man by another? One who will be influenced by me? Who will be imbued with my tastes, my intelligence – ?'

'We are *fond* of the king.'

'Pish! You have known him for so short a time.'

'And his father before him – '

'Do not forget that you would have great resources,' the Margrave went on softly, though his mouth was beginning to twitch rather, and his skin to go white in patches; it was plain that he was having to keep himself under severe control. 'Your schemes for poor children (I understand that you have some) could be greatly advanced. I shall have control of – '

'Stop! Stop!' cried Sophie indignantly. 'You are talking wicked, wicked nonsense. How can you? No possible persuasion would tempt me – or Simon. It is a *mad* notion. How can you entertain it? You look to me like a very ill man – and you are not young,'

221

she went on impetuously, 'you should be thinking of better things, using your power in a better way, especially if you have not much time left – ' ignoring the terrible look he gave her. 'Oh, I can't stand it!' She was half choking with indignation; she stood up, hardly aware of what she did. 'You should be ashamed of yourself; I had best leave you before I say what I really think – '

Only then did she realize that the door had opened and closed again behind her; two men had come in quietly and stood on either side of her.

'I am afraid, Dr Finster,' said the Margrave, 'that our charming guest is not to be persuaded; or not yet. Let her be secluded here for a further period of reflection; perhaps she may still come round to my way of thinking. Especially if she remembers that, otherwise, both she and her brother will certainly die; *that* is inevitable.'

Sophie turned – opened her mouth to scream for help – and almost choked on a large handful of dry bandage that was rammed halfway down her throat. Another bandage, wound vigorously round her head several times, held the first one in place.

The man with the grey cravat whom the Margrave had addressed as Dr Finster then bound her arms tightly together in front of her with more bandage, pinning it so that she could not reach the pin; she was pushed down into the pink marble chair from which she had risen, and her legs were fastened to its legs.

'There, Lady Sophie,' said the Margrave, who, though flushed and discomposed in appearance, took pains to maintain his calm manner, 'I grieve that you must miss the concert, but it is quite your own fault. Perhaps you will have had second thoughts by the time it is over, when I will visit you again. I do sincerely hope so. Otherwise I am afraid you will have to be removed from this pleasant room to one of our cellars under the Thames. There, I fear — in spite of all our efforts — large numbers of rats are to be found; so many, indeed, that any person left down there for more than a day or so is rapidly reduced to mere bones — but let us not dwell on such matters. I will see you later.'

As an afterthought he took the dead dove from the mantelpiece and laid it on her lap. Then he left the room, followed by the other two, Finster locking the door as he went.

The shock of the Margrave's disclosure, the suddenness of what had happened to her, and the extreme discomfort of her position, made Sophie feel so ill and strange that, for a short time after they left, her head swam and she lost consciousness. She had no means of knowing, when she came round, how long she had been insensible, for there was no clock in the room. No sound was to be heard; she must be a long way from the music room. She struggled, tried to push out the gag with her tongue, tried to wriggle her hands free — but without the least success; all she achieved was to slide down a silver bracelet which had been hidden under her cambric wrist-frill until it dangled uncomfortably over her knuckles. Perhaps I can bribe somebody with it, she thought rather hopelessly. But there seemed no possible way out of the trouble she was in. And that her brother was in.

223

What will happen when Mogg comes back to pick me up? I suppose they will tell him that I accepted a ride in somebody else's carriage? He will be suspicious, of course, but he will go back to Chelsea. When he finds I am not there, what will he do? Suppose Simon has not yet come home? Even if somebody does begin to suspect – begin to wonder if I am still here – what can they do? And even if they do inquire – by that time I may be in one of those cellars under the Thames . . . Her flesh crept on her bones at the thought.

Sophie was of a sanguine, cheerful nature, and not given to despair, but now she came very close to it. After a while, however, she began to be distracted by a shuffling, scuttling noise, fairly close at hand.

Rats! ran her first horrified thought. Even here – could it be? She was able to move her head, and did so, peering agitatedly about the room. The sound appeared to come from the direction of the elegant pink fireplace – but nothing could be seen there, save the stone pot of pale pink roses. These were suddenly displaced – the pot fell over – and a very dirty, angular black cat emerged from the chimney.

Even in her fright and distress, Sophie had to smile: the reality was so different from her expectations, and so different from her three frightening captors. Yet why should the sight of a cat be surprising? If there were so many rats under Cinnamon Court, there must be dozens of cats in the place too; it stood to reason. No doubt they patrolled it from attic to cellar.

Sophie was fond of cats, and would have liked to

call to this one — thin, scruffy, dirty as it was; but she had no voice. She made a muted noise in her throat and the cat paused in its inspection of the room and stared sharply at her. It had a thin, ugly face and large pale green eyes. No one could call you handsome, puss, Sophie said to it silently, but I am very pleased to see you, I'm glad you came here. Nice puss, good puss.

Now the cat, sniffing and peering as eagerly as a bloodhound, began to roam about, inspecting the room, plainly finding nothing that pleased it. By and by it passed closer to Sophie and suddenly noticed, for the first time, the white dove lying in her lap. Its interest at once aroused, the cat reared up on hind legs for a closer look.

No! was Sophie's first horrified thought. Was *that* what you came for, you wretch? You shan't have it! — not my poor dove. I suppose I might have known that a cat in the Margrave's palace would have blood-thirsty intentions . . .

But then, more soberly, she realized: this might be a chance for me. The only one. And it is merely the cat's nature, after all. And my poor dove is dead, nothing will bring it back.

Come here, then, puss, she called to the cat silently, in her mind. Come on to my knee. You shan't have the dove otherwise.

She laid her joined hands down over the dead dove.

The cat was interested; looked; hesitated; inched closer; jumped back. Sophie nearly went mad with impatience, remembering that the Margrave might return at any time. The hour was late, she felt certain; the concert must surely have finished long ago.

At last, coming to a bold decision, the cat leapt on to the arm of Sophie's chair, and reached a tentatvie paw down towards the dove, stretching out its thin neck and scrawny chin. By moving her tethered arms sideways, Sophie was just able to grab the cat by its scruff; and then, working as fast as she could, she shuffled the silver bracelet, with the fingers of her left hand, over her right wrist, and on over the cat's head. It let out a loud squall of indignation, wrenching itself free and jumping on the floor. Here then! Sophie said to it silently, and with her joined hands pushed the dove off her knee on to the green carpet. The cat, shaking its head furiously against the unaccustomed weight of its new collar, still could not resist the lure of the dove. With a triumphant pounce it seized the bird and retreated, growling and shaking its head, to the region of the hearth. Go on then! Sophie urged it in her mind. Take the dove away. Go, go quickly, before somebody comes back.

The cat glared at her with ears flattened, as if daring her to reclaim the dove; and then turned and sprang up the chimney, dislodging a cloud of soot, which fell on the overturned pot and scattered roses.

How long it was after this that the Margrave returned, Sophie had no means of knowing. A long, long time, she thought. Her head ached miserably, her throat felt dry and raw; she wanted to cough, but dared not in case she choked; the bandages bit into her arms and legs until she began to wonder if her feet and hands would rot and drop off; they felt perfectly numb. But even so, in her terror for Simon, she hardly noticed her own trouble. Where was he now? Could the Margrave, at this very moment, be arranging for his death?

At times, in spite of her distress, her head lolled forward and she dozed, or half fainted; it was in the middle of one of these periods of half consciousness that the door opened and the Margrave strode in.

He looked, Sophie thought, starting out of her doze in terror, even worse than he had before. The fear she had felt then was nothing to what she felt now. Something had made him frightfully angry; and a large portion of that anger was about to spill on to Sophie.

Indeed, he addressed her furiously.

'Stupid, brainless little chit! How could I ever have thought you worth inviting to join my scheme! How dare you say that I look ill – that I have not much time left? How dare you?'

Sophie, unable to reply, could only look at him helplessly over the bandage across her nose and mouth. But he did not wait for an answer. Plainly what she said had been rankling in his mind during the last hours.

'*I am not ill!*' he stormed at her. 'When *my* king is on the throne, my Chapelmaster's music shall be played continuously, for twenty-four hours a day – In any case, I am better already, I improve daily. I have many, many years of life ahead – I am only sixty! And let me tell you,' he went on, almost frothing at the mouth in his fury, 'a blind seer, a very well-thought-of person whose predictions have all come true forecast that in my sixty-first year I should have a great, great stroke of luck, of tremendous good fortune; the best thing I could ask, he said, the greatest blessing of my whole life. So what do you say to *that*, Lady Supercilious Sophie? Ashamed of yourself? In a few days I shall be the supreme power in this kingdom. I don't give *that* for your notions –' He snapped his fingers. 'Oh – ' impatiently, as she rolled her eyes, unable to reply; coming towards her he pulled out a silver knife. For a moment's heart-stopping terror she thought he was going to put her eyes out, but he slit the bandage behind her head, and thankfully she coughed and spat out the gag. 'Well? What do you say?' he asked. 'Will you change your mind? Have you thought over what I said?'

She shook her head.

A tap came at the door which the Margrave had closed behind him.

'Go away!' he shouted.

'Beg pardon, sir, but it's the midnight news. You said you wished to be – '

'Oh, to be sure. Bring it here, then.'

A red-headed page came in with the newspaper. When he caught sight of Sophie his face went wooden with shock; but he said nothing, only bowed and handed the paper to the Margrave, then left again.

'See!' cried the Margrave. His voice vibrated with triumph. 'I had heard a rumour earlier in the evening, but here is confirmation – '

He held out the paper so that Sophie could read it. Her appalled eyes took in the headlines:

DUKE OF BATTERSEA MISSING:
Feared killed in wolf hunt

'See!' cried the Margrave again triumphantly. 'My luck holds! Events fall the way I need them, I do not even have to act. Do you understand? Will you be persuaded now?'

Sophie's heart felt like a lump of ice inside her. But she said shakily, 'So far as I can see, my lord, the best piece of good fortune for you would be that you should die, *now*, before you can do any more harm. No; I will not join you.'

She shut her eyes, then, because she did not wish to look at his face.

A fearful silence followed. She heard him draw a deep breath – and waited in terror. But a heavy thud followed; she opened her eyes again, involuntarily, and saw that he had fallen to the ground.

Next moment Finster and a couple of pages rushed into the room.

11

The moon was high, now, and cast a silver glare over
the frozen snow, between the black houses. Wally's
shadow lurched from side to side as he ran, sliding
and stumbling, over the glassy surface.

'Died o' Fright!' he panted. 'Thank the lord I
caught ye! There's worrisome news.'

Behind Wally Dido then saw his brother Podge,
who, larger and plumper, found even more difficulty
in making his way over the slippery ground. He
waved to Dido and she called, 'What about your leg?
I thought it was busted for sure?'

He shook his head. 'Just a bit of a – bruise,' he
explained, getting his breath. 'Better – now.'

'Old Podge is made of gum arabic.' Wally gave his
brother an affectionate poke in the ribs. 'Takes a deal
to break *him*. Mends quicker than my coffee-stall, he
do.'

'What's the bad news?' Dido asked quickly. 'Not
summat to do with Simon or Sophie?'

'Aye, it is. Podge went over to Chelsea tonight – he
goes most nights,' Wally explained matter-of-factly.
'Even if he don't go in, he likes to walk around outside
o' Sophie's house, and think of her inside there.'

Podge became bright pink — this was visible even in the moonlight — and interrupted gruffly, 'Never mind that! I knew she wasn't in tonight — she was going to a party at the Margrave's — '

'What — not here, in Wapping?' cried Dido with the liveliest curiosity and astonishment. '*Sophie* was at that party? I never seed her! I was *there* — handing round the sherry cobbler and the larks on toast — I never laid eyes on Sophie!'

'Well, she went,' Podge said heavily, 'for old Mogg the coachman said he took her to the door. But when he went back to fetch her he was told she'd ridden off with the Duke and Duchess of Shropshire. Mogg weren't satisfied with this — off he goes to Shrewsbury House — and *they* tell him, there, that the duke and duchess weren't planning to come home after the party, but meant to drive straight down to their place in Wenlock Forest. So then Mogg comes back and he tells me — '

'It don't seem like Sophie, what I remembers of her,' said Dido, 'not to tell the folk at home before she'd go jauntering off like that?'

'That's what I thought too.' Podge's kind, plain face looked desperately worried. 'It's not like Sophie a bit. She'd have written a note for Mogg.'

'Where's Simon? Ain't he hunting for her?'

Podge and Wally looked at one another. Then Podge said, 'That's some more bad news. Simon went out after the wolves, and he hasn't come back. There were stories in the evening papers that he'd been killed by a wolf.'

'Oh, no!' Dido cried out in horror. Sophie was a

distant, though kind and gracious memory; but Simon she had *seen*, very recently; he had given her a sheepskin coat, they had made happy plans together –

'Oh, no!' cried Dido frantically. 'That *can't* be true.'

'Well he hadn't come home,' said Podge with gloom. 'Not when I was there. They sent off a rider to Wenlock Castle, but it'll be upwards of six hours before the man gets back– '

'And suppose all the time Sophie's shut up in Cinnamon Court by that murky Margrave?' said Wally. 'How'd we ever know?'

'Cinnamon Court's a plaguy great place,' Dido said. 'There's probably hundreds of rooms she might be in. Yes, and I remember – that old monster of a Margrave told his bully boys to shut up the old 'uns, the ones as let on to be sick, in the cellars under the river– '

'I've heard tell o' those,' shivered Wally. 'They say the rats will eat you alive – But why *should* he shut up Sophie?'

'What can we do?' demanded Podge, who looked distracted with worry.

At this moment a smallish black shadow shot up the front steps, past the three who stood talking, and vanished into Bart's Building.

'What was that?' said Podge.

'Oh, that's only Figgin. Little Is's cat,' explained Dido. 'She'll be rare and pleased to see him back. She was feared he'd been frizzled in the fire – '

'Oh, murder, you had a fire here, didn't you,' said

232

Wally, paying heed for the first time to the blackened, gaping windows and trampled sooty snow.

'That cat was carrying something white,' said Podge sharply. 'What was it?'

'Blest if I know – '

'I'd like to see what it was – '

'The cat brings her home all kinds of prog, so *she* says,' Dido told him. 'Most like it was a Dover sole, or a jellied eel – '

'Can I look at it?'

'Sartin sure. Why not? Let's find the mog.'

Dido led the way into the house. Figgin, having distastefully inspected the sodden basement and decided that his mistress could not possibly be there, had turned upstairs, and was wauling loudly outside van Doon's door.

'*Figgin?* Is that my Figgin?' came the joyful cry of Is within the room, and the door quickly opened. '*Save us,* what have you got?'

'Is?' called Dido. 'There's a chap here as'd like to take a gander at what Figgin's brought you – '

'Come in, and welcome,' offered van Doon, weary but hospitable. 'Indeed we were not asleep. The little one was too anxious; it is very good that her cat returned – '

The end of his sentence was drowned by the Slut's cry of utter wonder.

'Look ahere! A collar! Figgin's got a silver collar on!'

Icy white moonlight was blazing in at the large window of van Doon's room and throwing a great lozenge of light across the floor. Little Is and her black cat, squatting in this bright light, were like two characters on a stage. She pulled off the silver collar from the neck of Figgin – who at once rolled on the floor in great relief, then seized on his dove again, growling possessively.

'Sophie's dove!' whispered Podge, who stood behind Dido. 'Surely that is Sophie's dove? The one I gave her?'

'There's writing on this here collar!' announced Is. 'What do it say?'

She passed the silver band to Dido, who read in a startled voice: 'Henry Bayswater, it says. And Simone Rivière. Who in nature are they?'

Podge said hoarsely, 'Those are the names of Sophie's parents. It is her bracelet. I have seen it on her wrist a hundred times.'

'Oh, my lord,' said Dido. Gently she passed the bracelet to Podge, who stood turning it over and over in his hands. They all stared at Figgin, who, now that he had brought his dove home to Bart's Building, did not seem at all sure what to do with it.

'We still don't know where she is,' said Wally, after some thought.

'Figgin does get into Cinnamon Court sometimes,' said Dido after another pause. 'You told me that, didn't you?' to Is, who nodded.

'Once he brung me a cutlet wrapped up in a silk napkin – it had a hammer on it, in gold thread.'

'Well then,' said Podge strongly, 'we have got to go round there – rouse the porter – ask where she is.'

'At four in the morning? Suppose they say she ain't

234

there?' Wally looked dubious. 'They'd throw us in the clink – say we was drunk or raving.'

'*You* could go,' Dido suggested to van Doon, who turned pale at the thought. 'You know the Margrave, you came from there.'

'Oh, no, no, no, I must not!' the Dutchman said anxiously. 'His excellency expressly forbids me to go there, unless he summons me. I must not be seen – I must not disobey his excellency – ' He broke into a sweat at the notion.

'Oh; well, that ain't no use then.' Dido glanced at van Doon with slight contempt. She reflected, and said, 'I reckon we'll have to break in.'

'But – how can you?' Van Doon looked even more alarmed. 'There are watchmen walking up and down all night long in the street outside. I have seen them.'

'Aye, he don't stint on watchmen, the Margrave,' agreed Wally.

Dido said, 'But maybe if he got so many outside, he don't trouble to have guards around *in*side – '

'But how can we get inside?' said Podge.

'Over the roof? Down the chimbley, like Figgin?'

'No go. Even if you sent *her* down.' Wally nodded towards tiny Is, whose eyes grew round as saucers. 'I were a sweep's boy, when I were eight. Cinnamon chimbleys have to be swept with rods – they ain't wide enough for a person.'

'Then we gotta get in a window.'

'The downstairs windows are all barred.'

'You know a deal about it, Wally?'

Wally grinned. 'I were a cracksman's boy when I were ten. Till Dad put his foot down. But

235

Cinnamon's one crib we never cracked. Only the windows opening on the garden ain't barred – but you can't get into that garden, there's a twenty-foot wall with spikes on top; and it's guarded in the street outside too.'

'I know one lot of windows as ain't barred,' said Dido suddenly. 'I was looking at 'em only this evening when Pa's music was playing.'

What a long time ago, she thought.

'In the big salon? What use is that? Those look straight out on the river. You'd need a boat . . . ' Wally's voice died away as he considered the possibility of this; then Dido suddenly jumped up, exclaiming, 'No! We'd not need a boat! We'd need a ladder – I lay you a noble to ninepence! You got a ladder, haven't you?' she said to Podge, who, puzzled, replied, 'Sure; for sign-painting. I can bring it in ten minutes.'

'But where are you going to *put* the sorbent ladder?' said Wally crossly. 'I'm telling you the garden wall is guarded – '

'Come on!' Dido was at the door already. 'Let's go and look. That's one place they won't be expecting anybody.'

'I – I think I must stay here. This is no concern of mine? And I do not wish to anger his excellency,' van Doon said. 'The small one should stay with me also.'

Is looked a little rebellious, but Dido said kindly, 'No, mister, it ain't your jug o' gravy, you stay safe indoors and nurse your nose. And *you* stay to mind the house,' she told Is. 'You're in charge now.' Is nodded gravely.

'I still don't get the lay,' said Wally, as Dido and the two boys ran down the front steps.

'Why – this – ' Dido led them down the sloping cobbled slipway to the river, running past the end of the alley. 'See? Frozen solid, ten feet, fifteen feet out! There's a crust you can walk on, I reckon, all along the edge.'

She proved this by doing so.

'Jimbo! You're right!' exclaimed Wally, doing likewise. 'But will it take all three of us, *and* a ladder?'

'Can't tell till we try.'

Podge was a little harder to convince. He tested the ice; rapped on it; jumped on it; then he said to Wally, 'You'd better not come. Who'd look after Dad if we both drowned?'

'Hey, who are you talking to?' cried Wally, affronted. '*I'm* the best swimmer!'

'Oh, for Habakkuk's sake, fetch the ladder and stop arguing,' said Dido. 'It'll be daylight afore we're done if you don't bustle.'

'Not for another four hours,' said Wally, as Podge hurried off. 'Come on; let's see how far we can go.'

By river the distance to Cinnamon Court proved nothing like so far as it was by road, along the maze-like streets of Wapping, zig-zagging among docks and creeks and inlets.

Edging their way gingerly along the frozen crust, as close to the shore as possible, sometimes having to turn aside, skirting round gullies – but most of these were frozen solid – Dido and Wally took only seven minutes to reach the massive brick bulk of

Cinnamon Court. There, above them, they saw the great row of arched windows, shining silver in the brilliant moonlight; there, beyond, lay the snow-covered garden, protected from the river by a ferocious criss-cross of spikes.

'The window's our lay, no question,' whispered Wally, staring up. 'No one would be looking for a prig to come thataway. Do they open, those windows?'

'I didn't notice,' whispered Dido. 'Come along back; we best not stand here gabbing.'

'Lucky there's no river traffic,' she added as they retraced their steps. 'Anyone on a barge'd spot us; you can see clear across the Pool, bright as day.'

'I reckon the skippers are afeared of getting iced in. If this cold lasts – and Dad says it will – the river's likely to freeze right over. Dad says it did that when his great-granddad was alive; you could skate from Greenwich to Hampton, and they roasted an ox on the ice.'

'If it freezes, that'll be handy for the wolves in Kent; they can come over on the ice,' murmured Dido, and fell silent, thinking about Simon. When'll we know? How can they find out? she wondered. But, at least, we're doing our best for Sophie.

'Does Podge want to marry her?' she asked, out of this thought, and Wally, perfectly understanding her, replied, 'How can he? She's a duke's sister, he's a sign-painter. All he can do is give her presents.'

'That's rabbity!' cried Dido with scorn. 'You keep giving somebody presents – it makes you their *slave*. Or t'other way round.'

Wally glanced at her in surprise, but said no more, for now they had reached the causeway by Bart's Building, and there was Podge coming with the ladder.

'Brought along a couple of your old tools as well,' he said to Wally. 'Never know what you're going to need.' He had a small black velvet bag slung over his shoulder.

They each took a leg of the ladder, which was a fruit-picker's one, free-standing, with a third leg at the rear. Being wooden, it was quite heavy; Dido, secretly, was a little anxious lest it prove too much for the ice. Cinnamon Court, she had noticed, lay by an outer bend of the river-bank where the current cut in and ran swiftly; along the bank there, the ice was not so wide, nor, presumably, so thick. But she kept this thought to herself.

Reaching the wall of the Court they silently set up the ladder. Podge handed the black bag to Wally, who scurried up the rungs as quietly as a squirrel, inspected the end window, and set to work at its bottom right-handed corner.

Podge cupped a hand round Dido's ear and whispered, 'Diamond wheel. Cuts a hole in the glass.'

Whatever Wally was doing took a couple of minutes; meanwhile Podge was rubbing and kneading a lump of gum arabic in his hands, warming it and damping it with a pinch of snow. Wally reached down, took and delicately laid it against the circle of glass on which he had been working; then pulled; a neat glass disc came away stuck to the gum, which he passed down to his brother.

Now a similar piece had to be taken from the middle of the window, to reach the hasp. Wally could not reach high enough, so Podge went up and did it. After which he carefully slipped his hand through the hole in the glass, twisted, pulled, undid the catch, undid the bottom bar, and the casement came open. Podge then put a knee over the sill and vanished inside. Wally went next, and Dido followed; they had to be pulled up by Podge, as the window was well above the top of the ladder. As soon as Dido was inside, Podge carefully pulled-to the window again.

'Shows up like the very devil, an open window does,' he whispered. 'Now where?'

Dido was sorry that she had not seen more of the inside of Cinnamon Court; but she remembered that it formed an 'L', with the river passing one end, the street passing the other end, and the garden in the angle. Cellars were under the river, Wally said, so that meant they must be below the big salon where they now stood.

'Reckon we oughta go down,' she whispered, pointing, and Podge nodded. 'But let's look in all the doors as we pass.'

A wide, carpeted passageway, dimly lit here and there by wall lamps, led from the salon, turning left halfway along its length. Windows on the left looked into the garden. As they stole along, Dido reflected that breaking into a rich house was easy, for thick carpets favoured the burglar. She could not help being struck by Wally's expert way with windows and locks; at each closed door, if it would not open, he slid into the keyhole a slender rod with a prong like a miniature tuning-fork; delicately tried it, listening with his ear close to the lock; adjusted, twisted once or twice, and each time the lock came undone.

Reckon his boss musta been a topnotch cracksman, Dido thought.

The rooms they inspected were all smaller reception rooms, and had no one in them; they were dark. But, towards the farther end of the long passage, music was to be heard, issuing softly from behind a closed door.

'That sounds like my pa,' breathed Dido into Podge's ear. He nodded, and gestured her to put her eye to the keyhole.

When she did so she could see, as if at a penny peep-show, a small, round image of her father sitting on a gilt chair by a bed, playing softly on his hoboy. She could not see the occupant of the bed, who lay sunk among a pile of soft pillows; beyond the bed was the frowning, intent face of Dr Finster staring down at something; his lips were pressed anxiously together, yet there was an expression of hope and relief on his face. Pity if Pa's music is going to keep the Margrave from cutting his cable, thought Dido; if he was to kick the bucket a whole lot o' folk would breathe easier.

Her father's face made her feel sad; it was so weary and haggard, although it had a look of devotion, like the doctor's. Pa's tired to death, thought Dido; but nobody asked him if *he'd* like to lie down and sleep, he just has to go on playing and playing . . .

Moving on past the door she shook her head, beckoning the boys to follow.

They found a servants' stair and went down, past a duty room where a couple of footmen lolled, deep asleep, their heads and arms resting on a table. Empty bottles explained their slumber. Finishing up the wine from the party, thought Dido. Lucky for us.

The whole house, hereabouts, seemed drenched in slumber. Not a sound from anywhere. How can they sleep so? wondered Dido, when the moon shines so bright!

Down more, and steeper, stairs, and along another corridor, reversing the way they had come, stepping through squares of moonlight all the way from the windows on the garden side. Now they began to hear a soft, regular sound; Podge's face became alert, then angry, for it was the sound of sobbing they could hear; it came from behind a door near the end of the passage.

With immense caution, Podge opened the door, which was not locked. It gave on to a small room, all grey and pink, lit by a candle, where Sophie sat drooping in a chair while a kneeling page rubbed and chafed at her feet and hands. Scattered bandages lay on the floor.

The page jumped in terror as they came in; but at sight of Dido a look of huge relief spread over his face. He was the red-head who had given her his basket of programmes.

'Thank the powers it's you!' he whispered. 'Me and Boletus was told to carry her down to one o' the cellars, but Boletus is dead drunk and I couldn't –

wouldn't. You come to take her away? But how? She can't walk. Those bandages was tarnal tight. Her feet and hands are all numb.'

'I'll carry her,' said Podge, and picked up the half-conscious Sophie.

'We'll never get her out o' that window or down the ladder,' muttered Dido. 'It'll have to be the front door. – I know. I got it. You can put her in one o' them basket chairs they had for the sick folk; when I left they was still in the lobby.'

'But the front door's locked and barred,' said the red-headed page.

Wally silently exhibited his pick-lock.

'And there's guards in the street outside. They'll cop you for sure.'

'We'll need to entice them away,' said Dido. She reflected. 'Ain't there any other way out, bar the front door?'

'There's a stair from the cellar to the garden. And a door from the garden through the wall to the street. That's locked too. And guards outside.'

'Reckon we'll manage,' said Dido, and thought some more, while the three others watched her trustfully, and Sophie faintly moaned.

'Can you come by a skeleton?' she asked Red-head, who looked startled but replied, 'For sure; there's usually half a dozen in the cellars.'

'Prime. That'll save you a roasting. Can you take us to the cellars?'

He nodded.

'Right. Let's go. Front door first.'

As quietly as possible they made their way along

passages and down stairs to the lobby, Podge and Red-head taking turns to carry the inert Sophie. At the top of the main stair leading down to the vestibule they paused. There sat the night porter on his stool by the door, and he was wide awake, playing solitaire patience.

'Call him!' Dido whispered to Red-head, who nodded and called, 'Mr Chantrel – can you come and help me a moment.'

'What's the row, then?' asked the porter, yawning, and he came slowly up the stairs, rubbing his eyes. As he reached the corner, Podge rose from where he had been hidden behind the rail, hooked a foot under the man's legs, and threw him sharply to the floor. His head hit the post and he lay still.

'Is he dead?' breathed Dido.

'No; just knocked silly.'

'Better put him back by his stool. Now, unlock the front door, *but don't open it*. And lay Sophie in one o' them basket chairs.'

When that was done – 'You,' said Dido to Podge, 'stay here, with Sophie. And be ready to nip out the door and run like the devil when you hear us kicking up a row. Let's have Sophie's jacket – here – we can wrap her in this –' taking a silken Chinese rug from the floor. 'Understand? When you hear the ruckus – scarper!'

Podge nodded. He was very pale. He tucked the rug carefully round Sophie.

Dido and Wally followed the red-headed page, who led them through a green baize door, along a stone-flagged passage, and down a flight of stone steps to another, very massive door, which he unlocked; then he paused to light a candle.

'His Nabs gave me this key, and the one for the cellar where we were to put Lady Sophie.'

'Well, now we need to find a skeleton and put it there.'

The cellars were dank, disgusting places, even wetter than Mrs Bloodvessel's basement, most of them inches deep in river mud. Wally had to open the doors of several before they found a skeleton, half embedded in mud; they hauled it along to the cell which had been destined for Sophie, and dressed it in her jacket.

'Now lock up the poor devil again,' said Dido.

Faint cries and groans had been audible while they were doing this. Now, when Wally undid another door, they found the imprisoned children and Chelsea Pensioners, who were all in a miserable state of fright and despair; they could hardly believe – especially the old men – that this was a real rescue and not just another devilish trick of the Margrave's. But a few of the children knew Wally, and were prepared to trust him.

'Now you've gotta find us an axe,' Dido told Redhead. 'We'll be shovelling 'em up the stairs while you do that.'

'An axe? Where'll I find an axe?'

'*I* dunno. In the kitchen, likely. Look sharp about it!'

Wally and Dido shepherded the limping, bewildered group of captives up another flight of stone steps after Wally had carefully relocked the cell door.

At the top of the steps a locked, iron-barred gate led into the moonlit garden. Here they waited, while Wally worked on the lock and Dido counted the group; there were fifteen of them, she was relieved to find, the same number as had been at the concert.

'No one got ate by rats then?' she asked the tiny lavender-seller, who said, 'No, miss, but weren't the rats just something! We took turns shying bricks and rocks at 'em — otherwise they'd a had us for sure.'

While Wally undid the gate, Dido addressed the group in a whisper.

'Now listen: I want you to listen real hard. *Don't* go busting out across the garden as soon as Wally gets the gate open. Stay here in the shadow till I gives the word. Understand? We don't want nobody to see you till we got a way for you to go.'

Some of the children were sniffing back tears, and the old men were whimpering with fright and cold.

'Stow that row!' Dido hushed them. 'You're a sight better off than you was. Button up!'

Having opened the gate, Wally slipped along in the shadow of the house to inspect the row of spiked posts which protected the river end of the garden.

The sky was beginning to cloud over and more snow to fall, which Dido noticed with approval. Just so's it don't get warmer and the ice melt, she thought in sudden alarm.

'The posts are only wood,' Wally came back to report with relief. 'Steel heads to 'em, and bedded in brick, but with an axe I can chop out a couple in no time.'

Here, luckily, Red-head arrived with a meat-axe.

246

'Now you better mizzle,' Dido told him. 'Get back to your own quarters, fast. And thanks! Wally'll lock the gate behind you. Just tell His Nabs as how you put Sophie in the cell, and that's all you know.'

He looked a little wistful. Does he want to come with us? Dido wondered. But she was busy hushing the children and reassuring the old men; she had enough to worry about. Wally relocked the cellar gate, then hacked away two posts by the river, making a narrow passage through which the prisoners could wriggle through on to the ice. When that had been done –

'Now: *scarper*, all of you!' Dido told them. 'Away from here as fast as you can pelt. Wally and I will soon be coming after to help any that's in trouble – but help each other if you can – don't wait. Go on – mizzle!'

As soon as the last of them, puffing, straining, and snivelling, had been squeezed through the gap, Wally and Dido ran to the locked wooden door that led from garden to street. Wally began to batter it with the axe, Dido thumped it with one of the posts that had been chopped out. Both of them yelled at the top of their voices.

'This way! This way! Come along! Help, help! Save us! Hurray! Hurrah! Down with His Nabs!' And Dido added, '*Podge!* Now's your moment! Don't loiter! Beat it!'

They made a terrific row, banging and bawling; soon they heard alarmed shouts and running feet on the other side of the wall, as the guards came racing to see what was going on. By now Wally had made

247

a hole in the planking just about large enough to let a person climb through.

'Best we clear off now before they nab us,' said Dido, ramming her spiked post through the hole and into the stomach of somebody who had just arrived on the other side. 'Don't forget the axe, Wally!'

They scooted back across the garden to the gap in the line of posts and edged through. By now snow was falling fast.

'That's handy,' said Dido with satisfaction. 'It'll cover our prints, farther on. – Here, give us the axe, you take the ladder.'

Already she could hear the Margrave's guards, who had either broken through or opened the door

in the wall, and were now busy searching the garden
for escaped prisoners. It would not be long before
they found the gap in the river fence.

Dido, swinging the axe with all her strength, chopped a hole in the ice, which was not so thick here,
because of the fast inshore current; part of it suddenly gave way with a loud squeaking crunch, and
the portion on which she herself stood tipped
sideways; she only just had time to leap back to
safety. The hole she had made was about four feet
across. Stepping back, she began to hack at the edge
of it, and managed to dislodge another large section.

'Watch out, girl – don't take any chances!' called
Wally.

'Just a bit more – so they can't jump across – '
panted Dido, and whacked a third time with the axe.

A much larger piece came away, and tipped her
clean into the water – if Wally had not been
lightning-quick, thrusting the end of the ladder
against her, she would have been swept under the
solid ice by the current.

'Quick!' he yelled. 'Grab hold!'

'Thanks – blp – I got it – here I come – ' Dido
gasped, and, spitting out Thames water, was dragged
in triumph to safety, just as a group of guards came
scrambling through the gap in the fence and along the
ice – only to come to a dismayed halt at sight of a
twelve-foot stretch of black water which Dido's
chopping had created.

'Let's go!' she gulped. Wally and she scurried along
the ice, hauling the ladder between them. Despite its
weight they managed to keep up a good pace, and
soon overtook the group of escaped prisoners, who
were limping and hobbling amid moans and cries of
'I can't keep up!' and 'Won't somebody help me?'

'We'd best turn up here,' said Wally, at the first
creek. 'Don't take 'em to Bart's.'

'Where'll we take them then?'

'Once they're rested they can go to wherever they
came from; I don't reckon His Nabs will go looking
for them, do you? But they can come to my dad's
place for now,' said Wally.

12

'In the reign of Queen Anne, it all began,' sang the children, dancing in a ring in brilliant moonlight round the fountain in the forecourt of Bakerloo House.

'In the reign of King Jim, it was fairly grim
In the reign of King John, it still went on
In the reign of King Bill, it went on still
In the reign of King Fred, it came to a head
In the reign of King Bruce, they called a truce
In the reign of King Walt, it came to a halt.'

What the children were doing, Simon could not see, and hardly cared; he was greatly astonished to find them there still at this late hour of night.

'Don't you ever go to sleep?' he inquired, as they left their game, whatever it was, and came flocking about his horse, which had limped behind the hackney cab, all the way from Tower Hill.

'Can't sleep out o' doors this weather,' they told him, laughing, 'and you need a farden for a lollpoop's lodging.'

'Well – here – split this among you – that'll

house you all easily – ' and Simon gave the nearest boy a gold guinea.

'Lud love you, sir, if I was to give *that* to a lodging 'ouse keeper he'd think I'd prigged it; he'd turn me over to the rozzers and I'd be in stir before you'd had your breakfast! Anyhow this night's almost over; 'tain't worth a farden now till dayglim, thanking you kindly all the same – ' and the boy handed back the guinea. Simon searched for smaller coins, but recollected that he had used up all his supply of change on the mouse he had bought from Penelope.

'We ain't come to beg, but to give you a warning,' the boy said.

At this moment the door of Bakerloo House burst open and Dolly Buckle erupted from it, apron strings and cap ribbons flying distractedly.

'Oh, sir, oh, sir! Oh, your grace dear, oh, I'm that beshrought! Lady Sophie's never come home! And Jem's gone down to Wenlock and Mogg's gone to Bow Street – Oh, my lord, oh where can she be?'

Simon experienced a horrible sensation inside him, as if his heart had fallen through a hole into his stomach; now he began for the first time to understand what Sophie went through each time he went off hunting wolves.

'When did she go out?' he asked the tearful Mrs Buckle.

'Ha' past sivin – to a musical swarry at the Margrave of Hodmedod. Didn't I always say that man was no better than he should be?'

'I'll ride to his house directly – only I need a fresh horse,' said Simon.

'But Mogg's been there – to Cinnamon Court – and *they* said she'd gone to Wenlock – '

'Why in the world to Wenlock? Where is Mogg now? Oh, at Bow Street, you said – Well, I'll get a fresh horse – and clean clothes – then I'll go after Mogg.'

Simon rode to the stable, rubbed down and fed his horse (Sim and Sam being both in bed), went indoors for a quick wash and to change his torn and blood-stained clothes, then led out a fresh mount.

He had not altered his intention of going to Cinnamon Court, but Dolly Buckle, though a well-meaning woman, was a gabster; half Chelsea would, by breakfast time, know anything he told her. So he said nothing of his plans.

The children were playing a new game as he rode back towards the gate.

'Limbery, limbery, lag lag lag,'

they sang

'We'll put your head in the bag, bag, bag,
We'll turn you once, we'll turn you twice
And we'll send you off to Paradise . . .'

It seemed to be a kind of blind man's buff; a line of players ran through a 'gate' made by two others, who grabbed one of them and blindfolded him by tying a kerchief over his eyes.

As Simon mounted and rode towards the gate, one such blindfolded player came racing straight in the direction of his horse, who shied and snorted and had to be soothed.

'Hey! Watch where you're going or you'll do yourself a mischief!' called Simon, but the blind-folded person – it was a girl – continued running till she stood by his horse's rein, then said quickly in a low voice: 'And the same to you, sir! Cinnamon ain't a bit good for you, sir, not this time o' day. What *you* want is a nice drop of Early Purl.'

'Oh I do?' said Simon, staring very hard at the blindfolded girl. 'And where will I get that?'

'At the Two Jolly Mermaids in Wapping, sir; my uncle Benge keeps that tavern, and he makes the purl really arominty.'

'Thanks,' said Simon, 'I'll remember,' and he rode out once more into the black streets of Chelsea. A bank of heavy cloud had swallowed the moon and it was snowing again, hard.

Early Purl, thought Simon, riding eastwards, with the snow biting his face. Is that a trap, or is it good advice? On the whole he thought it would be good advice; he knew that the children were Sophie's friends.

The Two Jolly Mermaids turned out to be a sailors' tavern, open and active all night as men came ashore from ships that had just tied up in Shadwell Basin or the London Docks. A large bright fire roared in each tap room, and a bottle over the private bar contained a lifesize mermaid; Simon was interested to notice that it looked like Penelope Twite's handiwork.

When the landlord, a little brown gnome of a man, said to Simon, 'What's your wish, guvnor?' Simon said, 'A blindfold girl told me you make very good Early Purl.'

'Oh I do, your lordship, I do; the best you'll come

254

across this side o' the River Leafy. Just you give me five minutes with a red-hot poker and a dram o' wormwood . . . '

The little brown man bustled away, and presently came back with a steaming silver cup which smelt bitter and fragrant, like the bank of a brook in June.

'You look as if you've had a long night, your honour, but that'll wake you up for sure.'

Leaning close as he handed over the mug he murmured, 'Sampan Stowage, my lord. Off of Green Bank. My Bess'll show you the way; 'tis a mite hard to puzzle out, on a dirty night such as this.'

Simon drank down the Early Purl, which was amazingly powerful; paid for it, and left. Outside, holding his horse, he found a small girl, who looked extremely clean, as if she had recently been washed, hard, all over.

'You want to ride up in front of me?' Simon asked, and she said, 'Oo, that'd be lush!' and reached up her arms. Simon swung her on to the pommel – she was light as a feather and he noticed that she smelt strongly of lavender.

Fairly soon, in fact, Simon was obliged to dismount and walk, leading the horse, while Bess, in the saddle, directed him through narrow precarious ways, around boat basins, and along catwalks, behind warehouses and over footbridges.

'Shall you ever be able to find your way back on your own?' he said.

'Lord bless you, yes, sir, I've been scoffling round these parts since I was out o' my cradle. I sells lavender to the sailormen, see; they dearly likes a bunch to take to sea, or give to their sweethearts.

255

Here you are, your worship; now this-ere warehouse is Sampan Stowage, that's Mr Greenaway's place – and I thank your honour,' she added gravely, as he gave her a sixpence after lifting her down. She skipped away into the gloom, lifting up a small powerful voice in a piercing cry of 'Sweet lav – en – der!' just to keep in practice, Simon supposed, for there were no customers about in the snowy dark.

He found a place to tether his horse under a lean-to, then tapped at the big warehouse door that Bess had indicated.

'Who's there?' cried a voice inside.

'Lavender Bess brought me,' replied Simon.

'Oh she did, did she?'

With a grinding of bolts a small wicket door in the large one was slowly unfastened.

A tall, massive man stood in the doorway. Simon saw first that his hair, outlined against firelight which shone behind him, was white; next, that he was blind.

From over his shoulder a startled voice cried, 'Simon! Why, it's the Duke of Battersea, father!'

'Good lord, Podge, is that you?' exclaimed Simon.

'Pleased to meet you, young feller,' said the tall man, taking Simon's hand in one that felt like a large flexible rock. 'I've heard a deal about you from my son Dave here – '

A sort of human whirlwind at this moment hurtled forward and engulfed Simon; this turned out to be Dido.

'Simon! We thought as you was galloping twenty different ways inside of a pack of wolves! The papers said as you'd hopped the twig! My stars, ain't I just glad it's not so. And look – look who we've got here, just wait till you see – '

Her skinny hand pulled him forward across the floor of the warehouse, which was a vast, dark, warm place. Round the walls were piled coils of rope, every size from thin cord to massive cable as thick as a man's body; there were also chests and casks and barrels, many of which gave off a pungent smell of spice. In the middle a round brick hearth had its own chimney which disappeared upwards into the dimness. A space around it was kept clear, to avoid fire risk probably, and in this space quite a number of persons were sitting or squatting or lolling; some seemed young, some much older, wearing Chelsea Pensioners' uniforms; among them Simon was greatly amazed to discover his sister Sophie, reclining in a basket chair. A boy and a girl knelt beside her, rubbing her arms and legs.

'*Dearest* Sophie – am I glad to see you! How in the world did you get here?' asked Simon as Dido tugged him forward.

The blind man moved leisurely back to a great seat, obviously made to measure for him, from a massive oak cask divided into two semicircles which were nailed back to back.

'Simon! Thank heaven you are here! I am so very happy – ' Just for a moment Sophie's composure faltered, and a tear slid down her cheek. She clasped Simon's hand tightly, then said, 'Aren't we lucky to have found our way here? Mr Greenaway has been so kind – And his apple cider punch is like nectar,' she added, laughing.

'You, there, Wal – make up another jorum of apple punch for the dook!' instructed Mr Greenaway. 'And fetch him a bit o' bread-and-cheese – he looks worn to a ravelling. – We keeps apples and food-stuffs in the other shed, where it's cool,' he explained as Wally ran off. 'This loft has to stay dry, for the spices, you see, sir.'

Simon sat on an upturned cask and was given food and drink by Wally, while, in chorus, they all told him about the rescue of Sophie and the musical patients. At this recital he was so stunned that he could hardly speak – he hugged Dido speechlessly, and thumped Wally and Podge again and again, so hard that they almost fell down.

'If I'd only been there – ' he kept saying. ' – Not that you needed me, I can see that! You managed so cleverly. But – to think of that Margrave – just wait till I get my hands around his throat – '

'And just listen to *this*, Simon!' interrupted Dido. 'Listen to what Sophie was just a-telling us when you began rat-tatting at the door – listen to what His Nabs has planned!'

Sophie then described again the Margrave's design to replace the king with an exact duplicate, the change-over to be made during the Thames tunnel procession.

'He has it all completely arranged. Though where he can find a man who is the exact image of King Richard, I cannot imagine.'

'Oh, the man's found already,' said Dido. 'He ain't but a bowshot from here, lodging with my pa. I believe he don't exactly know yet what the Margrave has in mind for him to do; thinks it's more of a stand-in fit-up, I reckon; just for times, now and again, you know, when the king has toothache and don't want to open Parliament. He ain't a bad cove – Mister van Doon – but he ain't right sharp. My notion is that by the time he cottons on to what he's in for, then it'll be too late for him to get out of it.'

'We must let the king know at once!' said Simon, half starting out of his seat.

'Just a minute, young feller,' said Mr Greenaway in his deep voice. 'Before you go rushing off like a bull at a postman, we gotta reckon the ins and outs of this.'

Dido noticed how respectfully Wally and Podge attended to what their father said. Wisht I had a pa like that, she thought sadly. And she thought of her own father, sitting by the Margrave's bed, playing his hoboy, keeping the Margrave alive . . . Better he should let the pesky bloke die, thought Dido.

She came back from her reverie to find that Mr Greenaway was asking her a question.

'Lady Sophie allowed as how the Margrave suffered some kind of fit. But *you* said later on the doctor looked hopeful – as if he was mending?'

'Yes – he did,' Dido said slowly, remembering again the view through the keyhole. 'My pa's music seems to do His Nabs a power o' good. Dr Finster sets a lot o' store by it, I know. Maybe the guy just takes these fits every now and again; maybe they don't amount to much.'

'So we have to reckon that the Margrave will be back on his feet by tomorrow. 'Tis lucky you thought to put that skeleton in Lady Sophie's cell – we'll hope that makes him think she is dead. Any other road, her life'd not be worth a groat, now he's told her all that's in his mind.'

Podge's eyes grew huge at this thought. 'We've got to hide Sophie!' he cried fearfully. 'She can't go home to Bakerloo House. Nor stay here – it's too close to Cinnamon Court. But where can she go that's safe?'

'I think I know a place where she could go,' Simon said thoughtfully. 'But – Mr Greenaway, I see what you mean. If the king sends for Eisengrim and accuses him of the plot – of course he will deny it all – and there won't be any proof – '

'He'll ship van Doon back to Hanover directly –.' agreed Dido, nodding. 'And then he'll just wait for another chance. And, once he knows *you*'ve not been munched up by wolves, Simon, he'll be planning to do you in – like he done Lord Fo'castle and the Dean – '

'That's so; you'd best stay dead, dook, along with Lady Sophie,' advised Mr Greenaway.

'Put on a false beard,' suggested Wally, his crossed eyes sparkling. 'Podge can get you one. Podge is pals with a cove who sells false beards off a barrer. Or a wig – '

He and Podge began to discuss different methods of disguise for Simon.

Mr Greenaway said to Sophie, ''Twere a piece of luck, ma'am, that my boys were able to get you away from Eisengrim. The man come to me once to have his hand read; I can read a person's hand with my fingers, 'tis a gift came on me when I were a sailorman and blinded at sea; Eisengrim heard tell of it, and he come to me for a reading. He's a one that sets store by such matters,' Mr Greenaway said with a touch of contempt.

'Then I won't ask you to read *my* hand, Mr Greenaway! – He is a strange, dreadful man. I shall be grateful to your sons all my life – I would not *have* my life at all, if it weren't for them and Dido. What did you find in his hand? Oh, I believe I remember something – I remember that he said – he said it had been foretold that he would have luck in his sixty-first year – was it you who told him that?'

'Aye – that and the bird. 'Twas I who told him – ' Mr Greenaway was silent for a moment – 'I told him too – what I found plain in his life-line – that this way through the world would take a wondrous sharp turn when he found his path crossed by a girl who was dressed as a boy.'

'Then that was why he was so anxious to have me on his side!' exclaimed Sophie. 'I could not think why he should keep on urging me when I had made it so plain that I would do no such thing – And what about the bird?'

'The bird,' said Mr Greenaway, 'would be the last thing he saw.'

'No wonder he hates them so!'

'I've long wished to meet ye, ma'am,' said Mr Greenaway. 'My boy Wally – he conducts the children's birthday league, you know – he tells me he heard you were planning a scheme for homeless ones – '

'Yes, I am!' Despite the pain of her badly bruised and contused hands and feet, Sophie's face lit up with excitement. 'Next year when I am eighteen, Mr Greenaway – when my money comes out of trust and the lawyers can't stop me using it – I intend to start a series of houses where poor children without family may get decent food and lodging. Bakerloo House will be the first; I'm not allowed to use it yet – '

''Tis a grand scheme, missie.'

'Won't you call me Sophie?' she said, going a little pink. 'I – I feel I know your son Podge so well – '

Simon said to Dido: 'Just fancy, Dido! I've seen your sister Penelope!'

'Never! You've seen Penny? Where?' Dido was all eager interest. 'With her buttonhook beau? How's she doing? Is she better tempered than what she used to be?'

'No, the buttonhook dealer seems to have left her some time ago.'

'Oh, then she certainly won't be in good skin. Poor old Penny-lope,' said Dido, considering this. 'Where is she? I'd not be sorry for a sight of her.'

'I was wondering – ' Simon leaned his head close to hers and talked fast and earnestly, while Dido listened, nodding thoughtfully.

Podge said shyly to Sophie, 'I've a little ivory looking-glass for you, Miss Sophie – with roses round the frame; it's not much, I know you've plenty already, but I hoped you'd like it – '

Sophie said, 'Oh, Podge! You spoil me – indeed you do!' But her voice was a little sad.

Wally said to Mr Greenaway, 'Dad, how're we a-going to get all these folk away from here without His Nabs's guards smelling a rat? Or some o' those Bowmen bully boys? They're always about and they're hand in glove – '

'No dole, boy, don't you fret your head. The Canterbury carrier comes past at seven. He'll not have a full load, we can stow a good few among the casks and bales – '

Simon, overhearing this, said, 'Mr Greenaway, does the carrier go up over Blackheath Edge?'

'I reckon he would, lad – for the price of a pot of porter.'

'He shall have the price of a dozen pots – and gladly.' Simon then reflected and said, 'I wonder where I can get a china cup?'

'A cup, lad? I think I got a crate somewhere, real Chinese ones, come along with a load of spices from Poohoo Province; what you want a cup for?'

'If you have a crateful I might as well have several!'

Sophie said to Dido: 'As soon as it is safe for you to do so, I *long* for you to come and live with us at Bakerloo House. I so much want to hear all your adventures. The things you must have seen!'

Dido said rather gruffly, 'If you're sartin sure I won't be in the way?'

'In the way? I can't imagine anything more delightful! Simon and I rattle about like two peas in a pod in that house. And, next year – ' Sophie hesitated and then said delicately, 'If you do not wish to live with your father, that is?'

A cloud came over Dido's brow.

'No,' she said. 'No, I shan't want to live with Pa.'

Sophie thought how very sad it must be to have a father whom one could not respect. She too had noticed the deference and devotion of Wally and Podge to their father. Her own father had died in the Hanoverian wars when she was a baby.

Podge said to Simon, 'How do you plan to get a word to the king – if you can't be seen?'

Simon said, 'I've been thinking about that. What Wally said gave me a notion. Not false beards – wigs!'

'Wigs?'

'You'll have to help me, Podge.'

'That's of course.'

'Didn't you say you had a cousin who's a footman at St James's Palace?'

As Podge listened, he broke into a broad grin.

By degrees a dim, doubtful red glow began to show in the eastern sky – all there would be of a sunrise this wintry day. The snow had stopped for the moment, but cloud and fog hung low, and the cold was sharper than ever; on either side of the Thames the rim of ice now extended well out into the river, leaving only a narrow channel in the middle; soon that, too, would be frozen.

At half past seven the Canterbury carrier – a large hooded wagon which carried spices, dry goods, tea, and hides – paid its regular weekly visit to Mr Greenaway's warehouse, bringing him apples from the Kentish orchards, taking back goods for the shops of Tonbridge, Maidstone, Ashford and Canterbury.

The Margrave's guards, loitering about the streets of Wapping, let it pass unquestioned; they were accustomed to the sight of it.

Later Mr Greenaway, assisted by cross-eyed Wally and another lad, wheeled out his apple barrow into Wapping High Street. The helper, who wore the jacket, badge, cap, and leathers of a charity boy, then strolled away, and, by a circuitous route, down an alley to the river, and along the ice at the edge, made his way to Bart's Building.

The house was locked. Dido used her key to let herself in. At once the sour, choking smell of the wet wood made her cough, and a scared voice from upstairs called, 'Who's there?'

'That you, Is? It's Dido.'

'Oh, fank evvings! I was feared, all alone in the 'ouse.'

'Why, where's Mr van Doon?'

'There were a missidge come from His Nabs to go round to Cinnamon Court. To see 'ow 'e were getting on in his talk-learning. Off 'e went.'

'What about the lollpoops?'

'They took theirselves off, same time as usual.'

Dido noticed with approval that the lollpoops had tidied the rooms they used, and swept them too. Little Is had also done her best to clean some of the soot and grime from the rest of the house, and had washed the curtains in van Doon's room.

'D'you reckon the mister'll come back, miss?' she asked anxiously. 'He be a right nice gemmun.'

'I dunno.'

Tomorrow, Dido knew, was the day of the tunnel

opening. Presumably the Margrave had summoned van Doon for his final orders. Would he then remain at Cinnamon Court?

That would complicate the plan which had been worked out in Mr Greenaway's warehouse.

Looking at the sorrowful, anxious face of Is, Dido said kindly, 'Has he left his things?'

'Yus.'

'Then he'll be back for them, you may lay.'

In about half an hour, brisk footsteps could be heard approaching along the cobbles, and a voice raised in song heralded the approach, not of Mr van Doon, but of Mr Twite.

'Oh, riddle me riddle me ravity,'

he sang,

'And diddle hey diddle dye dum
I am known for my calmness and suavity
And the beautiful airs that I hum.'

He ran up the steps, opened the door, and looked around him distastefully.

'Hey-day! What a sordid scene!' He peered into the charred and blackened room that had been Mrs Bloodvessel's parlour. 'Could you not have cleaned it up – cleared it out?'

'Not without you pay for a joiner, and a plasterer, and a glazier, to mend the walls and the windows and the hole in the floor,' replied Dido.

'Ah well, ah well! 'Tis no great matter. – Hey,

266

you,' he said to Is. 'Run round the corner and buy two gills of hot coffee, a half quartern loaf, and one ounce of Vosper's Nautical Cut. And don't dilly-dally.'

When she had slipslopped off, Dido said. 'You heard what happened to Mrs B., Pa?'

'Ah yes,' he replied. 'I read it in the early editions, delivered to Cinnamon Court. A sad fatality, but – let us agree – a blessed release also. – Now, daughter,' he added, in quite a different voice, 'have you considered any further upon the matter I alluded to the other evening?'

'Which matter was that, Pa?'

'Tush, child. You know quite well what I mean.' He hummed, *Oh, how I long to be queen, Pa, and summon my troops to review, watching this soldierly scene, Pa, as I munch on a tasty ragout* . . . Married to Henk van Doon, who is, I daresay, as good-natured a fellow as ever rode down the turnpike, you would be queen of this fair land, your life would be nothing but garnets and gravy; furthermore you would be able to do your loving old pa no end of good turns. *Whereas*,' he went on warningly, 'in any other circumstances whatsoever, I fear that his excellency would consider it the part of prudence to have you eliminated – now that your task of teaching our Netherlands friend is complete.'

'Eliminated?' said Dido.

'As he would have eliminated your lamented friend Simon – only the wolves got in first.'

Mr Twite pulled an evening paper from his pocket and pointed to the headlines:

King Richard to lay wreath under Thorn Tree
on Blackheath Edge.

He read: ' "His majesty will today pay tribute to
the selfless gallantry of the Duke of Battersea who
died yesterday defending the capital from the assaults
of wolves – " Excellent valiant young man! He has
saved the Margrave a deal of trouble – '

'You mean,' said Dido slowly, 'You mean the
Margrave always did plan to kill Simon anyway?
When you promised me that if I stayed away from
Simon he'd be safe – when you promised that, you
were only codding me? You didn't mean it at all?'

'I had to enlist your support in the best way I
could, my chickadee.'

Dido had always known that her father was a liar.
But still she had hoped to be able to believe him in
this.

'Poor young fellow, cut off in his prime,' sighed Mr
Twite, and he sang:

> 'Oh willow, herb willow,
> Drop a tear on the pillow
> And toll out the knell, oh,
> For that charming young fellow!'

'Persuade your father, if you can, that you are still
ready to do what he suggests. That way, he may tell
you more of the Margrave's intentions,' Simon had
said to Dido, and she had promised to do her

best. – But now, faced with the flat fact of her father's falseness, she found that she could not pretend.

'Then I think that you're a pig, Pa, and I don't want no part at all in the business,' she said baldly.

'In that case, my dovekin, I can only advise you to make yourself very, very scarce,' replied Mr Twite, without any particular sign of dismay. He was wandering about, collecting such of his belongings as were undamaged, and stuffing them into a canvas bag. 'Yes indeed, I would certainly recommend that you leave the city without delay, or you are likely to meet with a fate similar to that of your red-headed young acquaintance.'

'What?' gasped Dido. 'Which one? What are you talking about, Pa?' – as the Slut came back with the bread, tobacco, and a tin jug of coffee. 'What do you mean?'

Mr Twite drank half the coffee before replying.

'Why, his excellency took a notion that the escape of all those young persons and elderly characters from the cellar had been somehow abetted by that red-headed boy – the porter revived and saw him running up the stairs, it seems, around that time – so they tied his feet together and dropped him out of the salon window; to see if he would break the ice. He did break it, and that was his finis, poor fellow. He went under and was seen no more.'

Mr Twite sang mournfully, with his mouth full of bread and coffee:

'Oh what a fearful finish
To sink beneath the ice

269

But let your tears diminish
He's now in Paradise.'

Dido was so choked with grief and indignation that she could not speak. Besides, what would be the use? The deed was done, nothing would bring the red-headed boy back to life. And I never even knew his *name*, she thought wretchedly. And he would have liked to come with us – I saw that. Why, why didn't I ask him? Now he'd be safe and well. Just wait till I tell Simon and he tells the king what that monster has done. Killing a person just like *that*. I suppose it's only one of dozens. But it seems different when it's a cove you know, as has helped you.

'Are you going away, mister?' asked the Slut timidly, observing that Mr Twite had now packed up all his things.

'That's the ticket,' he replied carelessly, draining the last dregs of coffee. 'I am va – ca – ting these prem – i – ses. And so is Mr van Doon from tomorrow. I shall be residing with his excellency. This house will be shut up.'

'What about *me*?' demanded Is. Her mouth drooped forlornly. 'Where'll I go?'

'Don't ask *me*,' replied Mr Twite airily, poking a couple of hoboys into the interstices of his bag. 'His excellency certainly don't want a little drabble like you about the place. You'd best go back where you came from.'

'But I never been no place but here!'

'Then you'll have to go on the streets with the rest of the lollpoops, I presume,' said Mr Twite indifferently, and he ran down the steps, whistling 'Calico Alley', without a backward look.

The two left behind stared after him, both through tears: Dido's of enraged grief, the Slut's of fright. Then they heard somebody else approaching, and saw Mr van Doon come gliding along the ice with the expert gait of a practised skater.

'*Oh mister! Oh mister!*' cried Is, and she ran to him joyfully. 'Oh, I was so feared I'd never see you no more.'

He patted her head very kindly, but the face he turned to Dido was white and haggard.

'What's up, then?' she asked him, though it was easy to guess.

'Come inside the house! It is too terrible to speak of in the street,' he said with a look of horror, and led them up to his room.

To help him, for he seemed tongue-tied, Dido said, 'His Nabs has told you all he plans to do?'

'And what he has done already! All those people he has killed. That page – ' Poor van Doon shuddered. 'And now he says I am in too far to draw back. Oh, I am on the edge of a deep, dreadful cliff. What shall I do? What shall I do now?'

'*I'll* tell you what you gotta do,' said Dido. 'Just you listen to me.'

13

The day of the Tunnel Ceremony dawned bright, fair, and bitter, bitter cold. Half London had lined up along the route of the procession, on either side of the Thames, and half London was half frozen, keeping itself warm as best it could, wrapped in velvets, in furs, in rugs, in rags, in old newspapers. Charcoal braziers and spirit lamps heated water for foot- and hand-warmers; hot cockles and hot pies and roast chestnuts had a nonstop sale. Wally had repaired and cleaned up his coffee-stall, and hammered out the dents, and was selling mugs of tea and coffee as fast as he could pour them, in a little alley called Glamis Gardens, not a stone's throw from where the new tunnel emerged into Shadwell on the north side of the river. In order to secure such an advantageous position, he had set up his stall there, with Dido's assistance, long before daybreak. Dido was helping him pour and sell his drinks, but an hour before the procession from St James's was due to arrive, he told her: 'You cut along now, young 'un – ' which made her grin, for she was several years the older – 'cut along, get yourself a spot by the road. You been a whizz at helping and I'll recommend you for the job o' Chief Coffee Waiter at the Pulteney Hotel any day you name, but now you want to hear your old man's music, so skedaddle! I'll see you at my dad's place, after.'

'You sartin, Wally? You'll never sell half so much, not without me.'

'Get along, girl! You want to see old King Dick riding in his gold coach – and Podge and Simon standing up behind. Give 'em a yell from me. Scarper now, or you'll never be able to fight your way to the front.'

'What I might do, after,' said Dido, considering, 'is cross the river on the ice and watch 'em come out the other side.'

'Blimey, kid, you sure that ain't a bit chancy? All the way over the ice?'

'I'm sure it's strong enough, Wally, I heard the landlord of the Jolly Mermaids tell your da that some bloke'd driven a curricle across at Charing Cross.'

'That may be,' said Wally doubtfully, 'but suppose half the crowd takes it into their noddles to do likewise? All those folk on it might bust the ice. Charing Cross is a lot farther west. It's rabshackle, to my mind.'

'The ice won't give, Wally. Just feel how cold it is – enough to freeze the feelers off a brass octopus.'

She waved to him and ran off.

Wally stared after her anxiously, then turned to dispense coffee to a waiting line of six impatient people jumping up and down and chafing their hands together.

Dido, accustomed to fending for herself, had no

difficulty in securing a place of vantage from which to see the procession. She wriggled, she edged, she slid, she nudged, she crawled, she slithered, and at last, with nobody even noticing that she had got ahead of them, she found herself perched like a house-leek, ten feet up, on top of the granite wall cutting through the bank, just where the tunnel road began its plunge to go down under the Thames. Her view could not have been better. Indeed, her only problem now was to keep the surging mass of people who were behind her on the bank from pushing her forward off the wall and under the hoofs of the processional horses. The hillside was all frosty and frozen, the ground like iron covered with snow; but the top course of the wall formed a slight ridge, a few inches above ground level, so she hooked her fingers and toes into this and clung as tight as a monkey.

After an immensely long wait, during which her fingers and toes gradually lost all feeling, and she began to wonder if they would freeze altogether and snap clean off, the sound of distant music began to be heard, and the beat of a drum.

Tum, tum, titherum, titherum, tum, tum.

Then the music became recognizable as Dido's favourite tune, 'Calico Alley' – played so joyfully, so liltingly, that *anyone*'s fingers and toes, even if completely frozen, would begin to clap, would begin to dance at the sound. In fact the crowds, lined up so thickly at the side of the road, did just that – they began to dance, and to clap, and to cheer and jump up and down as the forerunners of the procession came in sight – a drum major from the Household

274

Cavalry on a white horse, followed by a fife band, followed by the cavalry troops, with cuirasses glittering, and plumes flying, the red and gold of their uniforms glowing in the early light, and their horses moving so proudly and excitedly, lifting their feet high in the air, that they too seemed to be almost dancing to the music.

More and more troops of soldiers followed, in different uniforms, to different tunes, all Dido's favourites; then coaches, chariots, barouches, gleaming with gilt, with brilliant coats-of-arms emblazoned on the door panels, with top-hatted coachmen and white-wigged footmen, with postilions and outriders, with glossy horses and glistening harness, with flowers and rosettes and ribbons and fluttering flags.

And here, drawn by six black horses, came the king's ceremonial coach itself, very old and immensely grand, all constructed of gold and glass, so that he could be seen inside it; like a goldfish, poor thing, thought Dido, in his velvet cloak and crown with all them rubies in it; don't it look heavy, must be like carrying the kitchen sink on your napper, I bet it don't half give him the headache. And, perched up behind, two footmen in dark blue and gold, motionless as statues with white wigs and folded arms, whom Dido had no difficulty in recognizing as Podge and Simon.

'Hi-oh, SIMON! Hi-oh, PODGE!' she yelled at the top of her lungs, and thought she saw the eyelid of Podge, who was nearest to her, give just the faintest flicker as he went by, only five feet below her.

The royal coach rolled into the tunnel, to the music

of 'Black Cat Going Down Stairs', and vanished into darkness. Then the music changed to 'The Day Before the Day Before May Day', and here came an open coach with the Margrave of Nordmarck, refulgent in gold and white and diamonds, wearing a great ermine cloak; and opposite him in the open carriage sat Mr Twite, all dressed up in his best, severely beating time to the music with an ivory baton, and keeping a sharp eye on the band of the Household Grenadiers, who followed next – but with such a look of pride and bliss on his face that Dido's heart, in spite of herself, swelled in sympathy and admiration. Oh I don't know *what* to think about pa, she thought; he's a rancid liar, he don't reckon on nobody but himself, he was unkind to Ma and horrible to Mrs B., he never done a thing for Penny or me, but there's nobody in the whole world can make up tunes like his? Maybe his tunes'll go on for ever? Maybe folk will remember them long after they've forgotten Pa, and the bad things he done? Maybe the tunes is what's important, not Pa?

And then Dido wondered, for the first time, where her father had passed his childhood. He had never talked to her about it – never said a word. Maybe he had been a lollpoop, growing up in the street, spending his nights in a lodging like Mrs Bloodvessel's?

The carriage bearing the Margrave and Mr Twite rolled out of sight into the dark tunnel; Mr Twite had not noticed his daughter on the hillside above.

Now Dido turned and began to wriggle purposefully through the crowd, which swallowed her as the incoming tide swallows up a single grain of sand; slowly, doggedly, persistently, she worked her way up the embankment, through a thousand legs, always going uphill over the stony, snowy, frozen ground, on hands and knees, until the mass of people began to thin out, and at last she was away from the crowd, quite alone, on the bank of the frozen Thames. To her left were the masts and chimneys of the India and Millwall Docks; to her right the river stretched like a white velvet ribbon; far off, shining gold in the early light, she could see the spires of Westminster. And in front of her lay a quarter of a mile of ice.

Do I dare to go over the other side? she wondered.

Charing Cross is a fair step from here, it's true; the river's not so wide there.

Yes I do dare; that ice looks plenty thick enough to me.

Down below, along the procession route, the crowd was waiting, happily beating time and singing all the bits they could remember from Mr Twite's tunes, for the second half of the procession to begin appearing out of the tunnel in the other direction. Troops from the Bombardier Guards were now going in; they rode grey horses and wore huge white hats made of polar bears' fur, and white cloaks, and the music to which they cantered along was one of Mr Twite's most serious tunes, 'Three Herrings for a Ha'penny'. Quite soon, as the crowd knew, a troop of milkmaids and shepherds and hay-wagons would come dancing out in the other direction, to a different kind of music.

And there would be another coach following them, but who would be sitting in it? Would the king have changed coaches in mid-tunnel, as some thought, and come riding back to his palace at St James's, leaving the glass coach to continue empty to Greenwich? Or would Princess Adelaide of Thuringia be in it? (This was what another lot of people hoped and expected.) Or perhaps there would just be a *waxwork* king inside the second coach?

By and by, out it came. Londoners who had been alive at the coronation of Old King Jamie III recognized the vehicle; it was the one called the Royal May-Bogie, made expressly for that coronation, which had taken place at mid-summer; it was painted all over, most gorgeously, with coloured blossoms and leaves, so that it looked like a bunch of flowers travelling along the highway. The same two footmen – or two who looked the same at any rate – stood up behind, but now they carried huge bouquets of sweetpeas; and in the carriage, not quite so easily visible as in the glass coach, for the windows were smaller, but still easily recognizable, was the king himself. So he *must* have changed coaches in the tunnel!

'God save King Dick!' burst in a roar from a thousand happy throats. 'God save good old King Dick. May he never fall sick!'

Halfway across the ice, Dido paused, wondering if she had caught the sound of her name, called faintly in the distance behind her. She looked round. From here, in the middle of the great white highway which was the Thames, London seemed no more than a faint smudge; a cloud of smoke and a cluster of frosty roofs to the north and west of her. To the east there were masts, where ships lay frozen in at Greenwich and Woolwich; to the south, the hills of Kent glimmered in a frosty haze. Even the royal music, from here, was only a faint throb in the ice-cold air, sometimes to be heard from one side of the river, sometimes from the other.

I wonder what it's like, down there in the tunnel, thought Dido. Ain't it queer that, right under where I stand, perhaps at this very minute, Simon and Podge are changing over coaches. Oh I do hope it's all going as it should.

And then she was sure she heard her name again, clear and sharp across the diamond brightness of the ice: '*Dido!* Di——do!' And there, a small black speck making his way steadily towards her across the whiteness, was Wally.

Although dying to get on, and see the rest of the procession from the other side, Dido waited patiently until he had come up with her, slipping and sliding and panting.

'Why, Wally? What's amiss?'

'Had to catch you -- ' he gulped.

'What about your coffee-stall? You're losing umpty pounds worth o' trade!'

'One o' the lollpoops just warned me – van Doon sent word back to Bart's Building – he was in a mortal fright for ye – he heard the Margrave planning to *do* you – heard him giving orders – '

Wally stopped speaking. At first Dido thought he

had run out of breath. Then, seeing his face of stupefied horror staring over her shoulder, she turned to
find out what he was looking at, and saw the ice-
boat.

It was set on a triangular frame with an iron runner
at each corner and the point of the triangle at the
stern; there was a rudder, a mainsail, and a jib. The
sails were enormous, contrasted with the size of the
boat, which was hardly larger than a dinghy. Because
of the huge spread of sails, though there seemed little
wind, the boat was able to career along over the
frozen river at a startling speed, tacking vigorously
from side to side; now it swooped over to St
Katherine's Dock, now it darted south-east towards
Cherry Garden Pier; now it hurtled back to the north
side of the river; now it was coming straight for
them, like an arrow over the ice.

'It's the Margrave's ice schooner,' stammered
Wally with blue lips. '*Run*, Dido! Bunk! Mizzle! Best
make for the south shore!'

As the ice-boat careered towards them, Dido saw
the black hammer on the gold flag. And she recognized Boletus at the tiller and Morel standing in the
bows with a noose of rope in his hand.

'Run!' cried Wally again. But it was too late.

With a tremendous grinding roar, with a fizz of
pulverized, powdery ice, the silvery keel shot past
them, the noose, expertly flung, jerked them
together, and, gasping like fish on the angler's line,
they were drawn on board.

Tum, tum, titherum, tum, tum, sang the drums,

and the glass coach rolled out from the tunnel into Kent.

'Hooray, hooray, hooray!' yelled the happy crowd, as the horses paced forward, to the tune of 'Calico Alley', cunningly mingled now with 'Raining, Raining, all the Day'. And Mr van Doon, in velvet cloak and ruby-studded crown, bowed and smiled and waved to the populace until, unused to this exercise, his arm ached and his hand grew numb. Through Rotherhithe and Deptford, on towards Greenwich, the coach rolled, and gradually the crowds diminished until there was nobody left along the route. Then suddenly the glass coach turned aside, up Forest Hill, and over Black Heath, abandoning the rest of the procession, which continued towards Greenwich. By now the highway was a single road, then it became a farm track, then no more than a narrow glade between trees.'

'What is this?' called the occupant of the coach. 'Where are you going? Where are you taking me? This cannot be the right road. Stop! Stop I say!'

And he hammered on the glass panel separating him from the driver.

'We'll stop soon enough. Don't you fret your head,' replied the coachman, without troubling to turn round.

High on the hilltop, among the thorn trees, lay a thick, icy fog; the branches glimmered with hoarfrost, the birds were all silent. Not a sound was to be heard.

Presently the coach rolled to a stop; the horses stood giving off clouds of steam and vapour. A pair of men, who had been waiting there under the trees, walked forward; one of them took the bridle of the leaders.

'Nicely on time,' he said with a grin.

'Have you done the digging?' asked the coachman, dismounting.

'Ah. It's done.'

'Let's have him out then.'

Numb with horror and astonishment, van Doon heard the footmen jump down from the rear of the coach. The door was flung open.

'We need you out of there,' someone said, and rough hands dragged him out, so unceremoniously that he stumbled and fell on the frozen, snowy ground.

'What are you doing? You cannot do this to *me*?'

'Oh can't us, my codger! That's what you think!'

'But I – but I – '

He didn't know what to say. If they thought that he was the king – ? But, on the other hand, if they knew he was a van Doon – ?

'What are you doing? What are you going to do?'

The king was supposed to be taken to some island; where he would be imprisoned but not harmed; so the Margrave had said.

'You'll soon see, my cocky. You'll see soon enough, my fine majesty.'

His cloak, crown, and velvet jacket were taken off him. Somebody said, 'Tie his hands,' and they were grabbed, and roped behind his back. A sack was thrown over his head. 'Take off them di'mond buckled shoes,' someone said. 'He 'on't want 'em where he's going.'

Half fainting, cold and sick with horror, van Doon crumpled on the ground. He heard steps moving away.

'Let's see the hole — is it good and deep?' someone said. 'Might as well hit him on the head at once, then, and shovel him under.'

Then the coachman's voice: 'Nay, no, no, dag me, that ain't *half* deep enough. His Nabs'd have our guts for garters if wolves come along and dug him up again and he was recognized. Here: give us a shovel; it won't take but five minutes to dig out another ell or so — blow me, but this ground's hard though, ain't it — '

A sound of clinking, grunting, and panting.

Then, very softly from behind him, the paralysed van Doon heard a whisper.

'Mister! *Mister!* Can you roll over on your stummick? That way I can get at your hands to undo 'em.'

Hardly able to credit his ears, he rolled; and felt something tiny picking and sawing at the cruelly tight cords that bound him. It felt like a grasshopper's teeth . . . he could not believe than anything hopeful would come of it. But then an edge of metal snicked the ball of his thumb — like the sting of a hornet — and next moment his hands were free.

'Don't-ee move yet — now I'll do your feet,' said the hornet, and the sawing began again on the cords that bound his ankles. The sack was pulled off his head. Van Doon moved his cheek on the frosty ground, enough so that he could squint sideways and see who was working to release him.

It was the Slut.

'That'll do plenty, that's deep enough,' said a voice beyond the thorn tree. 'No wolf's a-going to dig him out of there.'

'Just a couple o' feet more.'

'What a one you are for digging! Ought to be king's gardener at Kew.'

'*Hup*, mister – can you stand?'

Hauled by two tiny hands, van Doon rose totteringly to his feet. Now the Slut was putting away a businesslike little pen-knife.

'That's the dandy. Now, you gotta *run*. Come on! Arter me. Fast as ever you can!'

Gulping in great lungfuls of icy, foggy air, van Doon set off clumsily, in his sock feet, after the Slut, who was barefoot. She sped away through the thorn-bushes, looking back every couple of yards to make sure that he was following her.

Quite soon they heard angry shouts behind them.

'Oy! Oy, lookit! The cove's scarpered. After him!'

Dido said to Morel, 'You'll be real sorry if you do any mischief to us, mister. The king knows all about His Nabs's little plan to do a swap-over in the tunnel; and it ain't a-going to happen. Or not the way His Nabs expects.'

'Really? Fancy that!' said Morel, smiling at her disbelievingly, as the ice-yacht continued to whiz along the frozen river, going eastwards.

'It's so,' said Dido. 'They done the swap already. The king went out to Greenwich last night, and rode in this morning. And van Doon went to St James's at sun-up and got in the glass coach. So now the king's riding in to London, and van Doon's on his way to Kent. And His Nabs is in for a mighty peck o' trouble.'

'You are a very clever child,' said Morel, 'and you made up all that out of your head, and there isn't a single word of truth in it.'

He folded his arms and continued to smile.

'What did the Margrave tell you to do with her?' croaked Wally.

'Take her down to Woolwich Basin, where the ice is thinner, and drop her in. He didn't tell us to do that with *you*,' – giving Wally a despising look, 'but, as you *would* come along for the ride, now you have to pay the fare.'

And he turned, whistling, to let out the sail, as the boat went about.

'I'd best drop Dad's sack over the side,' Wally murmured to Dido in a low tone. 'Maybe someone'll pick it up and find the gold key – '

'What's that about a gold key, my young shaver?' inquired Boletus alertly. 'You got a gold key in that there sack? And what would that be the key to, I wonder? Here, Morel, take the tiller a moment.'

He moved forward and grabbed the bag that still hung from Wally's shoulder.

'I don't see no gold key,' he grumbled, rummaging through its contents. 'But there's a very decent morsel o' cheese here, and a jug of what smells like real grade-A tipple – no sense in dropping that down to the fishes at Woolwich. Here, Morel – take a swig of this, it's right stingo stuff!' And he passed the flask to his mate, smacking his lips, then bolting down a large lump of cheese.

286

Too bad there ain't enough for you young 'uns,' remarked Morel, tossing down the rest of the drink and then munching the rest of the cheese. 'But there's no point in wasting it . . . Now where's this gold key you was on about?' he demanded of Wally, groping about in the bottom of the black velvet bag; '*I* don't feel any gold key. Are you trying it on? Because if you are – '

He stopped, suddenly, his face contorted into a mask of extreme agony.

'Jeeeee – rusalem! What in the wide – '

At the same moment Boletus let out a fearful yell of pain.

'Ohhhhhhh! Murder! There's a fire in my bread-basket!'

Both men doubled over, clutching frantically at their stomachs.

'What *is* it?' gasped Dido, utterly bewildered. 'What's got into 'em?'

Now the two of them were writhing in the bottom of the boat, rolling over and over like hedgehogs.

Wally moved to the tiller and took it, watching the men dispassionately. He said, 'It's Dad's apple-punch. You must never, ever drink it when you've eaten cheese. Or t'other way round. The two don't go together. Dad says it's liable to kill you. I don't know if he's right for I never see anyone try it before. But looks like he might be . . . Now we'd best be ready to jump; this seems as good a place as any. Are you game?'

'Y-yes,' stammered Dido, who was a good deal shaken by the speed at which all these things had happened.

287

The boat was rushing towards the Deptford shore. Just here, south of the river, was a small boatyard; by its entrance a great tangle of frozen nets lay draped over the bank.

'Aim for the nets!' Wally shouted as he put the tiller across. Dido flung herself out, and, ducking under the boom as it swung over, Wally followed her. Both of them rolled, winded, gasping, but otherwise uninjured, on to the pile of nets. And the Margrave's ice-yacht, with the two groaning men huddled on its bottom boards, sped on eastwards, towards Woolwich Basin, where the river was not yet quite frozen.

Dido picked herself up and said, 'What'll us do now?'

'Run like the very devil,' said Wally. 'See those black dogs over there? Only they ain't dogs – '

A sinister howling came to them over the ice.

'*Wolves!* Croopus, Wally!'

Since the wolves were north of them, where the river curved in a great U-bend, Wally and Dido ran southwards, towards the heights of Blackheath.

'They are going to catch us!' panted van Doon. 'I cannot run any faster – I have a bad pain in my side.'

'Then we must hide,' said Is, who had not complained about her bruised and bleeding feet. She looked around them at the wizened thorn trees, at the wild heathland, veiled in snow; she scraped the ground with her bare foot.

'Quick – lie down. What a mussy it snows so.' She pulled up armfuls of dead, frozen bracken and made van Doon huddle into the hollow she had thus created. Then she spread the bracken on top of him, thumping it down, flattening it, until it looked like any other part of the forest floor. Then she huddled down beside him, pulling more bracken over herself. 'Lucky those perishers ain't got bloodhounds,' she remarked, 'or they'd nabble us for sure. This way we got a chance.'

Indeed the coachman, gravedigger, and two footmen ran right past where they lay. One of the men trod on the Slut's hand. Soon they were out of sight and out of earshot.

14

At St James's Palace, a grand ball was being held, to conclude the day's festivities. Mr Twite's music was played. The king was there, looking a little awkward and melancholy, because he was acquainted with so few of the nobility and gentry who were gathered to do him honour. But he danced several times with Princess Adelaide of Thuringia, a plump, plain, kind-faced lady in orange satin and steel-rimmed glasses.

'Och,' he sighed to her, 'fine I wish I was back in bonnie Scotland and awa' from a' this clamjamfry.'

Princess Adelaide squeezed his arm comfortingly. 'Ach, never mind it, *liebster* Richart! We will come to know them together, these people, in a little time, you and I. When we are married we shall live among them very happily, you will see. They are all good, kindly people, I am sure.'

'All except *this* one,' muttered the king, as the Margrave, elegant in white satin and huge pearl buttons, approached him.

On his way, Lady Maria intercepted the Margrave.

'My *dearest* Eisengrim! Your *music*! Your musician! What a delight! What a rapture! We are exhilarated – liberated – transported! I, for one, believe that music could heal any trouble in the world.'

'Thank you, dear lady,' said the Margrave briefly, and moved on towards the king, who said, 'Transported! Yes, and that's just what *you* are going to be. And not before time.'

'Shall I withdraw, *liebster* Richart?' said the princess.

'Na, na, my lass, this will take but a minute. Ha! Eisengrim! I bid ye good evening.'

'Good evening, majesty,' said the Margrave. Then, leaning closer, he murmured, 'This party has now gone on long enough. Tell them to leave; I have several matters to discuss with you.'

'Och, no, I'll not bid them leave,' said the king. His tone was placid, but his gaze was steady and his mouth set very firmly.

Eisengrim's eyes flashed. 'You had best do as I order,' he was beginning, when the king, leaning forward, said to him gently, 'Tak' a gude, close look at my neb, Eisengrim. Do ye see a scar on it? No, ye do not. I think ye may be under a wee misapprehension. Ye may think that I am Maister van Doon; whereas, I am Davie Jamie Charlie Neddie Georgie Harry Dick Tudor-Stuart, very much at your service. *Now* do ye understand? I will end my ain party at my ain convenience, when I so choose, and at naebody else's bidding at a'. And as for ye, Eisengrim, ye may thank yer stars that ye are a Hanoverian subject and protected by diplomatic immunity, for, if not, ye wad be clapt in the Tower o' London afore ye could say Killiecrankie! But as matters are, these gentlemen will escort ye hame to Cinnamon Court, and I'll require ye to be oot o' this country, for gude and a', by sunrise tomorrow, or worse may befa' you. And now, I bid ye gude nicht.'

After saying which, the king very pointedly turned his back on the ashen-faced, speechless Margrave, and, still holding the arm of Princess Adelaide, walked away.

Four large, red-faced Officers of the King's Household, wearing kilts and carrying claymores, surrounded the Margrave and accompanied him to the door in close formation.

'I think we are lost, little one,' said van Doon, after he and the Slut had been walking through the thorny, snowy woods for a couple of hours.

'I think so too,' said Is.

'And night is coming.'

'Yus.'

'And I believe I can hear the howling of wolves in the distance.'

'Me too.'

'I am not at all happy about our situation.'

'Nor I'm not, neither. And,' said Is, 'I reckon we better run. Them wolves is getting tarnal close.'

'I do not think I can run any more. The pain in my side is getting worse. And,' said van Doon, 'I do not see the use of running if we do not know where we are running to.'

'Now hold up, mister,' said Is firmly. 'We didn't come all this way to knuckle under now, and get eaten by wolves. At least I didn't. 'Sides, I think I can maybe see a light over there in the trees.'

Dragging the Dutchman after her, she ran, slipping and sliding in her bare feet, through the snow.

While the ball was taking place in St James's, Mr Twite was conducting a concert in St James's Palace Yard, nearby. He had rather expected to be invited to conduct the musical ensemble provided for the ball, but, to his slight surprise, no such invitation had been received.

'It is of no account,' said Mr Twite philosophically. 'More people will hear my music outside,' and he had set up a platform in the middle of the Yard. Here, for several hours, the music that had already delighted the spectators along the processional route was played again, heard and enjoyed by a large enthusiastic crowd.

'More, more!' they shouted. 'Play it again!'

Standing on his platform, delirious with joy and success, waving his baton, controlling his players despite the snow and wintry wind, Mr Twite was probably the happiest man in London.

Yet gradually the crowd began to trickle away. The hour was late, the cold was severe and growing more so; by now the grand coaches of the gentry at the king's ball had all rolled off homeward. In the king's palace the lights began to dim and go out, all but the two that always stayed burning above the Royal Standard, which, fluttering red and white on the pole, showed that the king was in residence.

If they only knew what I know, thought Mr Twite, watching the crowd.

He had not observed the Margrave being escorted to his carriage by four burly Scotsmen.

As the crowd in the palace yard dispersed, it seemed to re-form again. Some people went away, but others came. The ones who left were all adults, and the ones who came were all children. Little by little the whole of the huge area was filling up with children.

Must be all the lollpoops in London, thought Mr Twite. I read somewhere there was ten thousand of the little perishers, and now I believe it. And they're all here, a-listening to my music. Very nice, to be sure! but not very remunerative.

But what the deuce! Eisengrim and I, between us, have got the king of England in our pocket. And *I* have got Eisengrim in *my* pocket.

For a long time the children thronging around Mr Twite appeared to enjoy the music every bit as much as their elders had done: dancing, jumping, singing, clapping and shouting.

After a while, though, there came a change. And this change followed a whisper, which started on the outskirts of the crowd and spread inwards and sideways with the speed of sparks through stubble.

D'you know what he did? That music feller — let 'is own daughter be scrobbled by the Margrave.

'E did? How?

Eisengrim sent an ice-boat with them two bad ones on board — Boletus and Morel. They picked up Dido Twite and Wally Greenaway and took 'em down to

Deptford where the ice is thin – dropped 'em in and drowned 'em like a brace of kittens.

How d'you know?

A message come to Wally, telling what they planned, and he told his dad, and his dad told my dad, and my dad told my mum, and my mum told Mrs Watkins, and Mrs Watkins told Peggy Watkins and Peggy Watkins told me.

Cor!

D'you know what that feller as calls hisself Bredalbane *did*? He drowned his own daughter. The one as is called Died o' Fright. Friend o' Wally Greenaway. He took and drowned the pair of them at Deptford. With his own hands.

That chap what's conducting the music – know what he did? He took and drowned *his own daughter*

As the whispers ran through the crowd, Mr Twite started to feel uncomfortable. Something was wrong, but he did not know what. His musicians, too, were beginning to look tired and nervous.

'Time to stop, guvnor,' they told him. 'We've just about played ourselves to a standstill.'

'Oh, very well. Very well,' conceded Mr Twite. 'But I wish to see you tomorrow, at Cinnamon Court, in the rehearsal room, at nine sharp. We are going to be very busy from now on!' He waved them goodbye, and they hurried thankfully away.

Mr Twite was about to follow them, but somebody stood in his path, and then somebody else jostled him. And a third person tripped him up.

'Now, what is all this?' said Mr Twite impatiently. 'Let me past, if you please. I am the Master of the

King's Music. I am not to be justled and hostled by a parcel of lollpoops.'

And he tried to hum with an air of nonchalance:

> 'Oh riddle me riddle me rassity
> And hey ding a dong ding a ding
> I am known for my sense and sagacity
> And the beautiful songs that I – '

A stone flew, and hit him in the mouth.

'Come, come, now!' said Mr Twite, wiping away mud, and possibly a tooth. 'I will say nothing opprobrious on this occasion because – but – '

Another stone flew, and then several more. Mr Twite began to run. He raced into the park, followed by the whole crowd of children. They yelled and flung objects – anything they could pick up – eggs, oranges, shoes. Mr Twite ran desperately across the park towards the river; but the storm of stones, shoes, and other articles became fiercer and fiercer. At last, he crumpled and fell to the ground.

At the sight of his fall, the children halted. They looked at him doubtfully from a distance. He still stirred feebly and moaned.

'Come out of it,' suggested a boy called Handkerchief Harry. 'We'd best leave him be. He ain't much hurt – I don't think. He'll pick hisself up, soon as we're gone. We don't want the beaks arter us, saying we done him in. We never. He's just a bit dazed, like.'

Everyone agreed. Without wasting a moment, the crowd of lollpoops took themselves off, disappearing speedily along alleys and narrow streets, drifting

rapidly eastwards towards the part of London they
had come from. In five minutes the park was empty,
except for Mr Twite.

But the wolves had come across the river, at
Charing Cross and Lambeth, at Westminster and
Millbank; roaming and sniffing, they scoured around
Victoria and Pimlico, along the Strand, up
Whitehall, and across St James's Park. They found
Mr Twite lying among the missiles that had stunned
him, and they quite soon finished off what the
children had begun.

Wally and Dido, running from the wolves across
Blackheath Waste, had several times to fight a rear-
guard action against their attackers, using what

weapons came to hand, fenceposts and branches and rocks.

'Murder!' panted Dido, warding off a snarling beast with a shrewd thrust from a holly-spike, 'I've never known the wolves so umbrageous as this. I reckon it's scanty pickings where they come from. They seem half starved.'

'Keep it up,' gasped Wally. 'Don't weaken! I see a light over thataway.'

'*I* thought Simon – puff – and his mates – puff – were supposed to have cleared all the wolves outa this part o' the country? All they seem to have done is *aggravated* them.'

'Maybe some more came over from France,' suggested Wally, dealing a hurried thwack at a large grey beast which was on the point of leaping at Dido from behind. 'This way – get closer to me! Now – a quick dash over the open space. That looks like a house – or a shed.'

'Thanks be!' panted Dido. 'Maybe it's where – my sis lives – must be – somewhere hereabouts – that Simon said she – '

The door of the building opened. Light poured out. A voice called anxiously, 'Come this way – *quick*! We have guns – but we daren't fire in case of hitting you – '

'*Sophie!*' shouted Dido in delight. 'Lawkamussy, am I glad to hear your voice!'

Ten seconds later, she and Wally tumbled over the threshold, with half a dozen wolves snapping at their heels. Sophie discharged her musket among the wolves and slammed the door in their faces.

Inside it took Dido's dazzled eyes several minutes to adjust to the light. (When Simon escorted Sophie to stay with Penny, he had forethoughtfully brought along a supply of lamp-oil, coal, flour, dried meat, books, and other supplies, enough to last for several weeks; as well as several new tea-cups.) As soon as their eyes stopped streaming, Dido and Wally saw a comfortable interior with beds, curtains, hangings, and a blazing fire.

In one of the beds lay Mr van Doon.

'Croopus,' said Dido. 'What's *he* doing here?' Then she saw her sister Penny. 'Wotcher, Penny? How's tricks? I'm right pleased to see you.'

'Well, Dido! How are you?' Penny said rather stiffly. But little Is rushed to Dido and hugged her about the knees.

'Dido! Poor Mr van Doon is proper poorly! Those chaps was a-going to kill him and I undid 'im and we run and run, and it give 'im a pain. Will 'e be all right?'

'Well I'm blest,' said Dido. 'How in turkey's name did *you* come to be on the spot?'

'I just followed,' said the Slut simply. 'When 'e left Bart's, I followed. And when 'e got into the king's coach, I watched my chance and hid in the boot. And when they stopped, I got out. And it was a good thing I did, for they was goin' to knock 'im on the head and bury 'im.'

Wally and Dido stared at one another.

'Lord amighty,' said Wally. 'So much for His Nabs saying he was a-going to ship the king off to some island. He never had no sich intention.'

'We might a guessed,' said Dido. 'Him and my pa's just about as crooked as a pair o' croquet hoops.'

The Slut began to cry.

'Now what's to do?' said Dido. 'You saved the feller, didn't you? You done real well for a little 'un. He'll be all rug, don't you fret, with Sophie and my sister Penny a-caring for him.'

But the Slut continued to sob bitterly. 'It's Figgin. My cat Figgin! There's nobody to feed him, the house is empty, and all those wolves about – what'll he do?'

'Oh, *scrape* it!' began Dido. But then she looked at little Is more gently and said, 'Don't take on so! That cat's as shrewd as he can hold together. He fetched you grub, didn't he? He went down the chimney of Cinnamon Court and saved Sophie? *He* won't be nobbled by no wolf, don't you worry. It's ducats to dumplings you'll get back and find him a-waiting for you.'

'But when?' demanded the Slut tearfully.

This was no easy question to answer.

For six days the blizzard raged without abating; more and more wolves found their way on to the heights of Kent. It was unsafe for the inmates of Penelope's barn even to step outside the door. When they fetched snow, to be melted down for water (since the well had frozen), they went in pairs, one with a pail, the other with a gun. But they were running short of ammunition; Simon, when he brought the supplies, had not reckoned on such a long visit. Nor on so many guests.

'One biscuit and one carrot a day from now on!'

announced Penny one evening, looking grimly at the depleted larder.

'Not for Mr van Doon!' wailed the Slut. 'He's too poorly. He can have my carrot.'

Penny's hard face softened a little as she looked from the anxious Slut to the ailing Dutchman.

'I am indeed grieved that I give you this trouble, Miss Penelope,' he said weakly.

'*You* can't help it, mister. I know that. Here, Is, you boil up Mr van Doon's carrot in a teacupful of water. He can take it easier that way.'

The Slut busied herself with cookery. Dido and Wally were sharpening spikes and hardening their points in the fire for defence against wolves when the bullets ran out. Sophie, always skilful with her needle, was at work helping Penny cut out and stuff more animals – seals, badgers, racoons.

Presently the Slut, having served van Doon his frugal meal, squatted down by his bedside and sang to him in a threadlike but tuneful little voice, while Penny absently joined in, supplying an alto part.

'Rum and rhubarb and raisins,'

sang the Slut

'Is good when you're under the weather,
Rum and rhubarb and raisins,
Taken singly or all together.'

'I was a-going to say that little Is could come and stay with my dad, when we get outa here,' Wally murmured to Dido, as they sat and whittled. 'If she got nowhere else to go. But maybe . . .' He looked at Penelope busily sewing by van Doon's couch and the Slut, cross-legged beside her.

'Penny allus was fond of cats,' said Dido thoughtfully.

15

During the night after the Tunnel Ceremony the Margrave of Nordmarck suffered from such a fearful series of spasmodic attacks tht Dr Finster, having bled him, drenched him by means of a clyster, attempted cautery, applied a cataplasm, and nine or ten leeches, was next proposing to go on and try lithotomy or dririmancy, when there came a violent knocking at the bedroom door.

'Do not disturb his excellency when he is in such an evil case!' angrily shouted Dr Finster, who had not been at the palace reception and knew nothing of the Margrave's disgrace. He himself had been out attending a meeting of the Royal Society and had arrived home very late, to witness his master's collapse.

'He has to be out of this house by dawn,' replied one of the Officers of the King's Household.

'Who the deuce are you? Are you mad? Leave my master in peace!' exclaimed Finster, flinging open the door. 'Go away! Take yourselves off! I cannot imagine by whose leave you are here, but you must be able to see that his excellency is a seriously ill man, he is in no – '

'We are here by order of his majesty King Richard.'

Finster gazed at them in utter astonishment. He had no notion of the turn events had taken.

But he knew his business as a doctor, and said severely, 'King Richard or no, what you say is quite out of the question. Look at the man! He lies at death's door. See for yourselves!'

The Margrave was indeed a ghastly spectacle as he reclined against his heap of silk pillows – his face waxen, streaked with sweat, his lips blue, his eyes sunken. The sheets were dabbled with blood, where Dr Finster's phlebotomy had gone a little wild, there were burnt holes in the pillow cases where the red-hot iron had slipped; leeches crawled about looking for their pond, and various green, black and yellow splashes showed where medicinal draughts had missed their mark. Dr Finster was at his wits' end.

'You his doctor?' one of the officers said. 'Well, fetch the bloke back to life. And make haste about it. He has to be oot o' the country before sun-up.'

Here the Margrave, roused by the voices, murmured, 'Bring me my Chapelmaster. Music – music – that is what I need.'

'Well, for Fingal's sake, let the Chapelmaster be fetched if that is what the man needs! Where is he?'

That was the problem. Bredalbane had already been sought through the whole mansion, but he was not to be found; the porter had not seen him come in.

His players were roused from their beds; they came yawning, glum and startled, and Finster savagely demanded of them where their leader had got to. 'He

304

has no right to absent himself at such a time as this!'

'Well he was a-coming along after us, that's all we know,' sullenly muttered one of the flautists.

'Play without him! Play something – anything!'

Nervously the musicians broke into 'Three Herrings for a Ha'penny'; but, without their leader their playing was ragged, off beat and off key; their instruments were only half tuned; they made a horrible noise.

With a face of anguish, the Margrave pressed his hands to his ears.

'No good! No good! Must have Bredalbane – ' he groaned. 'Air! Air! Open window and give me air. Air and Bredalbane!'

'The air is much too cold for you, sir,' Finster said anxiously. 'And Bredalbane is being urgently sought – he will be brought as soon as possible – '

'Air – must have air!'

Very reluctantly, Finster opened one of the large casements. A dark red dawn now mottled the eastern sky, indicating the probability of more snow. The air that rushed in was colder than the wing of a Valkyrie. Something else came in too: a seagull, dazed and frantic from the excruciating cold. It swung and veered wildly about the room, knocking over the lamp with a flap of its wings, breaking the mirror, beating down the bed-curtains.

'Get it out! Get it out!' shrieked the Margrave. 'Get it out of here!'

Even the stolid Scots guards were startled by the arrival of the gull.

'Och, 'tis an orra thing!' they said to each other, and tried to catch the bird, dashing about with towels and bandages. At last one of them succeeded in lassoing it with his plaid; by this time a good deal more damage had been done, various Meissen toilet articles broken, a gold ewer knocked out of shape, orange-water and seagull-droppings trodden into the Persian carpet. As the bird was finally hurled out of the window – 'Wring its neck!' gasped the Margrave; – 'Na, na, 'tis a fell unchancy deed tae kill a seagull,' one of the guards said firmly, closing the casement – a timid tap was heard at the door.

'Perhaps that is Bredalbane,' cried Finster. 'Come in, whoever you are!'

It was not Bredalbane, but one of the pages. He tremblingly bore in his hands Bredalbane's ivory-and-ebony conductor's baton.

'If you please, your excellency, a couple o' Bow Street Runners are downstairs. They just – they just brought this. They was given it by the constable who patrols around St James's Park. The constables – the constables found it – they found it – ' The boy gulped, and came to a halt. He could not go on speaking with the Margrave's burning eyes fixed on him.

'Come, speak up! Where did they find it?'

'There – there's a skellington what the wolves left, sir – ' blubbered the terrified page. 'They found *this* in its hand; and *this* was lying beside the – beside the bones – '

For a long moment the Margrave stared at the two

articles: the baton, and a little gold-and-onyx snuff-box with the Eisengrim crest on it which he had once given to Bredalbane as a token of esteem.

Then he let out a wail – a long, terrible, howling, keening, lamenting ululation – such as one of the wolves themselves might have given, robbed of its prey. 'No-o-o-o! Oh-o-o-o-o-oh! He is dead, he is dead! I have lost his music. Ah-ah-ah-ah-ah!'

And before their aghast eyes the Margrave began to shrink, to shrivel and dwindle; the lips pulled back from the teeth, the jaw fell open, the eyes glazed and filmed; with a final rattling gasp, which sounded like a wild ironic cackle, the patient writhed from head to foot and lay lifeless on his bed. And not merely lifeless: from the appearance, the chill, and the dreadful dank odour of the body, anyone just arriving in the room would conclude that the person lying there had been dead for several days, if not weeks.

'Gudesakes!' muttered one of the Scots guards, horribly shaken. 'What's come to the mon?'

'He has passed on,' coldly replied Dr Finster.

'Well – och, maircy – at least that saves us an errant. Best give him decent burial without delay. We'll grant ye an extension o' twenty-four hours tae see tae that. Then the rest o' ye's to be oot and awa back tae Hanover where ye belong.'

Shivering, Dr Finster drew the coverlet over the staring face of his dead master. Outside, on the frozen river, the wolves howled in lugubrious chorus.

In the courtyard of Bakerloo House, the children had

piled up a stockade across the gateway to keep out the wolves. They danced and sang:

> 'Heigh, ho, walk it slow
> Rub your eyes and cry
> Today's the day of the funeral
> You'll see us passing by
> You and Willie, me and Lily
> Hold the coffin high
> All the ones that knew him
> When he was still alive
> Come, come to the burial
> This afternoon at five.'

Several of them solemnly carried one of their number who lay limp and pretended to be dead. But then, all of a sudden, the 'dead' person, yelling 'Sticks, sticks, sticks!' would leap from the arms of the mourners and go chasing after them. The first one to be caught played the next dead person.

They were very serious about it and played it for hours until each in turn had played the part of the corpse. The words they sang went to Mr Twite's tune, 'Raining all the Day'.

Every man of the king's troops was now engaged in fighting the wolves; London was a besieged city with streets infested. Wolves made their way into Westminster Abbey, into the Law Courts, into Harrods, into Madame Tussaud's, into Astley's Amphitheatre, into Almack's Assembly Rooms. A wolf was hauled snarling out of the crypt of St Paul's, another found its way into the inner courtyard of the Tower, where it was set upon and pecked to death by ravens.

A Day of National Mourning came and went.

At last the weather improved and the wolves were on the run. They retreated to outlying suburbs – Primrose Hill, Putney Heath, St Johns Wood, Wandsworth Common. In dim sunshine, through melting snow, Simon, Podge and troops of mounted fellow-warriors followed and worried and harried and hunted them down.

On the day when they had finally fought their way as far as Blackheath Waste, Simon and Podge, without speaking to each other, rode faster and faster. They said nothing – yet both were dreading what they might find.

At last: 'Suppose – suppose there's no one left alive?' croaked Podge.

At the landmark where, rounding a corner of coppice, they came in sight of Penelope's barn, they slowed to a halt and waited, looking at one another. The barn stood silent and snowcaked in the mild sun; not a sound came from it. But a thread of smoke lifted from the chimney.

'There must be *someone* alive to light the fire,' said Simon hoarsely; he kicked his horse to a canter, crossed the open space, dismounted, and thumped on the door.

'Open up, it's safe to come out now, we've driven all the wolves away!' he called.

'Took your time about it, too, didn't you?' snapped Penny, throwing open the door. 'We might have starved to death in here for all the help *you* gave us!' And she was going on to give Simon a tremendous telling-off when, staring past her, with starting eyes and stammering tongue, he gasped, '*D-Did-Dido! And Wally!* You're alive! Why – why – you were given up for dead weeks ago. A Day of National Mourning has been held for you!'

'Go on!' said Dido, coming past her sister and giving Simon a warm hug. 'You're gammoning! You gotta be gammoning?'

'No I'm not. King Richard decreed it. Because you uncovered the plot that would have done for him. We believed the Margrave had you and Wally drowned.'

'Oh well; he meant to, and he would have, for sure,' said Dido, 'if it weren't for Wally's da's apple stingo. Just fancy, Wal, the whole country's been a-mourning for us. What'll they do now, when they sees as how we ain't dead after all?'

Wally grinned, his eyes crossing more than ever. 'Maybe they'll find the price of a new coffee-stall,' he said. 'I bet somebody half-inched my old one by now. I lay Dad'll be pleased to hear we're still kicking around. I'd best get to him fast.'

'He'll be pleased sure enough,' said Podge, and thumped his brother on the back. Then he saw Sophie, sitting at the far end of the barn, diligently sewing at one of Penelope's creatures. He turned pink, began to shuffle his feet in the snow, and pulled a little shell box from his pocket.

Dido's gimlet eye observed this, she grabbed Podge's arm and dragged him away round the corner of the building.

'*Don't* give that box to Sophie!' she hissed. 'She don't *want* it!'

Podge was horribly taken aback.

'Wh-what do you say? She don't want it?' He gave Dido a hangdog look. 'Wh-what *does* she want then?'

'She wants you, you clunch. You can give *me* the box, if you like.' Dido took it from his limp hand. 'Now, take her out on the heath and *ask* her – and don't come back till she's said yes!'

Podge gave Dido a dazed, radiant look and disappeared into the barn.

'Dido,' said Simon. 'I've got something dreadful to tell you.

The troop had brought sacks of food with them, to distribute to farmers and cottagers who had been under siege for weeks from the wolves. With some of these supplies, Penny and Is began to prepare a large and nourishing stew, helped by the convalescent van Doon.

'You're getting to be a right helpful little critter,' Penny remarked absently to Is. 'Reckon I'll miss you both when you're gone.'

A worried look came over the Slut's face.

'I'll be sorry too, ma'am – but I gotta get back and find my Figgin.'

At this moment Podge and Sophie came walking back out of the wood. Both of them were radiant now; they seemed to be walking six inches above the ground. And their arms were round each other's necks.

'We've fixed it up!' Podge called.'We fixed it up,

Sophie and I. She's going to be Lady Sophie Green-away!'

Everyone cheered, and there was a lot of laughter and hugging. In the midst of it Dido, who, though she had hugged them warmly too, was looking a little sad and withdrawn, suddenly said, 'What's that row? Not a wolf come back?'

'Oh, lord, I forgot!' And Podge, looking guilty, ran to his horse, which was tied to a tree, and brought back a basket which had been attached to the crupper. This he handed to Is. From inside it came a loud and furious wauling.

'Found him when I went back to Bart's looking for Dido and Wally,' he explained. 'Knew you'd be wanting him.'

'*Figgin!* It's *Figgin!*'

Out of the basket shot a furiously disapproving black form; but when Figgin recognized his owner, all his rage turned to ecstasy; he purred so loudly that, as Dido said, you couldn't hear the stew bubbling.

Now there were three radiant faces.

'I always did want a cat,' began Penelope thoughtfully. 'The fieldmice round here are something chronic; eat you out of house and home, they do.'

'If *I* stay, and *Figgin* stays,' said the Slut, looking her hard in the eye, 'Mr van Doon gotta stay too.'

'Who's standing in his way?' said Penelope. 'He can make himself useful, I daresay.'

Simon said to Dido, 'You'll still come and live at Bakerloo House, won't you, Dido? And, and perhaps – now that Podge and Sophie are fixed up – perhaps you'd think about being Duchess of Battersea one day?'

But at that, Dido burst out laughing.

'Me a duchess? A likely notion! I ain't half old enough – and I ain't half grand enough. *You* do all right as a dook Simon – you do fine – you was born to it, that's why. But I was born Dido Twite; I ain't cut out for parties at the palace and noshing with nobs. No, no, it wouldn't suit me a bit. I'll be your friend, Simon, from here to Habakkuk, like I've always been, for you're a real decent cove; but when you want a duchess you gotta look somewhere different. No hard feelings?'

'No,' said Simon sadly. 'I was afraid you'd say that, Dido, but I shall ask you again, by and by.'

Penelope called them: 'Come on, you two, dinner's ready.'

After dinner, while Wally was telling the story of their escape from the ice-boat, and Simon was telling the story of the Margrave's awful end, Podge said to Dido, 'Dido, I'm really sorry about your father.'

Dido looked at him, biting her lip. She said, 'He was a real bad lot. I *know* it's best he's gone. But it's – it was – his music; now *that's* all gone too – '

She had to stop; her voice dried up inside her.

'Have you ever thought, Dido, that perhaps you could make up tunes?' Podge suggested. 'You're his daughter, after all.'

Dido sniffed and wiped her eyes and said, 'No. I can't. I tried *ever* so many times. But it ain't in me. All *I* can do is make up tales. That's different.' Suddenly for some reason she remembered telling a story

313

about keys to the Slut. 'No,' she repeated. 'Pa's music is gone. It's gone. That's all there is to it.'

But over by the fire the Slut was singing,

'I love little Pussy his coat is so warm
And if I annoy him he'll chew off my arm – '

and Penelope, stitching away at a penguin, was absently putting in an alto part.

NEW, FROM JOAN AIKEN

LIMBO LODGE

An exciting new title in The Wolves of Willoughby Chase sequence

Dido Twite is abroad *The Thrush*, trying to return home to England after her adventures on the east coast of America (as described in *The Stolen Lake*). She is frustrated once again by orders the ship's Captain receives to find and bring home Lord Herodsfoot, who is away on a quest for rare games to cheer up the ailing English king, James III. His Lordship is said to be on the Pacific island of Aratu, 'Island of the Pearl Snakes'.

Snakes, however, are the least of the search party's worries as they land on the island at dawn, to the eerie sound of drumming. As Dido struggles through the jungle to find Lord Herodsfoot, she is helped by the spirit magic of the Dilendi tribe, but she is also confronted by enemies among the Angrian settlers who will stop at nothing to achieve their ends. And further dangers lie in store at that strange palace called Limbo Lodge . . .

ISBN 0 224 04664 0

Published in hardback by Jonathan Cape, priced £9.99

Book 1 *in the* FELIX TRILOGY

Joan Aiken

Go Saddle the Sea

Action-packed adventure, high-tension drama and heroic swashbuckling! Join dashing hero Felix Brooke as he boldly embarks upon the journey of a lifetime... Here's a taster to tempt you!

'Ye've run yourself into a real nest of adders, here, lad,' Sammy whispered.

'I know they are smugglers,' I began protesting. 'That was why the fee was low. But I could take care of my — '

'They are worse than smugglers, lad – they are Comprachicos,' he breathed into my ear.

'Compra — c-comprachicos?'

At first I thought I could not have heard him aright. Then I could not believe him. The I *did* believe him – Sam would not make up such a tale – and, despite myself, my teeth began to chatter.

THE FELIX TRILOGY by Joan Aiken from Red Fox

Go Saddle the Sea	£3.99	ISBN 0 09 953771 0
Bridle the Wind	£3.99	ISBN 0 09 953781 8
The Teeth of the Gale	£3.99	ISBN 0 09 953791 5

Book 2 in the FELIX TRILOGY

Joan Aiken

BRIDLE THE WIND

If you're an adventure addict then you'll love BRIDLE THE WIND – it's un-put-downable!

Here's a taste of what's in store...

Shipwrecked, imprisoned and then haunted by a ghoulish premonition – brave Felix may be down on his luck but he'll never, ever give up...

'*Oh*, but I don't want to die!'

And then, a second time, putting the fear of death, such as I had not felt, even through the shipwreck, into my own heart, '*Oh – but – I don't – want – to – die!*'

Petrified, I stared all around me. From where could the voice possibly come?

Trembling uncontrollably, I looked upward, and now, just for a moment, it seemed to my dazed senses that I could see something - some *body* - suspended from one of the arching boughs overhead, that I could see a thin form swinging, dangling at the end of a rope not three feet above me... It faded, melted, and was gone.

THE FELIX TRILOGY by Joan Aiken from Red Fox

Go Saddle the Sea	£3.99	ISBN 0 09 953771 0
Bridle the Wind	£3.99	ISBN 0 09 953781 8
The Teeth of the Gale	£3.99	ISBN 0 09 953791 5

Book 3 in the FELIX TRILOGY

THE TEETH OF THE GALE

*G*rab a copy of the thrilling finale of THE FELIX TRILOGY. It's an action-packed read – so hold on tight!

Pulses race when brave Felix leads a rescue mission with his sweetheart, Juana. It's a deadly dangerous task – will Felix keep his head and return a hero?
Here's a tingling taster...

'Juana! Keep very still!' I called hoarsely.

My heart seemed to fall clean out of my body into the gorge below. There she was, defenceless, in deadly danger, and here I was, strung on two ropes over the gulf, with my gun strapped out of reach, useless on my back; however fast I moved, I would never be able to get back in time to save her if the bear flew at her.

The massive bear turned, at the sound of my voice, and eyed me intently. I joggled frantically on the rope, to hold its attention.

'Bear! Bear!' I yelled. 'Look at me! Look at me on the bridge. Come and get me, bear! Here I am!'

THE FELIX TRILOGY by Joan Aiken from Red Fox